BRUSH

A NOVEL

PENN ANDERSON

Copyright © 2023 by Penn Anderson

All rights reserved. This book or any portion thereof may not be reproduced or used in any manner whatsoever without the express written permission of the publisher except for the use of brief quotations in a book review.

This book is a work of fiction. Names, characters, businesses, places, events, locales, and incidents are either products of the author's imagination or used in a fictitious manner. Any resemblance to actual persons, living or dead, or actual events is purely coincidental.

Printed in the United States of America

First Printing, 2023

Library of Congress Control Number: 2023913899

ISBN 979-8-9887493-0-1 (large print paperback)
ISBN 979-8-988-7493-1-8 (eBook)

www.PennAnderson.com

For Ray and Laura

Creation is a visitor.

*To be home when the bell rings is the
quad-shredding, smash-and-grab climb.*

*To have some pie to serve and a clean toilet.
At least.*

"You seem winded. Did you just get home?"

(Relax. Visitors don't leave when the answer is yes.)

"Do you need a moment? I could come back later."

"No, stay. Please. I have pie."

April

1

Chris used one hand to grab the pile of clothes from the large upholstered chair next to his bedroom window and fling them onto his unmade bed. He felt a splash of coffee hit the top of his bare foot and wiped it on the back of his calf. He needed to shower and get to work, but instead he sat down and watched the earliest warmth climb the side wall of the Lannon stone church across the street. The chair was old and comfortable, and drew him in every morning. His body filled in its negative space. Chris looked at his phone and gave himself five more minutes. Absolutely no worries for five minutes, and then he would get up.

A man stood in the church entryway and watered grass seed sprouts across the concrete using a metal hose extension. The water was failing to reach most of the grass and was forming a puddle in a low crack.

"Buddy, why? Jesus. Take a step forward, idiot," Chris said aloud. He looked at his phone and only had three minutes left. The man lifted the hose higher, pulling the stream even farther from the grass line. Chris took a deep breath, trying to calm his urge to open the window and call down to this guy. With only one more minute left, he took a long drink of his lukewarm coffee. Leaning forward to stand, Chris froze in place. From this angle he could see the solution to this one small mystery. The refraction in the mist of the hose water. The visible spectrum in the droplets. Chris realized the man had found his five minutes of peace while Chris had lost his own.

2

Jo pulled the warm blanket down to her waist and tugged her T-shirt up to cover her face and expose her bare chest. She stayed in that place, breathing through the cotton, while the sun began to dance through the curtains behind her bed and onto her body. Arms above her head resting on the pillow, she played with a tangle in her hair, working it with her fingers until it came loose. Her shirt began to fall below her eyes, and she pulled it sharply up again, higher now so it would stay in place. Her torso felt chilled and invigorated, while her warm face and legs stayed dormant and night-bidden. The effect was like vanilla ice cream between two oven-crisped chocolate chip cookies. Best devoured with no one watching. Jo liked everything about this moment. Thoughts of her workday ahead started to emerge, lists of projects and orders, but she held. Hearing the newspaper land on the stoop below, she wanted to go check the leaderboard in the Masters tournament, but she held. She reached a hand down to cradle her taut bladder, growing urgent, but she held. Looking through the stretched veil of her white T-shirt made Jo feel safe and simple. But without seeing the clock, she felt something in the light change, and bliss left the room. Like the instant a subway rider knows to start pushing because no one is stepping aside to let her off in time, the whitewashed bedroom view now felt claustrophobic and smothering. Shirt flipped back down. Big free inhale. Strong sit-up. The colors came rushing in and she was enrapt.

3

When Chris stepped off the elevator at the Milwaukee headquarters and walked past the cubicles to his office, he could tell immediately there was already a crisis. He only worked on-site at this building three days a week, but there was always a crisis. The massive wall of windows, designed in narrow vertical strips that highlighted (imprisoned?) the sparkling Lake Michigan view, did nothing to convince him this company was cool or well-managed. Any outsider would think it was both. Luscious plants, soft lighting, tapestries in Aegean shades of blue and green. Cucumber water at the front desk. An actual koi pond in the lakefront conference room. The investors and the girlfriends loved it.

Chris and two friends, Scott and Jared, had started FELL seven years earlier during a whiskey-blurred conversation around a fire pit after their college reunion. "Friends" was an overstatement. They had lived on the same dorm floor, played some euchre, liked the same girl, and were into computers. Video games, porn, and the occasional programming language to make sure they'd graduate. Sitting around that fire years later, they all had one more thing in common: the desperation for a change. All three had been working to exhaustion for software companies they didn't own. Long hours had turned into failed relationships, pale skin, and addictions to things that made them feel alive or dead, depending on the need. That night by the fire, they didn't say any of this to each other. Instead they name-dropped completed marathons and triathlons. They debated the value of the special edition Whistle Pig whiskey that was just released. Chris bragged about a threesome he stumbled into after his divorce. Scott had recently subscribed to monthly frozen steak deliveries and highly recommended it. Jared had gotten to play a round of golf at St. Andrews. As the night went on, and they ran out of topics, they talked about TV. "Have you seen…?" lasted twenty minutes. Finally, there was a long silence, and the men simply gazed into the fire. Someone leaned forward to add a new log and adjust the others. Sparks danced and crackled. Embers died by their feet. And then, maybe just to fill the silence, or maybe because the TV conversation had paved the way for any pedestrian topic, Scott mentioned he needed a tree cut down. He said he was worried it would fall on his house with the next big storm.

"It's really hard to find a guy to come do that kind of work," Scott said.

"Yeah, that's why I'm glad I rent instead of own. I have no time for all that homeownership bullshit," added Chris.

"Haha, same," Jared agreed. "I don't even have

time to take care of a houseplant."

"It seems like there would be plenty of arborists in a city as big as Milwaukee, but how do you find them? I don't want to reply to some sketchy ad and then have the guy get injured on my property or make a branch fall on my house."

"What about the big tree companies? Just Google it, dude." Chris laughed.

"Thanks, genius, I tried that. The wait times are long, and none of them want to take on these small jobs. And if they do, they want to charge $10k a tree."

"Shit," Jared exclaimed. "We're in the wrong business!"

"I'd love to see you climb a tree, buddy," laughed Scott. "The fire department would have to come get you down like a fucking cat."

Chris was quiet for a minute and then looked up at the men. "What you need is an app. Like an on-demand network of arborists. Like rideshare, but for tree work. I bet there are a lot of guys with the training who could use some side work."

Scott and Jared nodded. It was an idea that made sense. Oftentimes, tree work was time-sensitive and couldn't wait. A widow-maker branch hanging over a swing set. A downed branch blocking a driveway. The gig economy was a fledgling gold rush in every software engineer's mind, and the three men could readily see the immense scalability. Milwaukee. Statewide. Nationwide. Anywhere trees grow? Now, that's a market.

"I bet I could build that app in a week. It's actually incredibly simple," Jared asserted. Meanwhile, Chris had taken out his phone to search for competitors with this idea and saw none.

Scott chuckled, set his glass of whiskey down by his feet, and said, "You guys won't believe this, but I have a buddy who works at a forestry trade magazine. I bet he would know how to get the app on arborists' radar."

Nothing sobers up three men more quickly than fear. And this was good fear. The fear that makes a man need to try. The fear that makes his lungs expand with electric air and his heart thrust forth a sound like a giggle. Chris, Jared, and Scott made this tacit noise to each other, across the fire, with their eyes.

4

Mannequins of forsythia branches stood in a row of large glass vases against the front window of Jo's store. Some towering six feet tall and many others filling in the undercanopy, the light brown stalks crossing each other and themselves, forming a child's scribble with a sepia crayon. A customer would have to stand very close to see the pale green buds dotting the stems, and hear the whispers of potential they held.

Jo had worn snowboots the night before to cut these branches from an overgrown patch next to the parking lot behind the building. Everything was finally melting, but the northern corners still held mounds of dirty ice and rotted leaves. Before she brought the branches inside, she peeked around the fence to the garden to check for crocuses and snowdrops. Nothing yet that she could see, but it was getting dark at the time. She had made a mess hauling in the branches, cutting them to size, and placing them in the vases of warm water that she had prepped in the storefront. Despite the chore it had been, Jo admired her work now. The morning sun streaming in had already forced open a couple of tiny yellow flowers at the bottom of one stalk. Within a week, the entire floor-to-ceiling bay of three window panes would be ablaze in gold for the community of Mount Horeb to enjoy. Jo liked to think this tradition at her shop helped to signal the end of the darkness of winter, propelled passersby through those last few chilly days, and maybe taught them a trick they could do with woody, flowering branches from their own yards. Every year she noticed the same old man walk past daily and pause, noticing new buds pop wide as if from a magician's hand. She saw many children fall behind their parents' pace so they could look up at the blooming skyscrapers above the reflection of their open smiles. People between the ages of old and young rarely paused, and that was fine, too. Who can get to work on time, or meet with a tax accountant, or get to a dental cleaning while in a state of awe, anyway?

Jo turned to the back of the store to grab her purse and head next door for lunch but heard the bell that hung from the wood screen door and looked behind her. A young man in a camel hair sport coat, two sizes too big, strode toward her in a panic.

"Help?" he asked with desperation.

Jo cracked a smile. "It's going to be OK. You're in good hands."

The man smiled back. "You know my type, don't you?"

"I do," Jo replied kiddingly.

"Today is her birthday. My girlfriend. It's not that I forgot, so much as it is that I...forgot."

"It happens. Is there still time?"

"I think so. I'm meeting her for lunch at her friend's lake cottage. And I'm only ten minutes late so far."

Jo immediately started walking toward the glass doors of the cooler and thinking of the quickest arrangement that would still be thoughtful.

"I have these beautiful peach ranunculus that just arrived this morning. They're some of the first of the season. I think a full bunch of these in a milk glass vase would be lovely. Give me three minutes."

Jo grabbed two generous handfuls of flowers from the cooler and walked to the long stainless steel work table. She cut a fresh diagonal snip from the bottom of each flower and pulled off leaves that would fall below the water line. She spun the full vase around and analyzed the balance, then walked over to some galvanized metal buckets on the floor that were overflowing with soft, dried grasses she had collected the previous fall. Jo chose a few stems that were arched and which suited the vase to add to the ranunculus. The grass she picked felt like an angora sweater. Together, the peach flowers, the light tan grass, and the white hobnail vase pleased her in their simplicity and elegance. It looked like April. It felt like romance.

"This will be sixteen dollars, and you can choose a card from the bowl by the front desk." Jo carried the full vase over to the desk and set it down in front of him. As she walked behind the counter, he handed her a twenty. She watched as he took a ballpoint pen and wrote a message.

"HB, Sweet Tits. Love, me."

Jo pretended she was looking at the cash register and handed him his four dollars change.

The man finally paused a beat, forgetting his panic, and looked at the flowers. "This is absolutely beautiful. Thank you for making it so quickly. I know she will love it."

"My pleasure. I hope those last a good long time for her." Jo didn't know if she meant the flowers or the tits.

As the man rushed out, and the screen door cheerfully slammed behind him, Jo felt a hunger pang and remembered she had been on her way to lunch. She walked to the back of the store and turned up the staircase, taking the creaky steps two at a time. She opened the door to her apartment, grabbed her purse off the back of a kitchen chair, and quickly checked her face in a mirror by the door. Bounding back downstairs and across the worn maple floors of the shop, now nervous another customer would come in before her escape, she stepped outside into the perfect spring day, closing and locking the front door. The blue and white "Will Return" clock hung on the door and she adjusted the two red hands to give herself thirty minutes for lunch. Her finger slipped a touch and it became forty.

5

Chris thought back to that hopeful night by the fire and wondered how his life had gotten so darkly hectic again. All of the predicted satisfying elements of being the boss, instead of a cog in a machine, had turned out to be an illusion. Now he worked longer hours, tackled higher-stakes problems, and felt an emptiness of purpose that had no walls or floor. At the same time, he had to marvel at the wild success of the app, and he sometimes still had to pinch himself when he saw his bank balance. Jared and Scott had remained his co-owners, and FELL had a leadership continuity rare for most tech start-ups.

He remembered years ago talking to his mother, Eileen, about the chance to quit his job and start this company. She hadn't been thrilled. They had recently lost Bill, her husband and Chris's father, to heart disease. Eileen leaned on Chris for errands and support that he felt ill-equipped to give. He couldn't help but resent the burden of being an only child and the lack of empathy his mom had for his schedule. He loved her, of course, and she had always been a good mother, but their relationship was frustrating now and felt like a part-time job. It seemed like every one of their interactions was about clinics, doctors, insurance mistakes, moles of concern, or dead neighbors. When Chris did try to talk to her about anything in his life, she was never the unconditional cheerleader he often craved. Her reaction to the idea of FELL had been surprised, worried, and included too many annoying uninformed questions. But Chris did remember one thing she said that had given him pause and stayed with him to this day. She told him, "You can escape your situation, but you can't escape yourself." Now, seven years, 150 employees, and millions of dollars later, Chris was starting to understand what she had meant.

The office was a chaotic blur that morning as the press team was attempting to quash a *New York Times* story about unqualified arborists working on FELL jobs, following up on some tips a reporter had gotten. Chris was sure the rumors were bullshit, and these so-called whistleblowers were plants from new competitors. FELL had an airtight vetting system and multiple layers of site-based credential verification. A rating system and the ability to earn the coveted "FELLA" badge helped ensure high-quality work. Chris, Scott, and Jared met with their public relations director for two hours to hammer out the right quotes and intended response to the accusations.

Although Chris sorely needed some time in his office to catch up after the long morning meeting, the guys suggested walking to a brew pub in the trendy, historic Third Ward district for lunch to celebrate Scott's fortieth birthday. It was a beautiful day, and Chris agreed. On the twenty-minute walk, the topic was basketball and the season the Bucks were having. Chris half-listened while looking up at the mirrored reflections of the sunny blue sky and shuffling clouds in the skyscraper windows. The wind behind them coming off the lake was the wizard's wand of this dynamic spring day. He was glad he had come, even if this time away from the office meant he would be at work until 8:00 or 9:00 p.m. His phone vibrated, and he saw a call coming in from his mother, but he let it go to voicemail. The last time she had called, it was to ask him to bring her a new nightlight bulb. She had been sure to add, "When you get a chance. I know you're busy, dear."

The restaurant was half full, and Chris and the men got a big round table. The young redheaded waitress was promptly informed it was Scott's birthday, and within minutes the table had many mugs of beer and baskets of fried cheese curds. At least eight TVs were perched around the ceiling perimeter. The acoustics of the dark wood and industrial beams made for a loud room, and the men didn't hold back from making it louder.

"Anyone notice her ass?" Jared asked, unabashedly above the din. The men nodded and made noises of mock arousal that could have also passed for sounds of indigestion. Chris never had to wonder too hard why the women in the office didn't often come along for this type of outing. Although the common narrative was that they were all brownnosing grinds who never liked to have fun.

"Chris, get her number. We know you like redheads."

"Chris likes ALL heads, right, buddy?"

"Sure, sure, guys. I highly doubt she'd be interested. And don't you think she has to put up with tables like us all day? We can give her a break." Chris looked in her direction, and she was walking back over to take their orders.

"Hey, babe, what's your name, by the way?" Jared asked her.

"My name's Doyle. You guys about ready to order?"

"Doyle. Cute name. Is it real, or is that just your… 'stage' name?"

"God given, honey. It was my grandmother's maiden name."

"Whoa, fellas! She's giving us her security question answers! She must like us!"

Scott interjected, "Doyle, thank you, ignore these jackasses. I'll have the bacon cheeseburger."

The men went around and all ordered burgers, except one who ordered flank steak. Chris was last to order and asked for the chopped chicken salad with avocado.

"Whoa, whoa, whoa. Do you need a tampon, too, buddy?" Jared laughed.

"Jesus, Jared. Sorry, Doyle." Chris looked up at her and smiled apologetically. She smiled back, and Chris had to admit her blue eyes were magnetic. She turned and walked towards the bar, and all heads followed. Her butt did seem to defy the laws of physics.

"What, are you on a diet, bro? What the hell?" Jared slid a basket of cheese curds closer to Chris. Even though they made his gut hurt, he reached for some. They were no longer hot and had gotten soggy, and Chris couldn't believe he might have hours of stomach pain just to get the guys off his case for ordering a salad. But it seemed to work, and they moved on.

"Damn, it looked like you and Doyle had a little moment there. Go for it, man."

"Doesn't she look about my daughter's age, though?" inserted Scott.

"Scott, your daughter is eleven. You think the waitress looks ELEVEN?" Jared challenged.

"My daughter is thirteen, by the way, and you know what I mean."

"You know she's legal if she's serving alcohol. And just look at our boy Chris! Handsome guy. Nice car. Sweet condo. No baggage. Good teeth." Jared and the rest of the men agreed wholeheartedly on that last point. "Doyle should be so lucky to land a sexy geezer like Chris! She can count his gray pubes as foreplay," and the table erupted in laughter and exaggerated sounds of disgust.

Just then Chris's phone buzzed, and he could

see it was his mother calling again. "Sorry, guys, I gotta take this," and Chris stood up and walked quickly to the front of the restaurant.

"What's up, Mom? Everything OK?" he asked as he pushed open the door and walked outside.

"Oh, Chris, no, I'm so sorry, I know you're at work, I didn't know what to do."

"Slow down, Mom. Tell me what's going on."

"I can't find my pill case. I've looked everywhere. I tried to see behind the bureau, but I couldn't bend down that far. It might be down there. And now I missed my morning pills and my midday pills, and I think I feel my heart racing. I can't catch my breath."

"OK, Mom. It's going to be OK. Have you asked Martha to help you look?" Chris had helped move his mother into a retirement community after his dad died, and she had sold the house. Martha lived down the hall, and the two ladies had coffee together in the morning and worked on puzzles.

"Martha is visiting her daughter in San Francisco this week."

"Is there anyone else you can ask?"

"I've knocked on some doors, but no one answers. Chris, they're all so damned deaf! If I call the office, they will think I have dementia and make me move."

"Oh, Mom. That's not true."

"It is! I've heard they keep track, and if you screw up too many times, you have to go to assisted living or even memory care."

"Mom. Look. You didn't screw up. I misplace

things all the time. No one is coming to take you away. I'm actually pretty far from my car at the moment, but I'll get a cab and be there in thirty minutes. As for your heart racing, I think you just got yourself worked up. Can you do me a favor and go sit by the window while you're waiting for me? Just watch a bird or something."

"OK, honey. I'll see you soon. I'll go birdwatch in a chair and pretend I'm not an old lady who is headed for the granny tank."

Chris laughed, and so did she. He hung up and called an Uber to come to the restaurant. He walked back inside and straight over to Doyle, who was at the server's stand.

"Hey…sorry about this. I have to leave and go help my mom, but I'd like to take care of the bill for the table. Would you be able to run my card now?"

"Sure, no problem. Give me three minutes." Doyle reached just past him to grab the card reader, and Chris could smell her shampoo. "I hope your mom is OK. It sounds like you're a good son."

"Ha, thanks. I could do better." She handed him back his card with the receipt wrapped around it. Chris headed back over to the table to tell the guys he had to run.

"Give Eileen a big wet kiss for me, man!" Jared called after him.

"Dream on, idiot. Happy birthday, Scott. I'll be back at the office later if anyone needs me."

Chris walked outside to wait for the car. As he unwrapped the receipt to put his card back in his wallet, he saw Doyle had written her phone number with a smiley face. He folded it carefully and put it in his back Levi's pocket, hoping she was watching him through the glass doors.

When Chris arrived at the Liberty Acres retirement village, his mom was standing in the hallway by her door, hands clasped tightly under her chin. "Thank you for coming, honey. I'm so sorry about this."

"Don't worry about it." Chris walked past her and did a quick scan of the apartment. He half expected to see the pill case right out on the table. It took a few minutes of looking, but he found it in her bedside table drawer. He sat with her while she called the pharmacist to ask how to get back on schedule after the missed pills, and then he told her he should get back to work.

"Do you want some pie, honey?" she asked hopefully.

"Oh, Mom…I wish I could. I'm really under the gun today. Another time, OK?"

She was already wrapping Saran Wrap around a

slice of rhubarb pie on a paper plate. "I love you so much, Chris," she said, as she handed it to him.

"Thanks, Mom, I love you, too. This looks delicious."

As Chris sat in the cab on the way back to the office, he looked at the pie and knew he would devour it the second he sat down at his desk. He did have a lot to do at work, but he could have spent fifteen more minutes with his mom. Who was worse? Lewd Jared teasing the waitress, or someone who makes his own mother feel like one more burden on his calendar? Chris stared out the window and watched the buildings go by. The lower afternoon sun flashing between them onto his face felt like paparazzi.

6

Schubert's Diner had been operating in the same location on Main Street for over seventy years. Jo had only lived in Mount Horeb, Wisconsin, for ten years, but she felt like a part of the family in this restaurant. She was catching the tail end of the lunch crowd and recognized many friends and customers sitting in booths. Nods and smiles greeted her as she walked across the gray and white checkerboard floor to her stool at the counter.

"Hey, there she is! I thought we might not see you today. What can we get you?" Grant asked, tossing a towel over his shoulder and resting his hands on the edge of the counter in front of her. His arms looked tan and strong, veins visible in his forearms. His name was called from the kitchen, but his eyes and smirk never left hers.

"I've got this one, Romeo," Dag said while firmly nudging him out of the way, as only siblings could. "Hi, Jo. What can I get you today?"

"Dagmar Morrison, look at that haircut! You look beautiful. I truly love it," Jo gushed.

"Really?" She cupped her pageboy gently. "Not too short?"

"No way. It suits you perfectly. You might just inspire me to go short. You honestly look so free and...sexy," Jo said, whispering that last word.

"Jo!" Dagmar's face flooded in rose.

Jo, laughing, as it was always the most fun to tease Dag, said, "OK, OK. Sorry, but it's true! Let's see...I think today I feel like having the meatloaf sandwich. That fresh-baked bread smells too good to pass up."

"Oh, hon, don't forget it's…" Dagmar stopped herself. "Oh, umm, well, anyway…that comes with creamed corn, stewed rhubarb, or coleslaw."

Jo knew exactly what Dag was about to say: "Don't forget it's Friday." Jo had never been outspoken one way or the other about her religion, but she would think by now people would know she wasn't a practicing Catholic, if they even cared. Her parents had taken her to church in her childhood, but not regularly, and after they both had passed, any remaining obligation was gone. Anyone who works with flowers daily, including Jo, would find it hard not to believe in God, but that was an entirely different subject in her mind, and had very little to do with eating meat on Fridays.

Jo simply responded: "Rhubarb, please."

Grant came out from the kitchen again and delivered plates to a table behind her. She could feel his eyes on her.

"Whipped cream for ya on that rhubarb?" he asked in a low voice while leaning into the curve between her neck and shoulder.

He did push it a little far sometimes. "No thanks, Grant." Jo said, laughing a little. "Wait, what am I saying? That would be delicious. Yes, please."

Jo was never exactly sure of Grant's official job title at the diner. He cooked, baked, waited tables, fixed things, swept the front stoop, and made everyone feel welcome. His sister, Dagmar, had gotten him the job last year when he moved to Mount Horeb to help their parents. A lot of people in town were unemployed, and he was grateful for the work. Jo watched him as he moved deftly around the diner. She enjoyed her friendship with Grant and wasn't interested in anything more, but she had to admit he could wear the hell out of a pair of Levi's.

"Do you have any deliveries for me today?" he asked, now standing back behind the counter.

"Yes!" she said quickly, nervous he could read her thoughts. "I have six bouquets for you to deliver, and I'm sorry one of them needs to go all the way to Madison." Grant's shift at Schubert's ended at 2:00 p.m. on weekdays, and Jo had been hiring him for a couple of extra hours most days to do a flower delivery run. He seemed to like the extra money, and it helped Jo keep her store open more hours since she could stay on-site. "I have them all boxed up and ready to go."

"That's great. The more time, the better. I'm saving up for new golf clubs. Sandy Duncan and I will hit the open road when I'm done with my shift here." Sandy Duncan was what he called his sandy brown Oldsmobile.

"Have you been out to hit balls yet this year?" Jo asked. "I haven't had a chance."

"Not yet. It's still pretty wet. Maybe next week. Did you see that Tom Watson is only three back at the Masters?" he asked.

"I sure did! I'll be rooting for him this weekend."

"Here you go, Jo." Dagmar squeezed in front of Grant and set Jo's sandwich down.

Grant started to walk away to clear some tables and called back, "Sandy and I will be at your back door at about 2:15, ready to roll."

Jo paused and smiled before taking the first bite. "You're a gem, Grant! Thanks."

The meatloaf was warm and delicious, a gummy crust of baked ketchup on three sides. Her fingertips were gently buried in ten divots in the thick white bread, lightly toasted. She watched the homemade whipped cream slowly slide across the rhubarb in the little bowl by her plate, leaving a white film. Her eyes blurred for the smallest of instants as she thought of her parents. She had loved her mom's meatloaf, and she could still see her dad bent over the patch of rhubarb in their backyard, hacking off stalks to bring inside. They had been older, compared to her friends' parents, and they had just one child. But they adored each other, and the three of them had formed a very happy little team. Both heavy smokers, they had lost Jo's dad to lung cancer and her mom was diagnosed only two years after that. It all went so quickly. That time in Jo's life had been dark and lonely. Now she felt an occasional surprising tear well up, but the grief usually didn't derail an entire day anymore. Jo breathed deeply and went back to enjoying her lunch, feeling sated by the thoughtful care of her loving family, old and new.

Jo looked up at the ivory pressed-tin ceiling, admiring the detail and beauty, thinking about the craftsmen who had installed it long ago.

She looked at the black and white photo of JFK on the wall above the mixers. He had made a campaign stop at Schubert's in 1960. She thought about the times of fear and the times of celebration this place had seen. She thought about the thousands of malts made with those reliable little motors behind the counter, and the thousands of reliable little people who had enjoyed them. Jo closed her eyes and made a silly wish that this diner would be here forever. But anyone who works with flowers all day, including Jo, knew that nothing could last forever. Jo could only nurture this one moment. This one bloom. Imperfect. Impermanent. If a customer were to walk into Jo's shop and ask her, "What is most beautiful?" her truest and most heartbreaking answer would be: "The ephemeral."

7

The condo had been an impulse purchase. The "Rooftop Garden" model was what they had called it. The building was located in a great part of Milwaukee, near a dozen excellent restaurants and a lively public market hall. Chris could walk to Bucks games, concerts, the marina, and some of the greatest beer on Earth. He often drove to work because he loved his car, but he could walk or bike. Sixteen condos had been carved out of an old restored candy factory, with much of the original character preserved. Chris's modern furniture and appliances against the backdrop of exposed Cream City brick could have made for a striking magazine photoshoot. He was lucky to have a condo on the top floor, facing south, with a small garden just past the French doors of his kitchen. But the life he thought he was buying at the closing was not the life he was living, and there was no one to sue for fraud. After living there for a year, packing boxes still lined the spare rooms. One basil plant, long dead now, had been the only addition to the garden, a gift from an ex-girlfriend. The pot had frozen and cracked over the winter. He had yet to walk to a concert, and the restaurant food came to his door late at night in Styrofoam. Chris ended every week hoping a chaotic chapter was done. Hoping for a change in his routine, a change in the constant storm at FELL.

Chris sat against the headboard in his dark bedroom, only lit by three glows: the muted TV, his laptop, and his phone. Half a glass of icy Templeton Rye sweated on the bedside table to his right. He had learned the hard way to reply to emails only when sober, but he read through some messages and tried to get a picture of what the next week would look like. On the TV, a silent Bob Ross painted calmly. His palette rested on his arm with such ease, it could have been a sleepy golden retriever's paw.

"Bob motherfucking Ross. How do you do it, man?" Chris asked aloud and smiled ironically, shaking his head.

Chris picked up his phone to do another scroll through social media, seeing the same posts he had seen ten times already this night. The only new addition was an advertisement for a "Beginners Landscape Painting" online course.

"These phones hear everything," Chris thought to himself. His own company used a similar technology. If a person searches, speaks, or even texts something about tree work, FELL would make sure an ad would land in front of their face within an hour.

Chris opened the advertisement, even though he knew doing so would trigger more of them in his feed. Painting actually sounded really fun. His friends would never let him live it down, though. Chris could already imagine the Georgia O'Keeffe jokes. He wouldn't be able to use the restroom without a Jackson Pollock comment from Jared. He skimmed through the information anyway and looked at the supply list. He was surprised to see there were a few in-person meet-ups in the Milwaukee area. Do hot chicks paint? Chris guessed yes. He finished his whiskey and looked again at the class site. He looked up at Bob. Bob looked directly into his eyes, and although the sound was off, Chris could swear Bob mouthed the word "Fool."

"Oh yeah, Bob?" Chris chuckled. "You think I'm a fool? Join the club!" He was laughing uncontrollably now. "You dare me, big guy? You think I can't rock polyester pants like those? You feel a little threatened by the old Chrissy boy?" he asked the TV combatively as he grasped his phone. Feeling manic and possessed with slap-happy energy now, he clicked through the menus and signed up for the class. Then he ordered every item on the supply list, even the optional bamboo easel upgrade.

Chris closed his laptop, silenced his phone, and turned off the TV. He got up to pee, keeping the bathroom light off. He went to the kitchen and poured one more tumbler of whiskey. He got back into bed and sipped it slowly in the carbon-black room.

8

Most of the record collection had belonged to her father. Jo remembered him playing records each morning, singing along as he shaved his face and tapped the razor on the sink while she got ready for school. Fats Domino, Buddy Holly, Roy Orbison, Benny Goodman's *Carnegie Hall*. She had added her own purchases to the stacks over the years and organized them all by era. Jo selected Van Morrison's *Astral Weeks* and sat down on the sofa, putting her sock feet up on the coffee table. Next to her was a small stack of carbon copies from credit card flower payments she needed to get ready to drop at the bank in the morning, and she was waiting for her potato to finish baking. Jo saw the street lights come on outside her front window and stood up to pull her curtains closed. It was staying light much later in the evening now, and that made her feel relieved and renewed. Wisconsin winters were hard. Driving was difficult. Bundling up was a chore. Road salt coated doorways and pant cuffs. Jo was more limited in what she had available to sell in her shop and made less money in the winter, always thankful for the windfall of Valentine's Day. People tended to stay indoors unless they had children or skied. Welcoming spring was like hearing a bell ring at the top of a nearby hill. If daffodil yellow made a sound, it would be the sound of that bell, announcing, "This miracle still exists in the world, and so do you!"

Gratefully, in any season, Jo felt a coziness and joy in her apartment. It was warm and modest, decorated simply but comfortably. Ten years earlier, she had been a married woman living in a big house three hours north in Wausau, Wisconsin. She didn't know if anyone in Mount Horeb knew she was divorced, and she was glad she hadn't been asked directly about her past. With her half of the proceeds from the sale of the house, she had been able to buy this building on Main Street in a whole new town and make a fresh start. At first, Jo had thought she would rent out the second floor for extra income, but she fell in love with the space and ended up keeping it for herself. The apartment had a galley kitchen in the back, space for a small round table, and only one bedroom, but it had three tall, arched front windows and high ceilings that made it feel much bigger. It was all she needed. Being next door to Schubert's Diner felt like an extension of her kitchen, and living above her business brought many conveniences. Jo had been a little concerned she would have no feeling of closure to the end of her work day, but that worry had not come true. Some lines were blurred, of course, but it felt natural. She had made her apartment feel so homey that once she was upstairs for the night, she rarely went back down until morning.

One of her favorite memories in the apartment had occurred just a couple of months earlier, when a whole gang from the diner had clamored up her back fire escape and asked if they could watch the M*A*S*H series finale because it was too snowy to drive home. Winter parkas piled in mounds over chairs, Jo handed around bottles of Huber beer, and Saltines with cheese spread. Hours later, after the snowplows had come through and everyone had finally left, she burst into tears, not sure that night had even really happened.

Jo walked to the kitchen and took a potholder out of a drawer. She reached into the oven and gave her potato a delicate squeeze. There was a little crackle to the skin, and the inside was soft. Perfect. She set the potato in a shallow bowl on the counter and broke it open with a knife slit and a quick two-handed pinch. A sprinkle of salt and a generous hunk of butter disappeared into the pouch.

Jo walked back over to the sofa, setting her bowl on the coffee table to give it a few minutes to cool. She leaned over and filled out a form with her business details and folded it around the carbon copies, tucking it all into the deposit envelope.

"Sweet Thing" played on.

She sang along softly, knowing the lyrics better than almost anyone. Already in her pajamas, she walked back over to the kitchen, set the envelope on the counter and started to boil water for tea. Taking a cup of spearmint tea to bed with her was a habit she had picked up from her mother. Jo liked to get to bed early so she had a couple of hours to read before falling asleep.

"Madame George" played on.

Jo sat back down and let her mind float to lofty dreams for the summer ahead. Picnics and bike rides. Jumping from high rocks into Stewart Lake. Tan cheeks and shoulders. Sundresses and ripe peaches. The album ended and the arm lifted, reached back, and started over again. She picked up the remaining salty potato skin, wet with butter, and loosely rolled it up.

"Astral Weeks" played on.

Leaning back on the sofa, she took a bite, holding the bowl under her chin. Her unfocused vision extended deep into the watercolor painting hanging above her little TV. Jo could feel the long prairie grasses, the wildflowers in gentle pastels. The warm breeze. The sun-dried earth.

May

9

Work-from-home days were much easier now that Chris had his paintings to keep him company. His spare bedroom had become a makeshift gallery, with canvases at various stages of completion propped against the walls. When he needed a break from email or documents, he could go add some details to a landscape, or simply admire his progress.

Chris had been keeping up with the weekly online painting modules, but he hadn't yet been to an in-person meeting. These classes were organized one Saturday a month at the lakefront park, and Chris had been traveling to a forestry trade convention during the last one. For these meet-ups, students could bring a painting to get tips or critiques, and exchange ideas with other students. So far, they had been working from photographs of mountain scenes provided by the instructor, but soon they would be painting from their own choice of vista or from their imagination.

Chris had loved art as a child but hadn't picked up a paintbrush in over twenty years. He found that he took to it easily, and felt the worries of his day slip away when he mixed a color to his liking and spun the bristles across the taut canvas. He was learning simple techniques to create quick shadows and reflections, always aware of the light source in each scene. His teacher was accepting and encouraging, cheering on the bravery needed to pull a big tree trunk into the foreground of an already perfect scene. Chris had to stay loose and not take himself too seriously. The snow that he overworked never quite looked like snow. An overwrought waterfall looked like a lace curtain.

The feedback from Chris's teacher had been phenomenal, and she strongly encouraged him to attend the next meet-up. She also wanted him to try a plein air watercolor class she was teaching in the summer. It felt funny they had never met in person. With all the communication they had, it felt like a true friendship forming.

Chris had not mentioned his new hobby to any of his friends, and when he invited dates back to his apartment, he always kept the spare bedroom door closed. The only comments from the outer world had come from his downstairs neighbor when he laughed about all the boxes in the vestibule.

"Sometimes it feels like Christmas down here, right?" the man had joked.

"Haha, yeah, it's like no one goes to real stores anymore," Chris responded.

"Right? We've all become hermits and preppers. Someday we'll just 3-D print this crap right in our own condos and truly never leave."

"Scary but true, bro." Chris was stalling until the man turned and left, telling Chris to take it easy. This was the first conversation he had had with any other resident the whole year. When he was sure he was alone, he gathered up as many boxes as he could carry and brought them upstairs, coming down again a few minutes later to retrieve the rest.

Now he was on his seventeenth landscape painting, and he had found an art store down the street to replenish his canvases and the paint colors he used most often. The errand forced him to explore another part of his neighborhood, and he had found a great coffee shop, too. He was feeling even more guilty for how seldom he visited his mother, since this hobby proved that he really did have some extra time.

Chris saw three, then seven, then ten alerts

pop up on his phone. "What the actual fuck," he sighed. Before he had a chance to read the messages, a call came in from Scott.

"Scott, hi. What's going on?"

"Oh, man, Chris, the shit is hitting the fan with this *New York Times* reporter. Now he's saying some FELL guy cut down an old growth redwood outside of Santa Cruz and the neighbors there are going ballistic."

"How is that even possible?" Chris asked, frustrated. "Wouldn't that tree have been on protected land? Our GPS should have caught that and prevented the job from going forward."

"Apparently, it was on private property but adjacent to a preservation area. The owner is saying he never approved FELL to cut down this particular tree."

"This is not good." Chris put his forehead on the kitchen counter and set the phone next to him so he could still hear Scott.

"Yeah, man. This is not good at all. I think one of us needs to get to Santa Cruz. Like soon."

Chris returned the phone to his ear and stood up straight. "I'll go. I need to talk to these guys in person and try to figure out if there's any truth to what this reporter is digging up. I swear to God I can't read one more email from our legal department dumping more ink to cover these mistakes."

"OK. Yeah. I know what you mean. I'll tell Jared you're heading to Santa Cruz. Thanks for handling this, man."

Chris hung up and sent a message to his assistant to book the flight and hotel. He opened up his calendar app. Best case scenario, he would be back on Sunday, meaning he'd miss the painting meet-up again this month. Chris wished he could tell his high school self that someday skipping school would be what feels like confinement.

10

"Oh, Carol! The bounty!" Jo exclaimed as she looked through the buckets of tulips at her back door. Carol Strand was one of her favorite and most prolific flower farmers, growing unbelievable beauty on a few acres just outside of town.

"I hope you can use them. The warm-up last week made everything pop all at once," Carol lamented.

"No, it's actually perfect timing. I know I can sell at least 500 stems this week, and I'll take an extra hundred because my teacher friend, Martie, is walking her first grade class over this afternoon for a field trip. The kids will like to take some flowers home." Jo ducked back inside to grab her checkbook while Carol counted stems.

"Any preference on color, Jo?" Carol called after her.

"An assortment works great. Customers will love it. Nothing says spring like a cacophony of boisterous tulips."

Carol began to transfer armloads of bright yellow, red, pink, orange, and white tulips to Jo's waiting buckets that were filled with fresh water. She held out a few bunches of pale yellow, scented double tulips for Jo to smell, and they both sighed in ecstasy.

"I've waited many months to smell that scent again, Carol. I don't know how you do it. They're more beautiful every year." Jo handed Carol a check and they thanked each other a few more times.

"Wait, I have one more special thing for you. It's my treat." Carol reached into the back of her van, stretching far inside until one foot lifted off the ground. "This is for you, dear. I appreciate all your business." She handed Jo six delicate stems of small purple tulips, the top edges forming gentle cornered peaks instead of the traditional rounded petals.

"Oh, my. Now this is magic," Jo gasped.

"Just for you, though, OK?" she made Jo promise.

"Just for me," she said, and smiled. "These will go right upstairs on my own kitchen table." The women said goodbye, and Jo hauled the heavy buckets inside to start working on cleaning stems. Most of the tulips went into her big walk-in cooler, but a few dozen flowers stayed in the front of the store for display. She separated out some of the more ripe, open tulips to use with the school children later that day. Carol had included a couple of bunches of red-and-white striped tulips, which the kids might enjoy seeing as Wisconsin Badger team colors.

Before Carol had arrived, Jo had been in the middle of filling three large vases for orders that had been called in by phone that morning. One birthday, one anniversary, and one pet death condolence. She had already created a flouncy base of light purple lilacs in each vase, and now she was able to add the pale yellow double tulips. She tucked in a few thin stems of tiny multi-flowered creamy narcissus blossoms, leaving them a bit longer to float a couple of inches above the other flowers. She set the cards in front of each bouquet, lining them up on a long oak table behind the counter. The tabletop was actually just an old five-panel door that she had found in the basement when she moved in. She had always meant to get a proper display table for completed bouquets, but the door had become a character in the store and now she couldn't part with it. Sometimes she hung her sweater from the door's handle.

After each order had been picked up and Jo got

everything ready for the first grade class, she saw that she still had an hour until they would arrive, so she headed next door for lunch. Of course, the first person she saw when she walked in was Grant.

"You. Me. Nine holes after work tonight. What do you say?" he asked, eyes hopeful.

Jo paused and stood in place for a beat too long. She could feel eyes on her, conversations seemed quieter, and in her peripheral vision, she could swear she saw Dagmar lean forward over the counter.

"Umm. Let me think about work stuff for a minute…I have a classroom of students coming in this afternoon so I might be a little behind," she answered as she walked to her stool at the counter, Grant following her like the wake of a boat.

"Sure, think it over. Looks to be a nice night. I was gonna go play anyway," he said, a little dejected as he returned to the kitchen.

Dagmar walked over to Jo to take her lunch order.

"Do you have any of that Swedish rye today, Dag?"

"Sure do, hon."

"OK, great, I'll have turkey and cheddar on rye. And a Coke, please."

"You got it," and she walked away, a little coldly.

An older couple sitting at the stools next to Jo seemed to be looking at her and she turned her head to them. They were smiling at Jo and she recognized them but couldn't think of their names.

"He's a handsome one, yes?" the woman said.

"Oh, do you mean Grant?" Jo asked.

"Yes. Nice young man."

"He is very nice, yes," Jo responded, a little confused at this interaction.

"And helpful, right?"

Jo laughed a little. "Yes, ma'am, and helpful."

"Seems like he's sweet on you, dear," the woman added.

"More than sweet!" her husband interjected. "I'd know that look he gave her a mile away."

The woman swatted her husband with a napkin and turned back to Jo. "You want babies, though, don't you, dear? Old women know these things.

Take it from me. That man would make a good father."

Jo put her hands over her face. Fortunately, Dagmar returned with her sandwich and Coke just in time.

"Maybe Jo thinks she's too good for Grant," Dagmar said, looking at the couple but not at Jo.

"Dag! How could you say such a thing! You know I adore your brother. He's a good friend and a very helpful employee. Gosh, I mean, last fall he used a bucket to catch a bat in my store while I was screaming and hiding in the flower cooler. I'm so grateful for Grant in so many ways!" Jo blurted out, feeling rattled.

"OK, Jo, calm down. We're just teasing you a little. Everyone just wants to see you happy," Dag said warmly.

"Thanks, Dag," responded Jo, as she bit into her sandwich, a little stunned by the content of the last few minutes. What she wanted to say was, "But I am happy."

11

Within hours of learning about the redwood incident, Chris was standing in the doorway of a gorgeous mid-century home at the end of a long cul-de-sac, a fingerling jutting into a lush state forest, only a quarter mile from sea cliffs along the Pacific Ocean. The flat, low, staggered rooflines and natural stonework left a visitor wondering where the home ended and the forest began.

"Look, I appreciate the personal visit on this thing, but I don't know how you think you can help make this right. Nothing can bring back that tree," the owner told him.

"I know that. But I want to do what I can. And I want to figure out how this happened so I can try to make sure it doesn't happen again," Chris pleaded. "Our lawyers would kill me if they knew I was speaking to you directly. But I was hoping we could figure this out man-to-man."

"Ha, funny you say that. It's my wife who is most upset." As if on cue, Chris could see a striking, lean woman, six feet tall, walking down the hallway towards them. "Here she comes. I guess she wants to talk to you, after all."

"Come in," the woman commanded. "You've traveled a long way today. Sit and have some coffee with us."

The next couple of hours were illuminating for Chris. He had never interacted with an end user of his software in this way before. Not making excuses, he described to the couple what he had seen in the photo record that was left by the FELL worker. It showed a browning of needles indicating a disease common to redwoods that could have spread to other trees. The couple listened and asked good questions. He told them FELL should have gotten another set of eyes on the situation before work commenced. Chris also took responsibility for the contract confusion. The language they had signed allowed for arborist discretion, and Chris promised that going forward, any work near redwood groves would require visual verification from both the property owner and the FELL corporate office.

The conversation went better than he had hoped, and the couple agreed that FELL would make a sizable donation to Forest of Nisene Marks State Park, which was basically in their backyard. Together, the three walked around their property and found the site of the lost tree. One six-foot section of the trunk was lying on the ground, still needing to be hauled away. Chris had a sorrowful feeling looking at what remained of this grandfather of the forest. They were all silent for a moment, hearing only the leaves rustling around them. Chris felt like they were part of the undercanopy themselves.

"Let us make you a table." he said calmly, breaking the spell.

"What?"

"It will take a while to dry this wood. Maybe a year in a solar kiln. But let us cut this into planks and make you a table."

The couple looked at each other and the woman spoke first, her eyes welling. "Our son is getting married next year. That would make a very special gift for them."

"OK, it's settled then," Chris said. "I'll make the arrangements this week."

With no contract violation, ample photographic evidence of a diseased tree, and no angry party, the reporter backed off the story quickly.

Chris should have taken this as a big win, but something was nagging at him. He was a tech guy, not a tree guy. But from what he had read on the issue, this tree could have been treated with a fungicide and probably survived. Of course, he hadn't mentioned this to the owners.

Chris had done a thorough job. He had followed up with Scott and Jared, the FELL legal team, the California State Parks foundation board, an artisan table maker in Santa Cruz, and even the company that would be hauling the trunk off the property. He didn't have his assistant make these calls; he made them himself. But he knew there was one more conversation he should have had, but didn't. And that was with the man who had held the chainsaw.

12

"My brother has a motorcycle," the little boy had told Jo, when she called on his raised hand to answer her question, which had been, "Does anyone know what we call this color?"

"Well, that's nice. I hope he wears a helmet. Anyway, does anyone else know what we call this color?" She held the bright green foliage higher so everyone could see. "It's a more special word than green."

"Lime?" a little girl called out.

"Oh, that's a very good word for it. The word I was thinking of is 'chartreuse.' It's a funny word, isn't it? Can everyone say chartreuse?"

Jo looked over at their teacher, Martie, and they

smiled at each other as the children loudly said many versions including "chew shoes." Martie had been one of Jo's first customers and friends when Jo moved to Mount Horeb, and soon after, the two of them had concocted this field trip as a fun afternoon each spring for her students. The tradition was to walk next door to Schubert's afterwards, and each child could have a root beer float. Martie had told Jo this field trip had become more popular than the trip to see the State Capitol in Madison.

"I enjoyed having you all visit my flower store today. Thank you for being ever so careful when I let you open the cash register drawer. I hope you learned some things about working in a store and some things about flowers as well. The last thing we will do today before you go is to make a little flower present for your fathers."

"My father!" the students shouted and laughed. "You mean mother!"

"Oh, no, I do mean father. Men love flowers very much, and they don't get them as gifts nearly as often as women. We should help them today, don't you think?"

"Yes!" Now the children cheered the idea.

"And if you don't have a father in your house, then maybe you have a brother or a special uncle. That person will be for you to decide in your own heart. Over on the long silver table, there is a jar for each of you. You can choose five tulips from these buckets. If we see any of you pushing your way to the front of the line, you will go straight to the back and have to wait all over again. Does everybody think they can walk with quiet feet?"

"Oh, yes," the students nodded solemnly, knowing it was a special privilege to make their own bouquet. Jo walked amongst the group and helped to snip stems and pull off cumbersome leaves as needed. Earlier in the presentation she had told them she once found a toad hiding in a tulip, and she saw many of the children looking deep inside the flowers as if they were testing the nose on a glass of wine in Napa Valley.

Jo noticed one very small child standing still by her empty jar. She hadn't yet gone over to the buckets to choose her tulips.

"Can I help you get started?" Jo bent down to talk eye-to-eye with her.

"It's just...I don't think my father would like to have flowers," the girl said shyly.

"Oh, why not? They're so colorful. Men and women both love flowers so much," Jo insisted. Martie noticed the conversation and sidled closer to the girl.

"Miss Jo, this is Mai Lor. She has just moved here from Wausau and this is her first week joining our class. We're all so glad to meet our new friend."

"Wausau! My goodness, I used to live in Wausau, too!" Jo stuck out her hand and Mai placed her small hand inside. They shook hands like true business partners and smiled at each other. "It is a real pleasure to meet you, Mai. I just know you will love it here in your new town."

"Miss Jo?" Mai looked down and wrung her hands tightly. "It's just that…well…my father doesn't see very well. Some bad people hurt him during the war and his eyes don't work very well. I don't think he will enjoy flowers at all."

Jo and Martie exchanged a quick glance. "Oh, Mai. Your dear heart. I'm so sorry to hear that."

"Should I just make flowers for my mother instead? I know we're running out of time now," Mai asked in a worried voice.

"I have an idea. Stay here, I'll be right back." Jo jogged to the back of the store and opened the door. She crossed the back parking lot and pulled open the fence to her garden. It wasn't much, less than a quarter acre, but she had worked hard to bring it back from the scrub land it had been when she bought the building. It had a long way to go, but the plants there helped her fill in some foliage and special little gems in bouquets, to go along with all of the flowers she bought from farmers.

Jo pushed aside an overgrown bridal veil spirea and found just what she was looking for. She bent down and quickly but gently extracted twenty stems of lily of the valley, each stem no thicker than a toothpick. The beautiful gentle scent filled the air around her. She was kicking herself for already selling the scented tulips, but this would do nicely. She included a few of the dark green leaves in her bundle and hustled back inside. Martie was helping the students clean up their table spaces and line up at the door.

"Mai! You have to smell this!" Jo called as she walked quickly over to Mai and her jar of water.

"Oh! That smells wonderful! And look at the cute little bells!" Mai squealed.

"Do you think your father will enjoy this?" Jo asked as she helped Mai cut the stems to just the right size for the jar.

"He will love it. Thank you, Miss Jo. I can't wait to give it to him." Mai looked up at her so sweetly.

"I have one more thing to add," said Jo, as she tucked three stems of furry gray foliage into the jar. "This is called lamb's ear. Can you believe that name?" They giggled conspiratorially. Mai touched the soft leaves like they were a favorite stuffed animal.

As the children said their thank-yous and waved goodbye, walking single file out the door and turning left to go to the diner, Martie hung back to chat with Jo for a moment.

"Oh my, you handled that well. I was honestly so shocked when she said her father was blind; I didn't know what to say. You did such a special thing for her. Thank you."

"Gosh, it's my pleasure. That poor family. What a precious child."

"It's so unusual to have a new addition to the class this late in the school year. I really knew nothing about her family yet," Martie added, with a hint of defensiveness. "OK, love, I better catch up with these monkeys! Let's take a walk or get dinner one of these days." Martie dashed off and snaked past the last few students out the door to catch up with the front of the line. Jo truly didn't know where teachers found their energy.

She herself felt like taking a nap and she had only been "the teacher" for an hour.

Grant, who must have realized Jo's portion of the field trip had come to an end, ducked his head just inside the screen door. Jo looked up when she heard the bell. He was holding a small jar of red tulips, as he had apparently been one student's choice of a special man.

"Hey there, any decision yet on that round of golf after work?"

Jo did admire his persistence. But she felt so tired. She had lots of flower work to catch up on. She didn't know if her golf pants were clean. She had chicken and vegetables in her Crock-Pot upstairs.

"Hmm," Jo considered all of this for a moment. It would be so easy to say no.

"Yes."

"Did you just say yes?" He looked confused.

"Grant. Yes. I would like to play nine holes with you after work. Can we meet at 5:00?"

"Five it is." Grant turned and walked back to the diner with a victorious swagger, tulips in hand like an Olympic torch.

13

The black pearl Peugeot RCZ hugged the long curving road along the shore of sparkling Lake Monona. Chris had taken this slightly longer route from Milwaukee to Madison so he could enjoy the skyline view across the water as he came into town. The low white Frank Lloyd Wright convention center grounding the shore in the distance was flanked seamlessly by swirling parking ramps. It was designed in an era when automobiles were the biceps of America. And yet the design was a timeless and elegant architectural dame.

Chris had allowed an extra hour to walk around the farmer's market on the Capitol Square before his painting class. When he had messaged his teacher to tell her he would be missing another meet-up, she suggested he attend the Madison location, which was only one week later, instead of waiting another month. Chris had always loved Madison, and his car was a joy to drive. It also seemed like a good way to ensure he wouldn't run into anyone he knew.

As Chris walked around the four long blocks, slowly dodging strollers and lines for the most popular booths, he admired the bright displays of tulips on the Capitol grounds. He wondered about the arborists and groundskeepers who were state employees, and how many of them had done side jobs with FELL. The grand oak trees, some from the Civil War era, looked healthy and valiant. Chris guessed the trees had been getting regular injections to help direct energy to trunk strength instead of new leaf growth, as well as x-rays, pest inspections, and careful pruning. Did the arborists take the same care in their side hustles as they did in their 9-5 jobs, where their livelihood, health insurance and pensions were at stake?

Chris's attention was pulled to a corner up ahead. He could hear shouting and saw two graphic pro-life posters held above a table just off the square. People had gathered on both sides of the issue. Chris looked away, and reached the next block, walking past farmers with piles of asparagus, boxes of rare morel mushrooms, and long fresh garlic scapes. Tables of jams, soaps and wool tempted the eye on the way to ready-to-eat items like cookies and cheese bread. A banjo player stood on the next corner, just before the Veterans for Peace booth. Radishes, peas, leeks and bedding plants started to give Chris ambitious ideas for his own small garden. But the only thing he bought was a chocolate croissant, in honor of his best friend, the Peugeot.

Chris stopped back at the car to get his painting and some supplies out of his trunk. He tucked a portable easel under one arm and walked over to the small park by the lake. He was a little early, but the group was starting to gather. Bikers and joggers sped by on the path behind him. Paddle boards and kayaks dotted the water in front of him.

"Are you Chris?" A tan, silver-haired woman of slight stature approached him with her hand outstretched. "I'm Sue."

"Yes, I am," he said and shook her hand. "It's great to finally meet you in person. I appreciate your letting me join the Madison class today." Chris noticed in her an uncanny resemblance to his mother, Eileen.

"Oh my God!" Chris exclaimed.

"Oh, dear, what is it?" Sue asked.

"I just realized why so many people were walking around the farmer's market with flowers. This is Mother's Day weekend!" He clasped his hand to his forehead.

"Well, yes," Sue laughed. "You might have noticed a few advertisements lately."

"Sue, one thing you will need to know about me is that I am an expert at ignoring what's right in front of me," Chris admitted.

"Ahh, don't sell yourself short. I see a keen eye in your paintings. You're not the first son or husband to forget Mother's Day. And there is still time. It's tomorrow," Sue assured him.

The next two hours were possibly the best of Chris's adult life. He made friends, he felt competent, he learned, and he laughed. The wispy clouds hung in the blue sky over the lake that afternoon like a dream.

On the drive back to Milwaukee, Chris called his mom and asked her to brunch.

14

"You're in early today, Jo. We don't usually see you for breakfast," Dagmar said curiously.

"Yes, I have two weddings to prep today and figured I'd better not break for lunch later," Jo explained.

"That must be for the Peterson wedding...and who else?"

"Do you know Heidi McMaren? She lives in Chicago now but is coming back to get married at St. Ignatius."

"Sure!" Dag said. "She was in Grant's class."

"I hope she likes her flowers. We had to arrange

everything over the phone," said Jo.

"How could she not? You always do a gorgeous job," Dag reassured her.

"Oh, gosh, sorry I'm talking your ear off and you're so busy. I'll have a ham and asparagus omelet and fried potatoes. You can skip the toast."

"You got it," said Dagmar as she refilled Jo's coffee.

Grant wasn't in the diner. He was up north on a week-long trip with friends fishing for steelhead trout. It had made for a busier week for Jo since she didn't have his help with deliveries, but Grant never took a vacation and she was excited for him. The men had rented a cabin and the weather looked good. Grant had been waiting for his new waders to come in the mail for weeks, and they arrived, miraculously, the day before the trip. He had put them on and strutted around the diner, handing out hot, freshly fried doughnuts like a man who had just won the lottery and was quitting his job. Jo laughed to herself now, thinking of his theatrics.

Jo finished her breakfast and set cash on the counter next to her plate, making sure to catch Dagmar's eye and wave goodbye. Walking back outside and turning towards her store, she couldn't make sense of what she saw next to her door. It looked like a tall white fishing net, about four feet wide, and it was moving back and forth ever so slightly. Jo stood and stared.

"Miss Jo?" a tiny voice called from behind the net, which Jo now realized was actually a mass of flowering branches propped up from behind by a woman and a little girl.

"Mai? Is that you?" Jo started to walk quickly towards them to help relieve them of the awkward balancing act.

"Yes, it's me! And this is my mother. She wanted to give you these plum branches," Mai said excitedly.

Jo turned to face Mai's mother, whose head was bowed, and introduced herself. The woman did not look up but said "thank you" in a quiet voice. Jo helped gather more of the branches, the light sweet scent filling in the space around them like a misty morning.

"My mother is still working hard to learn English. I am helping her. Her name is Paj. She cut these plum branches this morning from our farm to say thank you for your kindness. My daddy calls me a good plum." Mai held the door for Jo and Paj as they carried the branches into the store.

"You are indeed a good plum, dear Mai," Jo said as she gently ruffled the hood of Mai's windbreaker. Mai skipped in a circle around the store showing her mother all of her favorite areas.

Jo filled three large pottery crocks with water and set them by the front windows. Together they lifted all the branches into the crocks and untangled some of the pieces, making sure every stem was under the water line.

"I don't know what to say. This is the nicest surprise. I rarely get to see flowering plum branches, and this color is so delicate and feminine. I thought it was white but now that I'm closer, I can tell it's the lightest of pinks. Like the blush on a porcelain doll. Simply beautiful. My sincerest thank-you for the gift." Mai tucked her head close to her mother and quietly interpreted Jo's comments. Paj smiled broadly and quickly raised her eyes up to Jo before looking back down again.

Mai asked if she could see where the lilies of the valley were growing, and Jo walked with them outside into the back garden.

"These are almost done for the year. You can see the little bells aren't pure white anymore and the scent has all but disappeared." Jo pulled one out for Mai to smell.

Paj was walking around the garden and gently tugging overgrown vines out of the way of other plants, giving them needed space and sunlight. She was very careful to step around new sprouts. She bent down and pulled a plank of matted leaves off of a cluster of green hosta nubs, and used a strong stick to extract a pesky thistle from the wet soil.

"This garden needs a lot of work. I just haven't had much extra time the last few years," Jo apologized.

Paj whispered something to Mai. "My mother says she can help you."

"Really?" Jo asked.

"Yes, she would like to help. She can come once a week."

Turning to face Mai's mother now, Jo said, "If it's not too much trouble, I would love the help. This garden has been overwhelming for me."

Paj nodded enthusiastically. When they went back inside, Jo wrote some information on a piece of paper so Paj could think about it and talk to Mai's father, too. Jo wanted to pay Paj five dollars an hour for her time, which was what she paid Grant.

After Mai and Paj had left, Jo stood admiring the plum blossoms for a moment before she started her workday in earnest. She had a peaceful feeling and was glad for the connection with this new family in town. A flashing image came into her mind of a completed, thriving, beautiful garden. It took her breath away, and the sound in her ears was like a child holding a sparkler.

15

"Well, I just don't understand why they wouldn't have one more person working at the omelet station. That line was ridiculous. You had to wait twenty minutes, Chris. Unacceptable."

"Mom, it was no big deal," Chris put his lanky arm around her shoulder as they walked down the hallway to her apartment. "I'm just sorry I kept you waiting at the table while your food was getting cold."

"Oh, I was having a fine time, just watching all the families and cute little kids. But I felt bad because I'm the one who suggested we try that place, and I had no idea you would be stuck in omelet purgatory."

"Eggatory?" Chris joked. His mom laughed as she finally realized Chris hadn't minded at all.

Chris took Eileen's Styrofoam container of leftovers from her as she unlocked the door. He walked into her kitchen and put the box in the refrigerator while she hung her purse and coat in the closet. The Hoosier green glass vase full of purple tulips Chris had brought earlier cheered her small round table. During the time they were out at the restaurant, the flowers had opened up to reveal their saffron centers.

Chris stood frozen for a minute, his instinct being to say goodbye. But instead, he walked over to the couch and sat down. Eileen looked over at him while she washed her hands and asked if he wanted a glass of water.

"Sure, Mom. Thanks."

Eileen brought it over to him and sat down in a

small brocade chair next to the couch. "What a wonderful day this has been, Chris. Thank you. I know how busy you are."

"My pleasure, Mom. We should do this more often," Chris said generously.

"I know I make the other ladies jealous when my handsome son comes to visit."

"Ha, really? Just wait until I make you a paint..." Chris caught himself.

"What, honey?" Eileen asked and leaned forward to hear better.

Chris looked down at his hands around his glass of water. He took a drink. He set the glass on a coaster in front of him and inhaled slowly and deeply through his nose.

"A painting. I...I've been taking painting classes.

I'm getting pretty good. I could make you a painting sometime. I don't know if you have any open walls, it looks like you've decorated really well around here. But even something small for the bathroom or above a lightswitch," Chris rambled.

Eileen was quiet, listening to every word.

"A painting class."

"Yes, well, it's online. But they did have a meet-up and I went to that. I finally met the teacher in person, which was pretty funny. She reminds me of you."

"Chris. I don't know what to say. I'm proud of you, honey." Eileen spoke carefully. It was so rare for Chris to share any part of his life with her. "I am maybe feeling a little surprised, that's all."

"I admit I'm surprised as well," Chris said.

"Do you know how much time you spent drawing as a little boy? You would sit at the kitchen table while I made dinner and go through sketchbook after sketchbook drawing lizards and sharks with your colored pencils. There was a whole month you only drew giant squid." Eileen smiled, remembering. "Then in junior high you made your own comic books," she went on. "Those I never understood, but the artwork was incredible."

"Ahh, you must be referring to The Adventures of Fart Man and his trusty dog, Bean." Chris and Eileen laughed.

"Yes, dear, that was the one."

"Wow, I haven't thought about that stuff in a long time," Chris said. "I always did love art. It's been a big learning curve in this painting class, but it's coming pretty easily."

Eileen sat up straight as if she had felt a sparkler graze the small of her back.

"You OK, Mom?" Chris asked, concerned.

"Yes…I just…remembered something," and she stood up and walked to the bedroom. When she came back, she was carrying a narrow leather pouch, about ten inches long. She sat back down in her chair, cradling the item on her lap.

Neither of them spoke. Eileen handed the pouch to her son and he took it carefully. He looked up at her for permission to open it and she gave a small nod of affirmation.

Chris slowly untied the leather cords and pulled up the long flap. With two fingers he reached inside and gently grasped a tapered ebony handle.

"Damn, this is cool, Mom," he said as he pulled

out a paintbrush and held it vertically in front of him. "Where did you get this?"

Eileen took her time answering. She swallowed hard. "It was your father's."

"You're kidding! I didn't even know Dad painted. Holy cow. That's unreal." He studied the brush closer. It had definitely been used, but he could tell it had been cleaned and stored with great care. Chris didn't know what the bristles were made of, but he guessed it was animal fur and not synthetic.

"The size of this brush is really weird, actually. It has a strong point for fine detail work but the bristles have enough thickness around this root circle that you could paint large sections." Chris showed his mom by pressing on the base of the bristles and fanning them out. "I wonder what he used it for," he mused as he tucked the brush into the pouch and returned it to his mother.

"That's yours to keep, Chris. Please, take it. What would I do with it?" She looked down.

Chris could tell Eileen had become melancholy. There were days when she would talk about Bill in a lighthearted way and tell Chris stories, and there were other days when the topic just made her sad. His death was still relatively recent and Chris knew it had been very hard on her. She was missing him and still adjusting to living alone. Chris missed his Dad, too. In a way, he had been too busy to grieve. It was like he had put a note on that expense to pay it in the next fiscal year.

"Wow, thanks, Mom. Sure, I'll hang onto it. Nice to have something of Dad's."

"He'd love to know you were painting, honey."

Chris just nodded, afraid if he spoke, his voice would break. It had been a good day.

16

Jo set her foot on the bumper of her Citröen LN hatchback and leaned over to tie her golf shoe.

"You know, maybe one of these times you'll let me drive you. Kinda silly to keep taking separate cars," Grant rolled his eyes at her.

"I think this system works just fine," she said as she put her golf bag over her shoulder and closed the hatch.

"Your clubs barely fit in that car," Grant teased.

"They fit perfectly. I used the hypotenuse," Jo said in a mock professor voice.

This was the third week Grant and Jo had played

a round of golf together after work. The nerves and formality of the first night were long gone. They were evenly matched at the game and these nights had been fun.

"I'll just play from the men's tees tonight," Jo said. "Then we can talk more."

"Remember that water on hole five, though...you sure you want to deal with that?" Grant asked. "I've hit it in the drink every week."

Jo thought about the distance over the pond and wondered if she could do it.

"I've got a better idea," Grant offered. "What if we both hit from the ladies' tees tonight. I really don't need to lose more balls in that pond. Come on, let me, it will be fun."

Jo looked at him, kind of amazed by him, really. Not many men would be seen hitting from the red tees. "OK, Grant. Thanks. I guess we'll really have a fair match tonight! May the best man win."

"I could shoot a hundred and still be having a great time with you," Grant said, meaning it.

Jo blushed and didn't respond. She took out her persimmon driver and walked up to the tee box, bending down to stick her tee in the ground and set the ball on top. She heard a commotion behind the tee box and stood up to see a foursome of men had just gotten there. They were grumbling and shaking their heads in frustration.

"Is there a problem, fellas?" Grant called back to them. "What could be wrong on such a beautiful night for golf?"

"Yeah, nice night. We don't exactly feel like waiting tonight," one of the men shouted back.

Grant walked closer to the men's tees and responded more to them, but Jo couldn't hear what he said. She suspected the men were agitated because they didn't want to play behind a woman, assuming it would be slow. They probably thought they should be invited to go ahead, even though no one had even started.
Jo took a deep breath and two practice swings. She approached the ball and set her stance. She looked towards the hole and lined up her feet and hips. Her heart was beating out of her chest. She looked back one more time at the group and saw Grant quickly make the sign of the cross, while smirking and winking at her. She looked back down at the ball and took a swing.

"Well, boys, looks like she'll be out-driving me again today! Enjoy your round, folks." Grant jogged back up to the red tees and quickly took his shot, also far and straight down the middle. It rolled to a stop about three yards short of Jo's ball.

They didn't talk much for the first two holes. The collaborative focus was on efficiency and building a buffer of space between themselves and the group behind them. They walked quickly between shots and didn't agonize over putts. When they had rounded the dog leg of the third hole and the men were nowhere in sight, they resumed their normal relaxed pace and banter.

Grant walked up to his ball and held his iron straight out to point at the hole about 150 yards away.

"What, are you calling your shots now like Babe Ruth's homers?" Jo asked.

"A little confidence never hurt anyone." Grant winked at her and took his shot. She was starting to think this man had an eyelid tic.

"Suck sand, bitch!" Grant called as his ball flew high and far towards the bunker to the right of the green. Jo doubled over laughing, and then hastily took her next shot, which was equally errant.

About an hour later, Jo was standing on the ninth tee box, waiting for Grant to return from the vending machine in the woods with two cans of Pepsi. The breeze had picked up a touch and she bent down to pull a few blades of grass, flinging them up in the air to see the direction of the wind.

"All tied up and one hole to go, folks," Grant approached behind her, using his TV golf announcer voice. "Jo Martin is hoping to overcome her inconsistent drive today. Grant Morrison shocked the world on eight, sinking a putt from a different zip code to tie it up."

"Inconsistent? Me? That's the first good putt you've made all day!" Jo countered.

"They don't ask how, they just ask how many, my dear." Grant and Jo both laughed, thinking about his sloppy style and her boring, dependable shots. Grant cracked open her Pepsi and handed it to her.

"Thanks, Grant," and she took a long drink. "Say, I forgot to check in with you about next week. Are you on for the afternoon delivery route every day?"

"You bet. I'd appreciate the hours," he said as they walked the long par five to their next shots.

"I've been meaning to ask you," he continued. "What's going on with that…person working in your garden?"

Jo looked over at him, disappointed, and also knowing this conversation had been coming for a while.

"That person, Grant, is named Paj. She's the mother of a student I met during Martie's field trip. She's been a huge help."

"But. Do you pay her?"

"Yes, of course I pay her."

"How much?"

"None of your beeswax," Jo stepped up to her ball and whacked it without taking any practice swings. Straight and far, right down the middle of the fairway.

"Wow, good shot. Yeah, OK, you don't have to tell me. But I could do that work for you. You don't need her."

"She and her husband have farmed for their whole lives. She has an immense amount of knowledge and I'm learning a lot from her."

"How? Does she even speak English?" Grant asked, skeptically and angrily.

"Grant. I must say I don't love this conversation. If you have to know, Paj was shy at first but her English is actually pretty good, and her daughter helps interpret. We talk a lot while we're working back there, and I hope I'm helping with her English skills, too. It has to be so hard to be thrown into a new culture. Have you ever really thought about what that would be like?" Jo asked assertively.

"Yeah, Jo, for your information I don't love this conversation either. I'm just trying to protect you. There are a lot of men unemployed in this town, and no one likes to see Viet Cong taking our fucking jobs." Grant was mad now, but shook his head in regret. "Sorry, Jo. I'm really sorry. Forget I said that." Grant struck his ball with anger and it burned low and fast, bouncing just up to the edge of the green.

"How can you say that, Grant?" Jo stopped, set her bag on the ground and turned to face him. Grant took off his bag as well. The two golf bags formed armor between them.

"That family has suffered as much as any of us from that damn war. He fought AGAINST the commies, Grant, right alongside Americans. And he was blinded by shrapnel doing it. They are refugees, Grant. Don't you get that?" Jo was frustrated at his ignorance.

"Jo, look. I don't know why they're here. I don't know why that man was fighting. They look like VC and that's all I know. My younger brother went to Vietnam and never came home," Grant's voice caught. "That's all I know." Grant's eyes were wet. He picked up his bag and started walking to his ball.

Jo grabbed her bag and caught up to him, setting her hand on his shoulder. "Grant. I didn't know.

I'm so sorry." Jo was thinking about Dagmar, too, and their parents, who were often at the restaurant. Her chest felt tight with heartbreak for them.

They walked quietly for the rest of the hole. Grant held the pin for Jo's last putt, which was long and made.

"It's a tie," Grant said, and finally made eye contact again. "I guess we'll need a rematch."

"I guess we will," Jo said, bending to retrieve her ball from the hole.

They both looked back 500 yards to the start of the last hole. The group of men was still nowhere in sight.

"Just be careful, OK?" Grant said quietly. "I wouldn't want you to lose customers over this. Or worse."

"I understand what you're saying, Grant. But you need to try to understand me, too," Jo said gently. "This is a man who lived in Laos and was recruited by our very own CIA to fight. When America cleared out in '75, these guys had the ultimate target on their backs. That's why they're here."

"I don't need to hear all this, Jo."

"No, I think you do. And I want you to tell your family or anyone who will listen," Jo implored. "He gets no veteran's benefits. No G.I. Bill. He won't even be buried in a military grave someday. But someone's brother did come home because he fought for us. Now his wife and daughter have to somehow keep that house together, put food on the table, and survive in a strange land."

Grant was quiet as they walked to their cars. The walk felt very long.

"Let me get those for you," Grant said as he took Jo's clubs off her shoulder while she opened her hatchback.

"You have a nickname for this car yet?" he asked.

"You mean like Sandy Duncan?" Jo gave him a half smile.

"Yeah, she's white and small. So maybe snowball. Or Betty White." he suggested.

"It should be something French, like macaron. And how do you know it's a she?"

"Macaron? Keep working on it, Jo," and they both laughed.

As they said goodbye and walked around to their car doors, Grant turned and looked over his roof at Jo.

"Look, Jo," he said. "I don't know if seeing those people working in your garden will get any easier for me. But you make me want to try. You really do have a big heart."

"So do you, Grant," she said without hesitation. And for a few seconds they just looked at each other. Maybe for the first time in their lives, they were aware of the cool, navy blue, bottomless depth of the inner life of a friend. Realizing the never-ending match play of forgiveness.

June

17

The blank canvas, only the size of a legal pad, and the travel-sized paint compact fit snugly in his briefcase. Chris had tossed in an extra tube of Titanium White before heading to the airport. After the stress of his last few work trips, he hoped doing some painting in his hotel room at night would give him needed respite.

The FELL corporate retreat in Alta, Utah was usually three very long days of meetings and forced fun. Chris dreaded it every year, but employees could bring their families and make a small free vacation out of it, so Chris could never realistically suggest nixing the event. Chris had to admit the food at the lodge was great, and they poured strong drinks at the bar.

"Alright, guys. It's been real. I'm gonna head

upstairs and turn in," Chris told the gang of FELL staff who had taken over the lodge tavern.

"Already? What, do you have a girl up there waiting for you?" asked Jared, slurring his words slightly.

"Just been a long travel day. I'm ready to hit the hay," Chris replied.

"Whatever, Grandma. You're gonna miss the best part."

"Oh, I don't doubt it, buddy," Chris laughed and shook both of Jared's shoulders from behind, a little too forcefully.

Chris stepped onto the empty elevator and felt it spin slightly. It was probably for the best that he stopped drinking when he did. FELL shuttles were departing from the lodge at 8:00 a.m. for a group hike, and he would rather not have a pounding headache on top of that huge waste of his time in the morning.

He looked at his phone and saw a message from his mom: "Have a great time in Utah." Airplane emoji. Mountain emoji. Heart emoji. It was too late to write back. She didn't turn off sound alerts on her phone, inexplicably, and he might wake her up.

Chris unlocked his hotel room door and saw his still-packed bag on the bed. He hastily hung his clothes on hangers and put his dopp kit in the bathroom. He went into the kitchenette and drank a full glass of water, refilling it and carrying it over to the desk to use for rinsing brushes. He opened his briefcase and took out his painting supplies, setting the small canvas on a desktop easel he had unfolded. Chris fished around both bags looking for his zipper case of paint brushes.

"You've got to be kidding me," Chris said aloud,

frustrated as he searched the bags again. He flopped back on the bed, rubbing the heels of his hands into his eyes, remembering exactly where he had left the brushes in his condo. This lodge was in the middle of nowhere, even if any store was open at this hour, and even if he was sober enough to drive. Chris scanned the hotel room looking for anything he could use as a brush. Washcloths, a pen, Q-tips, a toothbrush. He unzipped the deep interior pocket of his briefcase and plunged his hand inside looking for a black comb he used to keep in there. His hand pushed into a tube of soft leather.

"Oh, my God," Chris started laughing hysterically. "The brush Mom gave me." He pulled it out and tossed it on the bed. He had forgotten he stuck it in his bag when he got into his car after brunch with Eileen. "Pretty funny, big guy," he said, looking up at the ceiling. "Send me a brush that's too special to use, right when I'm desperate for any shitty brush. I didn't know you were such a fan of irony."

Chris unlatched his small paint palette and surveyed his options. He squeezed some Titanium White into a glass and squirted in a blob of body lotion from the sample in the bathroom, along with a little water. He muddled these together with the end of a toothbrush. Dipping a washcloth in the glass, he began to paint the entire canvas with a sloppy coat of his homemade liquid white base. He used the edge of his library card from his wallet to scrape gently up and down the canvas, creating a perfectly smooth, prepped surface.

Chris started painting a mountain landscape. It was going to be a scene from his imagination, incorporating many elements from previous favorite paintings he had done. As he struggled to use his makeshift tools, his eyes kept wandering to the leather pouch on the bed. He knew the brush had been used before. What was he saving it for? He could make sure to rinse it out really well. Still, something was stopping him.

He went into the bathroom and started to take the toilet paper off a roll, thinking he could fray the end of the tube with his toenail clippers and make bristles. With the toilet paper wrapped around most of one arm and spilling to the floor, Chris flailed his body in exasperation, breaking free of the absurd idea. He marched over to the bed and whisked the brush from its sheath.

"You're mine now."

18

Jo smelled the rain through the screen door before she heard it. She looked up from her work towards the front of the store and could see the sidewalk starting to darken. She walked over to turn on a small table lamp next to the cash register. The store felt cozy and safe. Jo had been listening to the news on the radio, but turned the dial to music now. Sam Cooke, volume low, filled the room. The rain fell slightly harder and coated the windows.

"Paj!" Jo exclaimed, remembering she was working in the back garden today. Jo ran to open the back door and called across the parking lot.

"Paj? Are you back there? Come inside!" After a few seconds, Jo saw the gate open and a small drenched lady emerged.

"Oh dear! Come, come, let me get you a towel."

While Paj hurried inside, Jo ran upstairs to her apartment to grab three big soft bath towels.

"Here you go, honey. I was so lost in my thoughts I forgot you were working today," Jo said, helping Paj find a chair and warm up with the towels.

"It is fine. I like the rain," Paj responded. "It helps the ground be soft to dig."

"Well, hopefully this blows over soon, but please wait inside with me," Jo said as she walked back over to her prep table.

"That is very beautiful," Paj noticed.

"Oh, thank you. These are for a wedding anniversary party tomorrow. This couple is celebrating twenty-five years." Jo filled a large vase with delicate green penny cress and layers of wild indigo. She placed five swooping stems of periwinkle lupine around the base. Next came the peonies. Light pink, fuchsia, and white. Still slightly closed but as large as softballs, they would be opened perfectly in time for the party the next day, exploding their frilly centers obscenely. Jo was glad she had cut dozens of extra peonies before the rain and stored them in her cooler.

Jo filled in the gaps with a few more stems of lupine and some small round aubergine allium. The jewel tones sang together. She went to the cooler to pull out three delicate branches of small white flowers.

"What is that flower word?" Paj asked.

"This? Mock orange. Isn't it lovely?" and Jo walked the thin branches over to Paj so she could take in the special scent. "I buy this from a farmer named Kate. She never has very much but she brings me what she can each year."

"Mock orange," Paj repeated. "You have that in your garden. Did you know?" Paj said, excitedly.

"Mock orange? I have this?" Jo asked, incredulously.

"Yes! It was tangled in the lilacs, but I have given it more sun now. Next year you will have mock orange flowers. I promise."

"Well, Paj, that's the best news I've heard all day!" Jo said as she finished the arrangement and spun it slowly around to check for balance.

"Paj, I've always meant to ask you about Wausau. You know I lived there, too, for a few years after college. It is a nice town. Can I ask why you left?"

Jo looked up at Paj and saw her head was down. A towel was wrapped around her shoulders and she was shivering.

"Can I get you some coffee or tea? Are you freezing?" Jo asked, concerned.

"No, no, I'm fine. You've been too kind." Paj spread another towel over her jeans.

"Wausau is a nice town, you are right," Paj continued, looking sad and worried. "So many people help us. Mai's teachers help us. And the church. We learned English and stayed warm through the winters," Paj paused. "But it was very hard."

"I can't even imagine, Paj. Your family is so strong," Jo said, hoping that Paj would continue her story.

"My husband is a proud man. He has a bad time

with his eyes. But he still wants to do everything himself. He does not want his wife and daughter to have a burden. And he did not want to go to the church. He said we would betray our ancestors. But the church help save us."

"Did people in town feel bothered when you didn't go to church?" Jo asked, beginning to get an impression of their life in Wausau.

"Many people were always kind to us. But some people did not want us there," Paj continued. "A group of young men would follow us if we were in town and sing 'Three Blind Mice.'"

"Uggh. That's terrible, Paj. I'm sorry."

"My husband is a cheerful man. He didn't mind too much. When we are sad, he will make us happy. He knows we are the lucky ones. So many Hmong people are still waiting at the camp in Thailand. And so many have died. We are safe and we are together. 'Three Blind Mice' do not bother him."

"Well, that's an incredible attitude, Paj. He sounds like a special man and I hope I get to meet him sometime." Jo felt like she was still waiting to hear why they left Wausau, and was hoping the rain would continue a little longer.

The two women were quiet for a few minutes. Jo set the finished anniversary bouquet on the floor of the cooler and started working on the next orders. "Cherish," by The Association, was playing on the tinny radio.

"My husband. Sawm is his name. He liked to go outside and do some farming late at night. We had a small piece of land we rented. He went out to dig after dark. He liked the silence. He used his hands to feel the rows and place the saplings."

"That's amazing," Jo marveled.

"We could grow food. We could sell some vegetables. Mai was growing strong. It was a good new life," Paj said quietly, remembering.

Jo turned down the radio and stopped what she was doing. She turned to face Paj.

"At first, he thought it was raining. He heard the sound of rain. All around him. But then he heard footsteps and laughter."

Jo's heart sank.

"Sawm reached his arms out into the darkness, and felt something like pebbles falling on him. He called out but nobody answered."

"Oh, Paj. How terrifying."

"He heard people running away. They called out angry words as they left."

Paj wiped her eyes. Jo wondered if she had ever told anyone this story before. Jo walked over and sat in a chair next to her. She wanted to reach out to take her hand, but didn't know if that affection was customary for Hmong women. Jo felt helpless to comfort her.

Paj took a deep breath and continued. "Sawm reached his hand up to his face. He tasted salt. The men had poured salt over the soil. Over all the saplings. Over Sawm."

Jo gasped. She knew what salt did to soil. The crops were destroyed. The plot of land would be worthless, possibly for years to come.

"Mai and I were inside when this happened. We saw the damage in the morning. They had used salt made for melting ice. It was everywhere."

"Paj. What terrible, terrible men. I can't tell you how sorry I am that happened to you. I feel ashamed those people were part of your introduction to America," Jo said, angry and apologetic.

"Sawm is our hero. He made us understand we would survive. He always makes jokes. He is always our sunshine." Paj smiled.

"I'm so glad you and Mai have him."

"We went to Mai's teacher and Sawm asked to feel the map that hung in the classroom. Sawm felt all around Wisconsin and picked this town. Mount Horeb. He said it felt like home." Paj laughed, remembering their adventure just a few weeks earlier.

"A relief map! That is called a raised relief map. This part of the state was never flattened by the glacier long ago, so it is much more mountainous. Well, it's very hilly anyway," Jo explained.

"Relief. Yes, it was relief." Paj nodded.

"Paj. Thank you for sharing that difficult story with me. You can always talk to me. I think talking helps. I'm very glad your family is here now," Jo said warmly.

"Miss Jo, why did you leave Wausau?" Paj asked shyly.

The absurdity of that question made Jo have to stifle an ironic laugh. Was she to tell Paj that she had gotten divorced and was a tad embarrassed? That she didn't want to see her ex-husband at the grocery store? Jo felt like a spoiled teenager, thinking about the triviality of it now. Would she say, "Look Paj, I know you didn't have any way to grow food, but can you imagine trying to go on dates with men who might know my ex? What could be more humiliating, right?" Jo just shook her head and tried to think of what answer she could possibly give Paj.

"Well. I suppose I just had always heard Mount Horeb was a beautiful place full of kind people. I wanted to see for myself," Jo told her.

Paj smiled ear to ear. "It is better to choose to run to something good than run away from something bad."

Jo nodded in agreement, astounded at the strong woman standing in front of her.

"I can see the sun now!" Paj exclaimed.

"So can I," Jo agreed. Paj was looking at the front windows, and Jo was looking at Paj.

19

Chris blinked and sputtered as drops of water flicked onto his face from the hiker in front of him on the trail, who had just squirted water onto his own forehead to cool off. For the last hour, Chris had felt like he was driving behind a car with misaligned windshield washer spigots.

"About five more minutes to the overlook, gang," Scott called back to the group. "Everyone hanging in there?"

Grumbles of affirmation rolled through the sweaty staff.

The assistant director of marketing, Nicole, caught up to Chris and walked beside him, breathing hard from the hustle.

"Oh, hey, Nicole," Chris greeted her with a light tone. They had dated briefly, against company policy, a couple of years earlier. Chris still saw her as a liability.

"Hi, Chris," Nicole responded professionally, while keeping her eyes on the trail ahead. "I just wanted to touch base quickly about the silent auction tomorrow."

"Jared's handling everything in the event hall tomorrow, as far as I know," Chris responded.

"Yeah. Speaking of Jared," she rolled her eyes. "He basically dropped this in my lap, like, yesterday. I'm trying to pull this thing together but we need more items in the auction. So I'm asking everyone in the C-suite to donate something."

"Huh. Well this is the first I'm hearing about a silent auction," Chris said, annoyed.

Nicole sighed. "Right. It's last minute. Like I said." Her words were pointed and exasperated. "Let me catch you up, Chris. We're getting slammed online for having zero diversity in our arborists. My idea was to create some scholarships for students from underrepresented groups to enter arborist training programs," Nicole explained quickly.

"Not a bad idea."

"Yeah, it's fine, but of course cheapskate Jared wants the staff to fund it, and he isn't even doing any of the work to organize the auction."

"OK, Nicole. I get it. What do you need from me?"

"Just come up with something, anything, by tomorrow morning, to put in the silent auction. It could be a gift card, a weekend at your cottage."

"I don't have a cottage."

"NOT THE POINT, Chris. Just think of something that people would bid on. Got it?"

"OK, Nicole," Chris answered, but she was already gone, moving with urgency up the mountain to talk to the other executives.

Chris took out his phone and recorded a voice memo to himself as a reminder about the auction item. His first thought as Nicole was talking had been the painting in his hotel room. It turned out great. When he had woken up that morning, he realized he had finished it, and when he saw it in daylight he felt it was one of his best. He wondered if he could enter it in the auction anonymously.

Chris fell to the back of the pack and saw a small trail veering off to the left. He quietly stepped off the main path to find a place to pee while the group was at the destination vista a couple hundred yards ahead. The trail quickly revealed itself to be merely an animal path, possibly matted by deer or even rabbits. It was narrow and rocky. Chris kept walking, stepping carefully, until he found a place he was sure he couldn't be seen. He was approaching the side edge of the extreme drop-off, and because this wasn't a human trail, there was no railing. Chris stood behind a large tree, letting the urine flow downhill from his feet.

Zipping up his pants, Chris walked closer to the edge. He took out his phone and held it up to take a picture. Chris froze. His hands clenched the sides of the phone and began to shake. The flawless familiarity of the image on his screen made a dissonant chord vibrate in his ears. He slowly lowered his phone and steadied himself.

The view before him was the exact painting that was back in his hotel room, drying. The painting he had made from his imagination. Chris rubbed his eyes, bent over to put his hands on his knees, and shook his head like a wet dog. He stood up and looked at the view again. The sun and shadows on the mountains. The placement of the aspen trees. The river in the center of the valley, dry in three spots. The small field of amethyst lupine flowers.

It was identical. It was undeniable.

The shock was like he had walked into his childhood home as an adult, and every piece of furniture, every knickknack, and even his young parents were there.

"It's the heat. It's the heat. It's just the heat." Chris turned to look into the woods behind him. He could hear his staff in the distance. He looked again at the vista. "I must be remembering it wrong." But yet every detail he focused on, he could remember the conscious decision to add to his painting. He remembered mixing the colors. He remembered the pressure of the brush.

"OK, God, I don't know if you're trying to send me a message, but I hear you loud and clear. Pretty cool trick, Cochise." Chris grinned at the absurdity of life, and the suggestibility of the human brain. He was sure when he got back to the hotel room the actual painting would look nothing like this place.

"You look like you've seen a ghost," said Nicole when Chris caught up to the group at the top. Someone was passing around mini-doughnuts, and another person was organizing a group sun-salutation on a plateau.

"Ha, yeah, I walked off the trail to pee and got a little too close to the edge," Chris explained. "I might be dehydrated," he said as he opened his water bottle.

Nicole looked at him like he was a trifling loser she had no time for, her eyebrows cramped in disgust. Chris remembered her annoying baby talk, messy apartment, and night gas, and shared the sentiment. After draining his water bottle and slamming four mini-doughnuts, Chris felt like himself again. He laughed quietly, remembering his delusional brush with the beyond.

20

Mountain Ranges of the World. The Legacy of Vietnam. Illustrated History of Modern China. The "T" World Book Encyclopedia. Migrants of the Mountains.

"Whoa, that's quite an armload!" Martie whispered as she walked down the stacks to where Jo was standing.

"Oh, hi, Martie!" Jo said quietly, feeling embarrassed. "Are you enjoying summer vacation?" Jo tried to get the attention off the books.

"Oh, it's lovely. So far I've been sleeping and sunbathing!" she giggled. "Next week I'll start working at my dad's orchard for a few weeks, but not full days."

"That sounds perfect." She thought how great it was that Martie seemed to love the school year and the summer in equal amounts.

"Hey, Jo, I'm actually glad I ran into you. The men are off playing poker tonight and I thought I'd host a bridge game at my house. Can you come? You know Dagmar, she'll be there. And our other friend Nancy Miller."

"Oh, yes, I know Nancy. She has bought flowers a few times. Well…sure, why not?" Jo said, feeling flattered at the invitation. "I will warn you I'm not the best bridge player."

The librarian walked past and the women stopped talking. Martie mouthed "seven o'clock" and Jo gave her the thumbs up as they parted ways.

Jo walked over to a big table and spread out her books. She was determined to learn anything she could about Hmong history and culture. She wanted to know about the resettlement camp in Thailand, having only read a small article about it in the *New York Times* months before. She knew she would need to visit the main library in Madison, but today she wanted to look at the geography and at least get her bearings on the timeline.

She started to page through a coffee table book with full-page photos of mountain ranges. Some of them were so beautiful, they looked like paintings. The Rocky Mountains. The Andes. The Himalayas. Each photo was more stunning than the last. Jo lingered in the section about the Swiss Alps. One photo showed brown cows wearing bells being led by a boy down a mountain path. It made Jo smile. Another photo was the Chapel Bridge in Lucerne, its long railing overflowing with bright flower boxes, Mt. Pilatus in the distance. Jo stared at the bridge and felt a yearning. She had never been outside of the Midwest, let alone the country. But for some reason, as she looked at that photo, she felt like she could do it. She felt like she wanted to do it, very much. Someday. Lucerne?

Jo indulged her daydream for a moment and then got back to the task at hand. Later, the librarian helped her find more resources, additional newspaper articles stored on microfiche, and a detailed map of Laos. Jo spent hours learning, and eventually walked up to the counter with three of the most useful books to check out.

"Hang on," Jo said as the librarian imprinted Jo's library card and stamped each book with the due date. She ran over to the travel shelf and quickly back to the counter.

"This one, too," she said, and set *Fodor's Switzerland* on the pile.

21

Back in his hotel room after the dinner banquet, Chris mixed Prussian Blue and VanDyke Brown in a rinsed out plastic coffee pod. He added dots of white until he had the shade of gray he wanted. Like weathered cedar planks. Like an old dock. He turned to his painting and delicately added a small cabin to the base of the mountain. He stepped back to make sure the scale was correct. At the risk of adding too much, he etched a small path from the cabin door down to the river. Then he added a window box full of red flowers, so small that he made the effect with the tiniest of brush dots.

"Because even a manly mountain hermit dude loves flowers," Chris said aloud, feeling like the painting was complete now.

He stared at it awhile, imagining living in such a little house. Fishing every day. Seeing every star at night. He wondered if there were any souls that time forgot still living up in the mountains just a few miles away. No technology. No barcodes. No plastic clamshell containers to throw away after eating a piece of fruit, forcing an ephemeral moment to last for a thousand years in a landfill. No dating apps. No cloud storage plan other than rain. Chris felt weak with envy.

He grasped the painting carefully by the edges and took it into the bathroom. He held it under the hair dryer for many minutes, and would do the same in the morning. His plan was to carry it downstairs to the event hall early and set it on the silent auction table with no accompanying information. If someone bought it, Chris would arrange for the hotel staff to send it to them by mail in a couple of weeks after it had dried completely. He hoped he could accomplish all of this without anyone from FELL knowing he was the artist.

Chris woke up hours before his alarm. It was that difficult time of morning when he didn't know if he should try to fall back asleep or just start his day. He turned on the light next to the bed and made a cup of coffee. He felt a nervous anticipation surrounding the painting, and took a long look at it again. The resemblance to the vista on his hike was truly uncanny, but he had been so rattled in that moment, he failed to take a photo, so he couldn't compare in detail.

"What a strange coincidence that was," thought Chris. "Damn, right down to the lupine. What are the odds?"

He shrugged off the unsettled feeling again and took a long shower. He shaved carefully, thinking his razor might have been a useful painting tool. He got dressed and sat on the bed, realizing it was still way too early for the breakfast buffet to be open. He decided the time was now. He grasped the painting by the back of the frame and quietly left his room. The painting wasn't the first item on the auction table, as people must have placed some things the night before. He saw a gym subscription, a basket of gourmet spices, and a massage certificate. The long table was covered with a white tablecloth, down to the floor, and Chris found a metal serving tray to set under his still-wet painting. He wished he had thought to use his tabletop easel.

Chris hustled back to his room and made another cup of coffee. He paced, and couldn't believe he had just done that. He wondered if this would turn into a huge embarrassment. He needed to get out of there. He went outside to his rental car and started to drive to get McDonald's breakfast. But something made him drive right past it, a few more miles, and park at the trailhead where he had hiked the day before. Looking at the time, he knew he could get up and down the trail and back to the lodge before his first meeting at 9:00 a.m. He didn't have any water but it was still cool, and most of the path would be shaded.

Hiking as if he were being chased, he made it to the summit in half the time it had taken the group. At first he walked right past the animal trail, but found it easily on the way back down. Chris paused before he took his first step inside that tight woods. His heart hadn't slowed down yet after his rush to the top, and the blood flow was causing a ringing in his ears. He tried to breathe slowly and calm himself down. He wished he had some water and an Egg McMuffin in his stomach.

Slowly and carefully, Chris walked to the overlook, stepping intentionally to avoid slipping on rocks and roots. As he reached the clearing by the sheer edge, Chris had yet to look up from his feet, but he knew he had arrived as the light changed. He remained in place, looking down, eyes closed, as he counted his breaths. Through his nose, out his mouth. Through his nose, out his mouth.

When he finally worked up the courage to raise his head and open his eyes, what he saw made him fall to the ground and let out a guttural call of agony into the valley. The rocks dug into his knees and he raked his hands through his hair, keeling and swaying in confusion.

"Stop! Chris! Stop this!" he yelled at himself. "You're losing your fucking shit. Get it together." On his hands and knees, he looked up at the view again. The dove gray cottage. The path to the river. The window box with the red motherfucking flowers.

22

"So, Jo. My husband said he's seen you out at the golf course playing with Grant," Nancy said, looking over the top of her cards.

"Here we go," Dagmar laughed.

Bridge night had been fun. Martie had a warm home and good wine. Jo hadn't played too terribly so far, maybe even good enough to be invited back.

"Yes, we've been playing golf about once a week. He's hilarious. You should hear the things he says when he has a bad shot."

Martie and Nancy exchanged a glance. "And then what do you do after golf?" the women snickered.

"Oh, it's pretty salacious," Jo responded. "Usually I drive home, eat a baked potato, and go to bed. But not always!" She looked at the three women, and lowered her voice seductively. "Sometimes, I warm up a piece of lasagna and watch Cagney & Lacey."

They laughed. "Jo!" Martie said, frustrated. "What do we have to do to get you to go on a real date with Grant?"

"Hey," Jo said, "it's not that I don't want to date Grant. It's that I don't want to break up with Grant."

"Don't you wonder what it would be like to have sex with him?" Nancy asked, giggling.

"Oh, my word, Nancy," said his sister Dagmar, covering her face with her cards.

Jo laughed. "I will admit it has crossed my mind

once or twice. Sorry, Dag."

"See? So why do you have to worry about breaking up? You guys would be a perfect couple!"

"But relationships DO end. Most. Almost all will end," Jo said, more serious now.

"Wow, that sounds like a line straight out of a fairytale, Jo. I didn't know you were such a romantic!" Martie teased her.

"That is exactly why I kept my last name. You have to be your own woman," Dag interjected.

"Morrison is a good last name to keep," Jo said.

Martie flopped her arms on the table in front of her and faced Dagmar in a comically dramatic fashion. "Dagmar, my dear. Not to imply that you don't blaze the trail of the feminist sisterhood, but is it at all possible…maybe just a smidge possible…that you didn't want your name to be Dag Haag?" Martie cracked up laughing and so did the rest of them.

"Maybe ten percent was Dag Haag," Dag said, trying to speak through her laughter. "Ninety percent was Gloria Steinem, I swear."

"Sure, sure, Dag." Martie patted her arm. "Just let us know when to show up for your bra-burning-Tupperware-party combo." Still laughing, Martie stood up to cut a slice of strawberry pie for each lady, carrying the turquoise Fiestaware plates over to the table on a wood tray.

"Yum," said Jo, as she admired the shiny lattice crust.

"I hope it's good," said Martie. "I picked so many flats of berries this year, I don't know what to do with them."

"Well, anyway, Jo," said Nancy as the women began to eat, "you can't go into something thinking it will fail. I say give it a try. Grant is a good man."

Jo felt her chest tighten. She didn't want to disappoint them. But she didn't want to be dishonest. She felt claustrophobic. She didn't want to be watched and judged. She wanted to feel anonymous, for once. Her father had always told her, "Live simply and let others simply live." Why was that never the way?

Jo knew her brain was starting to overreact. These women meant well. They were her friends. So much of her defensiveness was due to her divorce, which they knew nothing about. She took a deep breath and tried to articulate something she didn't even quite understand herself.

"Look. It's just…this might sound weird or hard

to understand, but I feel like dating Grant is a luxury that I can't really afford." Jo tried to choose her words carefully.

"What in the heck does that mean?" Martie asked.

"He's a good friend and makes me laugh every day. If it ends, I lose that. I love eating at Schubert's. It's next door to my shop! If it ends, how could I go back there? Grant is a rock solid help for my store. He does almost all of my deliveries. If it ends, that ends, too. Who could I find to fill his shoes? Who could I depend on so unfailingly? We both like to golf. We might go bowling this winter. It's just so good. He is one of my favorite parts of my life."

The women looked at her, quiet now.

Jo went on. Now unafraid that she would say too much, speaking something aloud that she had never known before. "I love Grant. Like actually truly love him. It would be a loss too great."

That night, her friends did start to understand Jo a little better. What she had described sounded like a good marriage, in fact. One without sex or children, but a marriage nonetheless. In a small way, they envied it.

23

Chris hastily parked by the front door in the spot reserved for veterans. Bursting into the lobby, he ran down the long carpeted hallway to the event room. People were just beginning to gather for the morning activities, but no one was looking in his direction. He swiped the painting from its place on the auction table, ran back down the hallway and took the stairs up to his room. He threw the painting on the desk and collapsed on the bed. He brought his knees up to his chest and hugged his arms around them. Turning his head, he could see the brush, still soaking in a glass of water, a beam of sunlight striking the ebony handle. He picked up his phone.

"Mom, it's Chris. Call me back, please. As soon as possible." He set the phone facedown on his chest and closed his eyes. After a minute, he picked it up again and sent her a text. "Mom, I need to ask you about something. Call me."

Chris stood up and closed the curtains. He walked to the door and engaged the deadbolt. He called Eileen one more time. "Mom, I don't want to freak you out. I'm fine. I just need to ask you about this paintbrush you gave me on Mother's Day. You said it was Dad's. Just please call me as soon as you can," he paused. "It's kind of an emergency."

Chris stood up and walked to the desk, his brow furrowed in anger. "What are you doing to me, you piece of shit?" he said while holding the brush as it dripped water onto the carpet. Sloppily dunking it back into the water, Chris used it to make long wet strokes up and down his painting. Over and over he dunked the brush in water and dragged the stream down the canvas, colors blurring and washing away. Murky water ran down Chris's wrist and onto his shoes. Then he heard something crack, the jolt of sound breaking his destructive trance. He threw the painting to the ground and pulled open the draperies. What had been a perfectly sunny morning was now dark as dusk, thick sheets of rain battering the earth. He couldn't even see the mountain ridge in the distance.

An hour later, Chris was sitting in the Salt Lake City airport, waiting to fly standby on a flight back to Milwaukee. He had been lucky to arrive safely after speeding through the meandering mountain roads in the storm. He sat at the airport bar, jittery, sipping a Maker's Mark and Sprite. When he heard the boarding announcement, he used the remaining drink to wash down a Xanax, and left one more message for Eileen.

Landing in Milwaukee groggy and starving, Chris pulled his suitcase from the overhead bin and deplaned. Food and sleep were all he needed. He wanted to get back to his apartment and put this nightmare behind him. He had left the painting in the hotel room trash can, and the brush was in its leather pouch, inside of a hiking shoe, in his luggage. He had debated throwing it away or snapping it in half, but he decided his own mental problems didn't need to be the reason for destroying family mementos. He just needed to talk to his mom.

As he walked through the terminal on his way to the parking garage, he took out his phone and swiped it out of airplane mode. Three texts, one voicemail.

From Scott: Where R U? Did presentation solo. Hope you're OK.

From Nicole: you had one job

From Jared: WTF dude. Thanks for ditching. You better have an amazing excuse.

Chris played the voicemail, which came from a number he didn't recognize.

"Hello, this message is for Christopher Schwarz. You're listed as the primary contact for Eileen Schwarz. My name is Jill and I'm a nurse at Liberty Acres. I'm sorry to tell you your mother Eileen has suffered a stroke. She is in intensive care at St. Luke's Hospital. Please call me at this number with any questions. Thank you."

24

"What's with the envelope?" asked Dagmar, as Jo sat at the counter finishing her Reuben and potato chips.

"I…uh…just have some paperwork to drop off for my bookkeeper after lunch," Jo lied. The manila envelope sat to the left of her plate, the address covered by Jo's billfold.

"Hey, Jo," said Bill, coming up behind her. Jo flinched in her seat, startled. Bill was a regular customer. "Do you have time to do an apology bouquet today?"

"Sure, Bill, no problem. Do you want that delivered or will you be by the shop to pick it up later?"

"Delivered, please. Bonnie's at home. I'm in the dog house and I'm keeping my distance for a few hours."

"What'd ya do now, Bill? Criminy. Give that poor woman a break," joked Dagmar from the other end of the counter.

"Hey! I didn't do nothing! She gets worked up over the littlest things. Says I never clean up after myself."

"Well, is she right?" Dag asked.

Bill shrugged. "Maybe not to her standards, is all. Says she doesn't want wrenches on the bathroom counter and my work boots on the sofa."

"Make it a big one, Jo." Dag rolled her eyes at Bill.

Jo spun her stool around to face Bill. "What would be good for the card, Bill?"

"How about just 'I'm sorry. Love, Bill'?"

"That works. I'll go make it now and drop it off for Bonnie this afternoon."

"Thanks a lot, Jo," Bill said as he handed her a ten dollar bill.

"My pleasure," said Jo as she spun back around and handed the ten to Dagmar. She got her change, picked up the manila envelope and walked back to her store. Any time people asked her about flower orders when she was outside of the shop, there was always a risk she would forget the details. She thought it would probably be a good idea to start carrying a little notebook with her, since this seemed to be happening more often. She went right to the counter and filled out a card with Bill's message, and then opened the cooler to start making the bouquet.

"All done for the day, Miss Jo," called Paj from the back door.

"Thank you! I'll see you next week. Remember to take your cash envelope by the stairs."

"Thank you, Miss Jo. I will see you next week. I think Mai will come to help me."

Jo clapped excitedly. "Oh great! I miss her!" she said as Paj waved goodbye and shut the back door.

Jo filled a tall cylinder glass vase with twenty long stems of bright blue delphinium, each stem covered in dozens of blossoms. They were perfect with no other flowers or adornments. Bonnie would be pleased and these would last many days before dropping petals. Bonnie and Bill only lived about six blocks away, so Jo decided to walk the bouquet over. She balanced the vase between her elbow and body, Bill's card and manila envelope in her hand while she closed the front door and adjusted the "Will Return" clock with her other hand.

The walk was a little longer than she thought. The sun was high and Jo felt sweat on her brow as she stood on the wood porch. She was hoping the flowers hadn't been too stressed by the heat during the walk when Bonnie answered the door. "Delivery for Bonnie!" Jo smiled.

"Oh, hello, Jo! This is a pleasant surprise," Bonnie said as she took the vase from Jo. "My, my, these are beautiful."

Jo fumbled with the two envelopes and handed Bonnie her card. "Just change the water once a day and keep them out of direct sun, if you can."

"Will do, dear. Thank you!"

Jo walked back downtown, going an extra block

to the post office. Her heart was beating faster now. She had gotten a photo the week before, carefully filled out the forms, and had her birth certificate submission notarized. This was the last step. She pulled the blue handle on the mailbox opening with one hand, and held the envelope tightly with the other while she set it on the metal chute. She breathed in through her nose and out through her mouth. She closed her eyes tightly, feeling a slight breeze pick up. She released the envelope and pushed the blue handle closed. Despite hearing the soft landing of her envelope on the bed of other mail, she pulled the handle to tilt open the box again. The envelope was gone. Jo knew with a deep clarity that her life would never be the same. In a few weeks, she would have a passport.

July

July

25

The microwave beeped twice and Chris reached up to the open shelf to grab a white plate. He used one finger to quickly roll the nearly-scorched burrito onto the plate and carried it over to the coffee table in front of the sofa. Every day after work for two weeks, Chris had gone to the hospital to spend time with Eileen. She was out of intensive care and starting to do a few things on her own, but the stroke had taken so much from her, and recovery would be long. It was hard and confusing to see her so helpless. The first few nights had been the darkest because Eileen had not been able to swallow on her own. This was something in her advance directive that Eileen required in order to be kept alive. Chris held her hand for hours, willing her to swallow. He didn't know if his intensity of encouragement was a reflection of how badly he wanted her to survive, or merely because he didn't want to have to live with the fact that he stood by while his mother died of starvation. A few times in the last two weeks, he had been grateful he had no siblings. He alone could process the information, and he alone could make the decisions. But there were also a few times in the last two weeks when he would have given anything for a sibling.

The nurse at Liberty Acres had told Chris they didn't know how long Eileen had been on the floor next to her bed. Her friend Martha alerted the staff when she didn't show up for their card game, and they made the decision to enter her apartment. That was the part Chris couldn't think about. Everything else was just lists and check marks. He had gone to her apartment to sort through her bills and water plants. He tossed some food from her refrigerator and raised the temperature on the air conditioning. He talked to Liberty Acres about scheduling in-home nursing care for when she was back at her apartment, even though he had no sense yet of when that would happen.

Chris finished eating and walked into his painting room with a thick-bottomed glass of Macallan Single Malt, neat. He hadn't touched anything in there since he flew home from Salt Lake City. The brush in its leather pouch was on top of the bureau. His paintings were all dry now. His regular brushes were in the zipper pouch, still right where he had forgotten them on the windowsill. The room didn't feel spooked; it felt welcoming. Chris knew he had been dehydrated and drunk in Utah. He felt silly now, and was grateful he hadn't decided to destroy his dad's brush. He set his glass down and took the brush out of the pouch. He held it under a floor lamp bulb and looked at it closely. The ebony was beautiful. The curvature of the bristle mound was unique, and it had come clean easily.

Chris carried it over to his easel, where he set a

fresh canvas in landscape orientation, but then quickly turned vertically to portrait.

"No landscapes tonight," Chris chuckled. "Maybe no landscapes for awhile."

He sat down in the chair and took a long sip of Scotch.

"Nothing to fear, Chris. Just a brush. Just a canvas. Just paint. These are your friends. Think of something beautiful, and start."

26

"You sure you just want that cup of soup?" Dagmar asked.

"Yeah, I love hamburger barley."

"But is that enough? No cheese sandwich? Maybe a biscuit?"

"I wanted to save room because I saw on the board you have cherry cobbler today."

"Still warm!" Grant called out from the kitchen window.

"Yes, we do. You might not know this, but it's still warm."

"OK, great," Jo laughed. "I guess I'll take a piece

right now, then."

"Vanilla ice cream?"

"Of course."

Jo got back to reading her newspaper and finished her cup of soup. Dagmar set the cobbler down in front of her, with a slight nod of her head at the man standing next to Jo. Jo turned to him and realized he might need a seat, as the counter was full today.

"Oh! Would you like to sit down? I am basically done. I can just take this next door to eat. It's no problem!"

"No, ma'am. Awful kind of you to offer. I have a table back there," and he pointed to a booth along the wall. "My brother over there said you're the florist. I just stopped by the store and no one was there." He scratched his bald head and put his hands in his pockets.

"Oh, sorry, yes, just on my lunch break. Can I help you with something, though?" Jo asked, seeing her ice cream melting in her peripheral vision.

"Well, you see my mother just got home from the hospital." He lowered his voice and leaned in to add, "She had her last chemotherapy today."

"Goodness. I hope this is the beginning of a healthy new journey for her."

"Well, me, too. The doctors just don't know. I suppose they did what they could. My brother and I were hoping to send her some nice flowers today. She sure has been through a lot."

"Yes, I can do that. Just need to know where to deliver and what message you'd like on the card."

"Yes, ma'am. I'll draw you a map." He walked

to the end of the counter and took a paper placemat menu from the stack, and a pen from his lapel pocket. "We sure wish we could be there with her today, but we're just passing through on a route for Anheuser Busch. We'll be back in town next week."

Jo wondered why they couldn't stop by on their way through town, but it wasn't her business. Her job as a florist gave her a window into all sorts of family and relationship dynamics. She had learned to just do her job and not spend too much time playing soap opera writer in her mind.

"Just one thing," Jo stopped him. "Is she OK to come to the door? Sometimes flower deliveries and doorbell rings for sick people just disturb their sleep."

"My mother? Ha! You'll understand when you meet her. I just called her on the pay phone and she was ironing quilt squares. She said she had to go because her bread dough needed punching."

The man handed Jo the map. "I put the message for the card up at the top for ya."

Jo saw that it read, "To the best mom in the world. Save us some jam. We'll see you soon. Love, Mouse and Rat." She had to smile at these adult boys.

"It's out in Cambridge. So ya see, just take 92 to Lincoln Road, and then ya get over to A. Just don't miss the north on Highland," he said as he pointed to his pen scrawlings on the back of the menu.

"I...I just...I didn't know...hang on one second, can you?" Jo slid off her stool and walked to the back of the restaurant where she saw Grant going through receipts.

"Grant," Jo hissed quietly. "That man back there

just asked for a delivery to Cambridge today! It takes over an hour to get there. How much time do you have for a route today?"

"Shoot, Jo, I can only do the normal two hours today. I'm going fishing tonight with my midgie friends and picking everyone up in Sandy Duncan." Grant had once explained that he called these guys "midgie friends" because they had so many rum and Cokes that the midge flies on the river enjoyed drinking their hangover sweat. Jo never quite understood men, but enjoyed them nonetheless.

"OK, don't worry about it...how about you do the other deliveries and get back in time for fishing, and I can do this one. I'll just close up from two to four, and maybe stay open later tonight. I can't say no to this guy. He drew a whole map and everything. His mom has cancer." She too whispered the word.

"You sure, Jo? I can cancel. We can fish any old night."

"No, this will work. But thanks for offering, Grant. I'll have the rest of the flowers by the back door for you."

Jo walked back to confirm the details with "Mouse." She wanted to tell him she would have to charge him a little extra for the distance.

"Where did he go?" Jo asked Dagmar.

"He and his brother had to get rolling, but he left you this." Dagmar handed Jo a hundred dollar bill.

27

Chris woke up to hair across his mouth. A lot of it. A warm astringent feeling in his jaw and abdomen. His thighs lightly immobilized. Two hands pushing against his chest.

"Is that good?"

He didn't speak, just nodded his head. He opened his eyes to see alabaster skin, full breasts, long auburn hair, a shadow on a graceful collarbone. He lifted his arms to hold her waist. It seemed to be the last hour of night or the first hour of morning. He reached his thumb down to touch her. The first glow of lavender light passed over her shoulders. He lifted his thumb to his mouth and collected a pool of saliva on his tongue, returning the wetness to her, gliding it up and down. She leaned back and used one hand to brace herself against the mattress, looking away from him. He licked his thumb again and continued, his movements small and focused.

"Keep going. Keep."

Chris realized it was Doyle. The waitress. The day in the brew pub. More light entered the room now. With his free arm he reached around to hold her undulating ass, his hand overflowing. He couldn't last any longer and he came deep inside of her, his body shivering. She collapsed down onto him, her hair falling across his face and the pillow. Her soft breasts filled the space between them. He gently rolled her to his side, onto her back, and continued to touch her.

"That's OK. You don't…"

Chris took one of her legs and pulled it towards him, draping it over his knees. He could feel her foot flexing against his calf as he touched her.

She had pulled a sheet up to cover herself and he tugged it back down slowly. He licked and sucked her nipples, as the rest of morning arrived.

Later, standing in the kitchen with coffee, she asked him about his art.

"What do you mean?"

"Last night I got up for water and saw your paintings. The door was open. I hope it's OK I looked."

Chris didn't reassure her it was OK.

"You're quite the artist, Chris."

"Thank you."

"Even some DIY porn in there, huh?" she said with apprehension and a grin.

"What?"

"The woman. The redhead. Is that someone you know? It's a really beautiful portrait."

Chris set his coffee down and walked into the spare bedroom. On the easel was a finished painting of a naked woman, a thin wisteria sheet draped around her. Deep curves and glowing shadows. Her back was arched and her face was turned to the side, hair covering most of her features.

"No one I know. Just taking a break from painting landscapes." He saw the brush, soaking in a glass next to the easel. His jaw clenched and a wave of fear shot through him.

"Well, they're all really good."

"What day is it?" Chris asked in a monotone, looking at her like she was an apparition.

"Wednesday," she replied, looking back at him curiously.

Chris walked out of the room and Doyle followed him. He reached back to close the door.

"Right," she said. "Wednesday. Work day. Got it. I'll get dressed and head out."

Chris dumped out his coffee and stayed facing the window above the sink, arms braced on the counter. He lowered his head and counted breaths. In through the nose. He could hear Doyle gathering her things in the other room.

"OK, Chris," she said. He turned and she was standing by the front door grasping the handle. She was wearing jeans and a mint green tank top. He felt it was the first time he was seeing those clothes.

"Sorry if I did something wrong," she looked at

the floor as she spoke.

Chris turned back to face the window over the sink. He heard the door close behind her.

28

Lost. Truly lost. Every tree, every curve, every four-way stop looked alike. Jo pulled over to check her Gazetteer again. She was down to less than a quarter tank of gas. She compared the page in the map book where she thought she was to the drawing the son had given her in the diner. She couldn't find Hwy A and wondered if she had crossed into a different county. Now the least of her worries—the flowers—were probably melting in the back of the car. She turned up the A/C but it was weak, and the sun in the back from the west was more intense with every passing minute.

Jo decided to do what she should have done a half hour earlier. Stop for directions. She set the large flat of maps on the passenger seat and pulled back onto the road. Her dress felt damp in the small of her back. The hair around her temples was curling.

After about a mile, she came to a gravel driveway and she turned in slowly, tires crackling up a hill through dense woods. The drive wound majestically in switchbacks, bordered by elms and dogwood. The shaded edge of the road and rocky outcroppings were dashed with interesting ferns, and looked prehistoric. Through the trees in the distance she could see open fields of prairie grasses, dotted with sumac. Her excitement grew as she expected to see a mansion soon. And she felt relieved it would probably be a safe place to stop for directions.

After another minute, to her surprise, she came to a parking lot. Off to the right was a small white house with a wood porch and painted sign next to the door. It looked like a list of rules and Jo was getting the impression this was a private club. She parked and got out of the car to go read the sign. As she walked clear of another grove of trees to her left, she could see about twenty white campers and RVs. She heard voices, what sounded like radio music, and water splashing. In the distance, the sound of a lawnmower.

"Come on in, we'll get ya signed in, ma'am," a man called to Jo through the screen door. Jo walked up the three wooden steps and smiled at him as she went inside. He was shirtless, standing behind a desk with a cash register, and Jo was now pretty sure this was a campground. On the side of the room, snacks and pop bottles lined a cooler. Sandwiches wrapped in waxed paper, jars of cut melon and grapes, and chocolate bars on one shelf. Cartons of milk, beef jerky, and long whips of pulled mozzarella on another.

"Day pass, ma'am? That'll be six dollars," he said.

Jo turned to him and this was the moment she realized he wasn't just topless. He was bottomless. She stood, paralyzed. She looked at his face. She looked quickly down at the white hair coating his very round stomach. She looked at his face again and regained her composure.

"I'm lost. I was wondering if you could help me with directions." Jo set the hand-drawn map on the counter.

"Sure thing, let me take a look here," and he reached for a pair of glasses.

"Ahh, the Gableman house. You're not too far. Just go out from where you came and turn right. After about two miles, you'll see an orchard on your left. Start paying attention because Dave and Marie's house is just past there. They're on about ten acres and it's set way back from the road."

"Thank you very much," Jo said. "I'm so relieved I'm close." She picked up the map and turned to go.

"If you get to the service station, you've gone too far!" he called after her.

"Great, thanks. I need gas, too!" she laughed.

Standing on the wood porch outside, she turned to read the painted sign.

Maidenhair Fern Recreation Club

Please respect the rules of our small rustic nudist club, for people who desire an escape.

1. Register upon arrival.
2. Alcohol permitted in moderation. Illegal drugs will not be tolerated.
3. No sexual activities or propositions. This will result in immediate dismissal.
4. Physical contact limited to simple greetings.
5. No cameras allowed at any time.
6. Nudity is required for use of the pool. This is not a clothing optional club.
7. Showers are required.
8. Enjoy your day in peace and amity.

Jo sat down in the driver's seat and gave herself a look and a small laugh in the rear view mirror. She couldn't wait to tell Grant what she had accidentally stumbled upon. The sound of the mower approached to her left and when she looked over at the lawn, she could see that man was naked too, but for Nikes.

After parking in the beautifully landscaped turnaround at the Gableman house, Jo opened her hatchback and was thrilled to see the flowers still looked perfect. The fresh lemony scent of the light green bells of Ireland greeted her, the salmon lilies and textured yellow basketflowers were vibrant, and blue bachelor buttons added a regal touch. Pink cosmos reached and trailed around the bouquet in every direction. July's riot of color and vitality would be sure to give this mother a moment of joy.

Jo stood at the door and heard footsteps. She saw the curtain next to the door shift ever so slightly.

A beautiful older woman with paper-thin skin and high cheekbones opened the door.

"What do we have here?" she said warmly.

"Flowers for Marie."

"From whom?" she asked, tickled.

"Here is your card, ma'am," said Jo, maintaining the ruse that the delivery person hadn't read, let alone written, the card.

"I bet this is my boys," she said, putting her hand over her heart. Jo saw age spots and bruising, places on her arm where someone had worked hard to find a vein. The tone of her skin reminded Jo of her parents in their final months. Jo inhaled sharply and felt a burning sear behind her eyes. She exhaled slowly and looked down to suppress the tears.

"Bells of Ireland. I haven't seen these since I was a girl. What a treat this is." She leaned her face deep into the bouquet, inhaling with eyes closed.

"They're an old favorite of mine, too," Jo agreed.

"I'm surprised you found us, way out here."

"No problem at all. I had a good map."

"Oh, wonderful. A map is needed in these parts. I think the town skips a few road signs on purpose sometimes," the woman laughed. "Keeps it interesting."

Jo turned to leave with a smile and low wave.

"Enjoy your day now, dear. And thank you," the woman called after her.

Jo sat in her car at the Conoco station while the service attendant filled her tank with gas. Jo thought about her delivery. The house, the land, the woman. Jo had been around enough death to recognize it. To see it hanging like fog, even on a hot sunny day. She had a strong feeling that the woman did not have very much time left.

Jo paid the man and gave him a generous tip. She rolled up the window, put the car in drive, and saw him hold out a hand telling her to stop. He cleaned her windshields, even though that was not the reason for her tip. As she watched the water run down the window and the clear crisp rectangles form as he dragged the rubber blade across, she felt adrenaline start to flood her body.

The mother in the doorway had said, "Enjoy your day. Now. Dear."

Jo turned out of the service station and headed back to the Maidenhair Fern Recreation Club.

29

Chris took the stairs instead of the elevator up to Eileen's apartment after the care conference at Liberty Acres. Chris had brought Eileen home from the hospital that morning and gotten her settled in bed watching TV. The staff had been nice enough to hold the meeting the same day so he could work out the details for Eileen's coming needs. He stopped to catch his breath on the landing and looked down the stairs behind him. Hearing no one coming, he sat down on a step. It was dusty and echoey. He reached a hand across his neck to knead the opposite shoulder. He pushed both hands firmly across the tops of his thigh muscles. He bent over and put his head between his knees, twisting to stretch his obliques. Flashes of Doyle's body kept coming back to him. He wasn't sure what happened to him the night before, but he knew he didn't get much sleep.

Chris took out his phone and looked at the photo he had taken of the next quick painting he made after she left his condo. It looked like a page from a children's book about pirate ships. A wooden chest overflowed with ropes of gold, coins, emeralds and sapphires. A diamond-encrusted crown set atop.

"It was worth a shot," Chris said aloud, rolling his eyes.

Not able to delay the rest of the staircase any longer, Chris stood and made his way to Eileen's floor. Walking slowly down the carpeted hallway, he stopped to take a strawberry candy from a bowl a neighbor had set out by the door. As he unwrapped the green and red cellophane, he saw something shining on the floor down the hall towards Eileen's apartment. It looked like a pinhole of light from the floor below. He walked closer and realized it was just a new penny. He picked it up to set it on a small table by the nearest door.

"Ha, wait a minute, what am I doing? This is my treasure! I painted this, didn't I? I have a magic fucking paintbrush, right? That's what you think, Chris? Isn't it? Well, take your damn riches then, you all-powerful lunatic."

"There he is," the nurse Jill said as she opened Eileen's door and looked into the hallway. "I thought I heard something. We were wondering what happened to you."

"Sorry. I'm here," Chris said, tucking the shiny penny in his pocket. Jill held the door as he walked past her into his mom's apartment. Chris could see Jill had already rearranged some furniture to make things easier for Eileen, and set up a communication log on the kitchen counter for the various staff members who would be checking in during the day and night.

Jill gave Chris more information and made sure he had everyone's contact info. She eventually left to help another resident, and Chris stayed with Eileen for two more hours. She slept most of the time. Jill had indicated she would be back to help Eileen with eating dinner, but Chris still felt like he was abandoning her as he walked down the hallway back to the parking garage.

"Hey."

Chris turned to see Jill coming down an adjacent hallway carrying a clipboard.

"Oh, hey," Chris said, relieved to see her on her way back to Eileen.

"How are you hanging in there?" She stopped, letting the clipboard rest in one arm by her waist.

"Hmm. Hard to say. Kind of running on empty, to be honest."

"This is a tough time," she said, looking him directly in the eye.

"Yeah. Feels that way. Thanks so much for your help."

"Chris," she paused. He looked at her face, and noticed for the first time that she was very pretty. Not his usual type. Boyishly athletic and clean-scrubbed. Straight blonde hair in a low braid. He guessed she was about his age. She didn't flinch in his gaze.

"Can I give you some advice?" she asked.

"Always," he said, trying to be self-deprecating. But she didn't smile.

"This is a tough stretch. Really tough. This is not where you want to be on a Saturday. Or the next many Saturdays."

He looked at her, interested. Taken aback by her familiarity. She spoke as if she truly cared.

"But there's no route that goes around this mountain. There is no shortcut. And I've seen this play out enough times working here to know that any shortcut you attempt, you will regret when she's gone. And what I mean is a stronger word than regret."

Chris stayed quiet, his arms crossed in front of him, car keys dangling from one hand.

"Try to give yourself as few of those regrets as you possibly can. You might think you can't climb this mountain. But you can. You can do right by your mom."

Chris inhaled and chose his words. "I hear you. I appreciate it."

"OK. We'll talk again soon. Try to get some rest,"

she said as she walked quickly past him. She smelled like lemon.

Chris sat in the driver's seat and took a drink from the old coffee he had bought on the way to the hospital that morning. He looked at his phone and pressed "play" on a voicemail from Jared.

"Brooooooooooooo," Jared laughed. "I love making this phone call. Are you sitting down?" he laughed again. "We just got Q2 numbers back and sales are unreal. Looks like profit sharing will be in the eight figures this year. YOU get 10 million, and I get 10 million, and Scott gets 10 million," he shouted into the phone. "That emerald ash borer mutation in the Midwest has been PAYDIRT, BABY. Alright, man, go car shopping or get a hooker, I'll see you next week. By the way, are you ever gonna put in a full day at the office? Ha. Later, man."

Chris set his phone down and looked over at the red light of the fire alarm box on the wall of the parking garage. He stared for minutes, until his vision blurred. He turned his eyes back to the white wall in front of him. Only one word was in his mind: Emerald.

30

"Back so soon?"

"Yes, and thanks for the directions to the Gablemans' house. I found it."

"Are you a member of AANR?"

"What? No. What's that?"

"American Association of Nude Recreation. Just askin' because you'd get a buck off."

The man handed Jo her change and went over the rules. He spun a laminated map around and helped orient her to the features of the club.

"The pool house is about a hundred yards down the path behind us here," he pointed. "Then if you want to get out of the sun, we have a trail through the woods that goes around the perimeter of the property. It'll only take you about twenty minutes to walk the whole loop, but you don't want to miss it. Any questions off the bat?"

"Umm. No. I think I've got it. Thank you." Jo turned to leave as a young, naked, extremely tan couple walked in. Jo didn't know if naked was the right word, since the man was wearing a cowboy hat.

"Propane's out in village three, Tim," she heard them say.

Jo stood outside on the wood porch collecting her courage, and Tim called after her, "Fresh towels in the blue cart on the pool deck, ma'am!" Jo turned and nodded back at him.

Sitting on the toilet in one of the restroom stalls,

pretty sure she was alone in the pool house, Jo untied the belt of her green jersey cotton dress, crossed her arms and pulled the dress over her head. She folded it carefully and put it in her handbag. She snaked each sandaled foot out of her underwear and stuffed those in the folds of her dress. She had been surprised there was a men's room and a ladies' room, but appreciated the gesture, especially as a first-timer.

The two shower spigots faced each other, with only about a four-foot span, and Jo was grateful again she had the room to herself. As she stood under the shower, she thought about what it would be like if another woman were taking a shower there at the same time. Nothing very different from school gym class, she rationalized. And yet. She had a feeling she would think about this more later.

Dripping wet, she stood looking at herself in the full length mirror next to the doorless entryway to the pool. Sun on one side of her body, the darkness of the locker room on the other. The deep shadows highlighted her curves and imperfections. She looked like a grown woman, a fact that still took her by surprise sometimes. The chiaroscuro of middle age. She wished she had skipped the cherry cobbler as she looked at the small roundness of her abdomen. Her long wet braid was matted and flat, and she regretted not combing it out before taking a shower.

Looping her sandals over one finger, she held her purse and dug around looking for sunglasses, but realized she must have left them in the car.

"All in," she said aloud to herself.

Adjusting her posture and holding in her stomach, Jo inhaled and walked out of the pool house onto the hot concrete. Off to the right, a white arbor covered with hanging wisteria led the way to a shaded area with tables. She saw some groups playing cards. A few people had cans of beer. She continued straight, making no eye contact, and walked the length of one long side of the pool, finding an empty lounge chair. She set her bag down and took a towel from the bin, unfurling it on the chair ungracefully. When Jo sat down and realized no one was watching her, she finally exhaled.

After about thirty minutes of sunbathing, alternating between paging through a *Reader's Digest* and sneaking glances at other people, Jo was getting very hot. In just that short time, she had released any feelings of arousal or exhibitionism. In fact, as more time passed, the club seemed to be one of the more asexual settings she had ever visited. Enjoying the pool that day were people of every body type, ranging in age from 20 to 90. A man walked past her who looked like he had recently lost hundreds of pounds, skin hanging slack around his strong body. A woman with one breast sat next to Jo working on a crossword puzzle. There was no perfection, no lurid glances, only acceptance and joy. Survivors, all. The only detail that made Jo feel different was her tan lines, forming the outline of a one-piece swimsuit. It definitely gave her away as a novice. But she realized she was more self-conscious in regular clothes at the grocery store than she was here. It felt revolutionary.

Jo set the *Reader's Digest* on the small glass table next to her chair. She stood, again ungracefully, wondering if the towel folds had made marks on her skin. About ten people were in the pool, swimming and chatting. She walked over to the pool edge, and in what felt like the most ridiculous moment of her life, turned her butt to these strangers and used the metal ladder to descend into the pool. She laughed quietly and shook her head.

But then. Euphoria.

Jo spent the rest of the late afternoon and sun-kissed evening at the pool. She walked the wooded trail in her sandals, and wondered how she had made it thirty-eight whole years, as a mammal, having never walked in a forest naked. Now, that seemed to be the absurdity, not this. After showering again and getting back in the pool, Jo was comfortable making more eye contact and saying hello.

"Will you be at the car show next weekend?" a woman had asked her.

"Oh, uh, I don't know about the car show."

"You can pick up a flyer at the front desk on your way out if you want. It's always a fun day. But if you come, just remember it's a potluck."

"OK. Will do," Jo responded, thinking about how food planning was an unrelenting chore in life, even for free spirits. She didn't guess she would ever be back to the club, let alone for a car show, but it was still fun to think about this community. She overheard conversations about bike rides and volleyball. She had learned some of the campers stayed for the entire summer, closing out the season with an evening bonfire in September before driving back to all parts of the country. The club seemed like a hidden utopia, and Jo felt welcomed.

Jo stood by an orange beverage cooler, the kind they have on the sidelines of football games, dispensing lemonade into a paper cup. She drank it while looking out over the waning crowd. The sun was low and sparkling over the top of the pool water. She bent down to fill another paper cup. Any worries of grace or holding in her stomach had slipped away hours before. The feeling of anonymity at this place had been exhilarating. She watched as the last few people climbed out of the pool and went to dry off.

Jo knew she had time for one more dip, and then she too would head home so she would have some light left for driving.

She lowered herself down into the pool, not using the ladder this time. She went all the way under and pushed off the edge, revolving her body in barrel rolls, back arching and arms at her sides. She came up for air and went down again, tucking her legs in for a backwards somersault. Her eye caught a shiny penny on the deeper end of the pool floor. She used a breast stroke motion and frog leg kicks to propel herself to the penny, water pressure tight on her ears. As she picked up the penny, it floated briefly out of her grasp. She reached for it again, holding it more securely this time, as she felt her braid come undone. Hair swirled around her as she played for a stolen moment in the dying beams of light.

August

31

Remembering the service would be spotty during the second half of the hike, Chris checked his phone as he slowed on the trail and replied to a text from Scott. He saw another text come in from Doyle and decided to delete and block her number. He called the Liberty Acres nurse's station hoping to leave a message.

"Liberty Acres, Jill speaking." *Fuck.*

"Hey, Jill, this is Chris Schwarz calling."

"Hi, Chris. I just left your mom, actually. She's doing well. I've got her set up listening to an audiobook at the moment."

"Oh, great, thanks. That's good to hear. I'm just calling to let you all know I have to go out of town for work for a couple days."

"OK. Should be fine here. Eileen has PT coming in during the mornings this week and OT in the afternoons. Everything is covered for meals and bathing. I'll just be in touch if anything comes up."

"Thanks. I appreciate it."

"You sound out of breath," Jill said, with a hint of a smile.

"Yeah, I guess I've just been running around packing."

"OK. Well, everything is being handled here." Her tone indicated she needed to get back to work.

They hung up and Chris continued his ascent. It bothered him that Jill seemed to be able to see right through him.

Chris had flown back to Utah to try to shake the absurd notion about the paintbrush once and for all. His loss of grasp on reality had started to affect his life at work, with his mother, and obviously in the bedroom. He needed to snap out of it.

Once again, Chris reached the terminal overlook having missed the small trail entrance, and had to retrace his steps to try to find it. Walking slowly and looking carefully, he couldn't locate any path into the woods. The underbrush was much more overgrown than it had been in June, but he didn't see any opening at all. Sweat poured down his back. Chris took a long drink from his water bottle, determined to do this hydrated and sober.

Chris turned and walked back up the trail, even slower this time, searching for any break in the forest. He reached a small bend in the path and saw matted grass that formed a plausible opening. He thought he recognized the rock formations as he stepped with difficulty into the woods. He ducked his head slightly and squinted, putting his arms out in front of him to bend branches out of his way.

After a few minutes he reached the clearing and was sure he recognized the tree he had peed against. Shaking leaves and clinging vines off his shirt, he slowly approached the edge.

"Ha. Not even close," he laughed, relieved. He looked over the valley and saw a dry river bed. No flowers, no aspen trees, only drought-stricken pines, and what looked like a small electrical substation. He could see a green soda bottle in the rocks next to the riverbed. It was nothing like any painting he had ever made. No cottage, no flower box. No utopian mountain man. Not by a long shot.

Feeling saner than he had in months, Chris hacked his way back through the woods to the main trail and headed back down to the parking lot. He drained his water bottle while standing by the car. Feeling famished and elated, he drove directly to dinner at a pizza place he had seen when he came into town. Candlelit red-and-white checkered tablecloths, Italian music, and great smells greeted him as he waited to be seated.

"Just one?"

"Yeah, just me tonight."

"Right this way."

Chris was seated at a table for four, and the waitress quickly brought a basket of bread and removed the other three placemats.

"Anything to drink?" she asked.

"Sure. A house red would be good, thanks."

"Cabernet OK? Glass or bottle."

Chris nodded. "Bottle."

Chris drank his wine and looked at the menu. Everything looked amazing. He was feeling renewed and finally free of his mental albatross. Ravioli, lasagna, chicken parmesan—it all sounded delicious.

He expected the waitress to come back to get his order soon, but instead the host walked over to his table.

"Hi, how are you enjoying your wine, sir?"

"Uh, fine," Chris answered, slightly annoyed.

"I'm sorry about this, but I was wondering if I could move you to that smaller table over there," he said, pointing to a table for two by the front door. "We have a big group that just arrived and we'd like to push these tables together for them."

Chris stared at him, slightly incredulous. Eating alone was already something that moved the needle on the humiliation meter, but he had never been bumped before.

"Oh, sure, no problem," Chris responded politely, knowing there was really no other option. He watched as the host gathered up the basket of bread and bottle of wine to carry to the new table. He didn't want to look at the faces of the patrons sitting around him, feeling like he had stepped into a middle school lunchroom movie scene.

"Actually, hang on," Chris stopped him. "Do you serve food at the bar?"

"We do. Would that be preferable?"

Chris nodded and carried the menu and his glass

over to a leather stool at the bar. He sat down and made eye contact with the bartender, glad to have his back turned to everyone else.

"Looks like you've got your drink all set for now. Can I bring you something to eat?" the bartender asked kindly.

"Yeah, thanks. I'm thinking the fourteen-inch sausage pizza sounds good."

"Perfect. I'll put that right in for you."

Chris looked over his shoulder to see the party of ten now seated behind him. A few wrapped presents were stacked at one end of the table next to an older couple. Men and women of various ages were laughing and talking. One woman held a baby on her lap. Two waiters were filling waters and taking drink orders.

Chris filled his wine glass again and the bartender

set the pizza in front of him with a smaller white plate and utensil set. Chris pulled the first piece away from the pie. The thick cheese was gooey and pliant, sauce steaming through the strings. He folded it in half and took a huge bite. The blistered bubbly crust was chewy but crispy on the bottom. He congratulated himself for ordering well. The noise from the party behind him had grown louder. Other tables in the restaurant had also filled up, and the place was ringing with energy and familial exuberance.

Chris poured another glass of wine and ate more pizza. He was knocked slightly in the shoulder blade as a couple walked past side by side behind him. His throat started to feel dry as he tried to swallow. The pulsing force of togetherness around him grew stronger and pushed his solitary spirit into a smaller and smaller space. A space with no oxygen. Chris finished his pizza, washing it down with the last of his wine and signaled for the check. A man at the party table behind him let out a sudden booming laugh that cut through the room. Chris startled in his seat.

Chris put three twenties on the bar and stood to leave.

"Hey, man, you OK to drive?"

Chris's chest felt tight and his face was hot with embarrassment. He couldn't speak. His gut pain was searing on the right side of his body from the greasy cheese. He pretended he didn't hear the bartender, walked outside into the sweltering night, and drove back to his hotel.

32

"Dag? Can you hear me?"

"Jo, is that you? Guys, it's Jo calling! Shhh. Grant, it's Jo!"

Jo smiled, about to tear up hearing her friend's voice. It had been a very long day. Two days, really.

"Yes! I'm in Zurich. Can you believe it?"

"You did it, lady! How was the flight? SHHHH guys, come on."

"It was just fine. No hiccups so far. I'm just trying to stay awake now. I still have a train ride to Lucerne in about an hour and then I can check into my hotel and finally sleep."

"What time is it there?"

"It's 3:00 p.m. I made the mistake of taking a little boat tour when I arrived and the rocking almost put me right to sleep. I had to do jumping jacks when I got off the boat."

Dag laughed. "Oh, my gosh, Jo. I still can't believe you're doing this. Now be safe, do you promise me? We can't wait to hear all about it when you get home. Say hi, everybody!"

Jo could hear a whole gang shouting in the background and it warmed her heart before hanging up the phone in the cafe lobby. Even though the suffocating feeling she sometimes had in her small town was part of the reason she was taking this trip, she missed them all already. She handed the restaurant host Swiss francs equal to about ten US dollars, which they had agreed upon for the favor of placing an international call.

"*Danke*," Jo said and held up her finger, indicating she would like a table for one. He escorted her to a small table outside on the patio by the Limmat River. Just needing to stall a bit before her train, she ordered a glass of Riesling, quickly realizing her waiter spoke perfect English.

"Can I bring you some bread, miss? Or pastry?"

"Yes, bread would be wonderful, thank you."

"American?"

"Me?" Jo chuckled, knowing full well it was obvious. "Yes, I'm American."

"I have been there. To New York City," he said.

"Oh! How exciting. I've actually never been to New York myself!"

"Next I want to go to California. I want to meet Gidget."

"Good choice," Jo laughed. The waiter left and Jo looked out at the boats on the water. She had explored the old town area for a couple hours after arriving from the airport and was already in love with Switzerland. She had climbed up a narrow winding staircase of the Grossmünster church tower and gotten a panoramic view of the city. She really wasn't sure yet if she was dreaming.

The waiter set down her glass of wine and a plate of bread with a little pot of butter. The weather was warm and calm. Jo felt so content and comfortable, she wished she had more time before departing for Lucerne. A dark-haired man seated to her left wearing a suit and tie stood up quickly and swatted his napkin at her table, dismissing a honeybee. Jo was startled and the man apologized.

"The bees, I am so sorry. It is the only problem with this summer."

"Thank you," Jo said, realizing he must have overheard her speaking English.

"Did I hear you say you are American? On holiday?" he asked.

"Yes. Just taking a vacation."

"Long way to travel, no? What part of the United States?"

"Hmm…I live a couple hours north of Chicago," Jo replied, not sure how to describe Mount Horeb in a general context.

"Ahh, yes, I have done work in Chicago. Also in San Antonio. I like America. Will you be staying long in Switzerland?"

"Just one week, but I hope to see a lot."

"Only a week! Yes, I have heard Americans take

such short holidays."

"Haha, yes our bosses do not like to let us go very long."

"Is your boss very demanding?" he asked.

"My boss is actually quite nice," she replied, smiling to herself.

"Well, I would like to thank him for letting you free for one week so I could meet you. To your boss!" He held up his glass to toast and Jo reached hers between the tables to meet it.

"Yes, to my boss! Cheers." Jo and the man turned back to face the river. Jo started to butter a piece of bread.

"Pardon my interruption again. Might I ask if you have dinner plans this evening? It would be my great pleasure to help you with ideas for your upcoming week. I know Switzerland very well. And of course I would enjoy the company of such a worldly bon vivant."

Jo took another sip of wine and kept her eyes on the river, shocked and flattered, but cautious. Her nostrils flared trying to suppress a laugh that he had called her worldly. She wondered if it would be smart to end the conversation and take her leave. But then again, he was incredibly handsome and she enjoyed the low timbre of his voice. He smelled like aftershave and sunshine.

"I apologize for my English skills," he said.

"Your English is perfect! What do you mean?" she looked at him, surprised.

"Oh, no, not at all. I struggle to find the right word. English is my fifth language."

"Did you say fifth? What are the other four?"

"German, French, and Italian, of course. And I lived in Amsterdam for a year, so also Dutch."

"That's amazing. Who needs Esperanto when you know them all!" He looked at her blankly, not understanding her joke.

"Well. Let's see. I do like dinner. But I don't know the first thing about you," Jo said, turning in her chair to face him fully now.

"My name is Micha. I am pleased to make your acquaintance." He held out his hand.

"I'm Jo," she said, reaching to shake his hand. His skin was warm and dry, his grasp strong.

"Oh no, what am I thinking!" she exclaimed. "I am leaving for Lucerne this afternoon. I won't be back in Zurich until next weekend. Back Saturday and flying home on Sunday."

"Can I take you out to dinner next Saturday on your final night? It would be my absolute pleasure."

"OK, yes. Perfect. I can tell you all about my week. I would have to meet you in a public place. For safety."

"I understand. Let's meet here at 7:00 p.m. and we can walk to one of my favorite restaurants."

"I like that plan." She smiled at him, wondering if he would really be here next week, and knowing it didn't matter.

"Oh!" he put his head in his hands and looked distressed. "This is terrible. I just remembered next Saturday is my birthday."

"Your birthday?"

"Yes, and I'm so sorry my mother always makes

a big dinner and I will be there with my brothers that evening. My sincere apologies."

"Oh, please don't worry. I understand!"

"Tell me where you will be during the week. Maybe I could meet you."

"Let's see. I will spend three nights in Lucerne. Then on to Interlaken on Wednesday. Thursday and Friday I will be in Bern."

"You will have an enchanting week! That is a very nice route. I imagine you are taking the Golden Pass scenic train?"

"Yes, exactly," Jo said as she reached into her backpack and pulled out her train pass to show him.

"Actually, I won a design competition a few years ago in Interlaken and I have been meaning to get down there to check on it. Can I meet you there for dinner Wednesday? 7:00 p.m.?"

"OK, yes. That would be fun. I'm staying at a place called Balmer's."

"A classic! I will meet you in the Balmer's biergarten at 7:00 p.m. and we can walk to find a delicious dinner. I can hear all about your adventures thus far."

"We have a plan," Jo smiled to herself at the absurdity of the idea that this man would take a two-hour train ride to meet a stranger for dinner. But she was enjoying playing along as if it would happen.

"Can I ask what you design?" Jo inquired.

"Gardens. I'm a landscape architect." He pointed across the river to a set of terraced steps and benches, with a fountain surrounded by planters full of verbena and geraniums. "That is one of my designs, actually. It was another competition last year."

Jo was speechless. He set money on his table and stood up to leave. "Lovely Jo, until we meet again." He bowed slightly at the waist and turned to go. Jo watched him walk across the restaurant's cobblestone path, cross the street, and drive away on a Vespa, powder blue with a leather seat. Jo was sure she would never see him again, but greatly enjoyed their brief encounter. She wondered what other sparkling moments this jewel box of a country held for her.

33

Chris plunged his arm into the popcorn bag and brought another big handful up to his mouth, a few kernels spilling over the sides and landing on his jeans. His frothy beer sat on the cement between his feet in a plastic cup. His flight back to Milwaukee wasn't until 7:00 p.m. so he had driven to the airport, returned his rental car, and taken the TRAX train to a Salt Lake City Bees Minor League game for the afternoon. Chris and his dad, Bill, had traveled to minor league parks all over the Midwest when he was a kid. Sometimes Bill would take Chris along on work trips and he would get to catch a game in a different part of the country, but he had never been to Smith's Ballpark.

A man and a young boy, about ten years old, were sitting in the row in front of Chris, sharing a black pen to track the game in a spiral-bound scorebook. Chris watched over the boy's shoulder as he traced his pen carefully around the diamonds and his father helped point out a few details he missed in the chart. Chris had done this same type of scoring as a boy, Bill by his side helping him learn. He hadn't seen a paper scorebook like that in years. This one looked well-loved.

"Hey, can I ask where you got that book?" Chris leaned into the dad's shoulder.

"Oh, sure. It's this company called Numbers Game. They're printed in Milwaukee. Pretty great, huh?" The man twisted his body to turn to Chris, marked their page with his thumb and flipped the front cover closed to show him the design work.

"Yeah, very cool, thanks. I'll have to order one. I used to do that with my dad. We're from Milwaukee, actually."

"Oh really? Big Brewers fans?"

"Ha, you know it! Brewers, Bucks, Badgers, Packers."

"Yeah, you cheeseheads are something else. I went to college in Minnesota."

The man and his son cheered, and added the run to their grid. Chris remembered that feeling and was hit with a sentimental and emotional surge. He inhaled sharply through his nose to bury the tears. The man turned around to face him again and Chris quickly grabbed his sunglasses from the neck of his shirt and put them on.

"Yeah, we've been giving these books to everyone. Maybe your dad would like one for Christmas or something. I don't know if it's because of the hipsters, but hand scoring is getting really popular again."

"Good idea. He would love it," Chris said, knowing there was no need to tell him his father was gone. No need for the young boy to overhear that fathers go.

"Have the Bees been having a good summer?" Chris asked, changing the subject.

The boy turned around with a very serious face and proceeded to give Chris a detailed account of the season. After a few minutes, his dad had to pat him on the leg and remind him the game was still going on and he needed to attend to his scoring. The dad mouthed "sorry" to Chris and they smiled.

A thought entered Chris's mind about his ten million dollars that could be coming in a few months, and how he would easily trade every last dollar for one more baseball game with his dad. No question about it. He wondered if he could take a picture from behind this man and boy, and paint it when he got back to Milwaukee. Could he bring Bill back? Maybe he could find a good photo of a young Bill at his mom's apartment and get his features just right. Could they be sitting in Davenport, Iowa along the Mississippi watching a River Bandits game with fireworks in the background? Chris could paint that. He could make it real. The thought scared and excited him. But he also remembered the hike the day before when he had convinced himself the brush held no magic.

Chris took off his sunglasses and rubbed his eyes, digging hard into the tops of his eye sockets. He felt like he was losing his grip again. All of these swirling ideas and emotions. Nothing was making sense. He had only cried a handful of times in his adult life, and lately he was crying every day. He reached down for his beer and took a long drink. He decided he had to leave.

"Aww, can't stay for the end?" the man turned to ask.

"I wish. I gotta catch a flight," Chris said. "Nice to meet you fellas. Numbers Game scorebook, I'm gonna remember that."

The young boy turned to wave and Chris gave him a salute. He jogged down the wide steps and walked towards the park exit in the direction of the TRAX station. He felt his phone vibrate, and saw an unknown number calling from Wisconsin. Thinking it might be about his mother, he answered.

"This is Chris."

"Chris! Glad to catch you. This is Sue Donovan, your painting teacher."

"Sue!" exclaimed Chris, caught by surprise and feeling guilty for having missed so many sessions.

"Hey, I hope it's OK I called. I actually just wanted to check in on you. See how you're doing."

Something in the purely honest tone of her voice hammered a tiny fissure in Chris's iron walls. In all of his instincts to lie to her. In all of his ready excuses. A tiny sliver of authentic light pierced through the dark room of his self protection. Chris burst into tears.

"Oh! Oh, dear. OK."

She waited while he sobbed.

"Chris. It's OK. Listen to me. It's going to be OK."

"Sue. I don't know what's going on with me," Chris said, trying to gather his composure. "I keep thinking about my dad. Missing him. I'm a mess. I don't feel like myself. I have this damn paintbrush my mom gave me..." Chris started crying again and then fell silent.

"Chris, are you there?"

"Yes," he sniffed. "I'm here."

"I'm listening," she said.

"Sue…do you ever…I mean, when you're painting…painting a lot. Do you ever…imagine things? Like, think you can change things? I mean…never mind. I don't even know what I mean."

Sue was quiet for a moment.

"Chris, I probably should have talked to the class more about this before we began. Look, painting can bring up a lot of stuff. Stuff we haven't looked at in a long time. Maybe ever. Stuff we didn't even know we needed to deal with. It can be confusing and it can be emotional."

"Yeah, that's an understatement," Chris agreed.

"But it can also give you a bridge to get to a

healthier and more authentic place in your life." She paused, waiting for him to share more, but he didn't.

"Here's the thing, Chris. When we paint we're finally creating instead of consuming. Just think how much we all take. Constantly taking and consuming. Media, binging, scrolling, buying, eating, drinking, getting. But now. Now, see, you're putting something in. You're making beauty where there was none. And sometimes, as artists, we even make horror where there was none. Of course you feel turned upside down. It's powerful."

Chris felt comforted by her words. He wanted to keep talking. He was embarrassed for breaking down, but not as much as he thought he should be.

"I don't want to pressure you to come back to class. You have to know what feels right and follow your own timeline, OK?"

"Thanks, Sue. I do want to come back. I've honestly never felt more like myself than when I was with you all, doing this thing that I love."

"That's great to hear, Chris. Look, you men have a way of not talking when you need to. I've never understood it, but it just seems to be how y'all are built. When we hang up, I'm going to text you the name of a therapist in Milwaukee. He's fabulous. I think talking to him would do you a world of good."

"Oh, you don't have to…"

"Zpp zpp! It's just a text. Do with the information what you will. I'll never know if you go see him or not, OK? I'm just sharing his contact info with you. Zero pressure."

"OK. Sue, thanks. I appreciate it."

"Hope to see you soon, friend," she said.

Chris hung up with Sue just as he reached the platform and stepped onto the train. He put his phone in his back pocket and held onto a bar, using his sleeve to wipe his eyes. He felt the text come in from Sue. The train slowly started to move.

34

Jo had to break out of her optical trance staring at the Swiss countryside from the windows of the train to unwrap the brown paper around her croissant. Tiny pastry flakes fell onto her royal-blue sundress and she looked around guiltily. In the last few days, she had learned that the Swiss people were tidy, punctual, and followed rules. She reached into the top zipper pocket of her backpack for her silk scarf square to spread on her lap. As the train rounded an extreme mountain pass, she could see the last few train cars whipping around the curve behind her. Verdant rolling hills dotted with charming wood chalets, glassy teal lakes, dramatic mountain peaks, and the early morning sun filled her view. Leaving Lucerne had been bittersweet. Walking to the train station at dawn, she had only seen one other person, a workman using a sharp metal poker to collect trash in the street into a bin he carried. Lucerne had been more exquisite than she had even imagined in her dreams, and the photos in her library books did it weak justice.

In the past three days, she had taken a steep cogwheel tram to the top of Mt. Pilatus and enjoyed a cold radler while looking out over a network of hiking trails. She had met another woman traveling alone from Lawrence, Kansas, and they exchanged cameras to take photos of each other standing in front of the Chapel Bridge. She had stored her handbag in a locker at a beach house and swam out to a floating platform to jump off, laughing and talking with travelers from around the world, glad she had packed a bikini on a whim. Every meal had been better than the last, and she ate a different kind of milk chocolate bar every day. On the train now, looking out the window at the glorious moving postcard, she wondered if the best part of the trip was over, and if she might regret not spending the whole week in Lucerne.

"Fahrkarte!" Jo startled as a tall man in a white shirt and black vest stood next to her seat. She quickly reached down and grabbed her rail pass to show him, and he moved on to the people behind her.

Hours later, she was seated on the alpine patio of a small family restaurant in Gimmelwald, enjoying a well-earned hiker's lunch of rosti. The cast iron skillet of potatoes was covered in cheese, vegetables and pieces of steak. She hesitated for a second seeing the onions, remembering she might have a date that night, but laughed at herself and dug in. If one man who lived 4,000 miles away remembered her as having onion breath, that was a penalty she would gladly absorb for enjoying this delicious hearty food with abandon. Hang gliders floated across her view, looking like colorful birds against the sheer gray facets of the mountain valley. The peaks were snow-covered and Jo sat above and below wisps of clouds in the blue sky.

After lunch, Jo hiked for a few more hours. Walking through another small carless mountain village, a young girl in a traditional Swiss dress and apron passed her on the path, leading a cow with a large bell around its neck. On the side of the path was a stone shed with a sign written in German. Jo used her pocket translation book to read it as "Bottles of fresh milk. Leave money in the box." Jo felt as if she had stepped into a storybook.

Always clicking in the back of Jo's mind was the series of gondolas, trams and trains she would need to unwind her day's journey in order to get back down to Interlaken where she had quickly checked in to Balmer's Hostel and dropped off her backpack. It was a transportation puzzle worthy of Jules Verne. She had to concentrate to make it work, and not be stuck on the mountain overnight. But wanting to enjoy every possible minute high in the Berner Oberland, she waited until almost 5:00 p.m. to begin her descent.

Walking into her private room at the hostel, she collapsed onto the bed with relief. She was proud of herself for all that she had navigated in a day that felt like four separate days. She only had about fifteen minutes to get down to the biergarten on the off-chance that Micha showed up. She used the bathroom down the hall and then came back to her room to use the small sink there. She quickly washed her face and armpits with a bar of Dial soap and brushed her teeth. She changed into the same sundress she had worn on the morning train and touched the bar of soap behind her ears, wishing she had brought perfume or any sort of make-up. She swiped a dab of Vaseline on her lips and looked at her reflection. Her cheeks were sun-kissed pink, her skin tan. Her eyes looked bright and her hair, while slightly windblown, had summer highlights that helped her look American, if nothing else. She pulled it into a low ponytail and tied it around into a loose bun. One last regret was not bringing earrings, but this was as good as it was going to get living out of a backpack at the end of a day of hiking, so she left her room and went downstairs.

The garden courtyard was lively with travelers. Jo knew she brought the age up by about fifteen years, but she delighted in watching the youthful freedom. There was a grassy area with lawn games, a covered alcove with hammocks, and an outdoor bar. Jo found a seat at a shared wood table with a group of backpackers from Italy. No longer surprised by this, she learned their English was also perfect.

"Jo?"

She looked up. He was even more handsome than she remembered. Light tan low-slung shorts.

A navy blue T-shirt, snug by American standards. A small leather satchel strapped across his chest. Aviator sunglasses tucked in the neck of his T-shirt. He looked strong. Stunned speechless, Jo could only smile at her situation. Micha walked closer and stood in front of her. She stood up and they faced each other, standing one foot apart. They lined up well. She could smell his cologne.

"You came."

"So did you."

Jo and Micha left the courtyard at Balmer's and spent the next hour walking around downtown Interlaken. Micha told her all about the history of the city and pointed out interesting architectural features. They talked about differences in the United States, and the challenges for bikers and pedestrians in large cities from the design prioritization of cars. Being sensitive to the slight language barrier, they spoke simply about broad ideas. Micha was kind and intelligent, and he led a fascinating life. He told her he was thirty-five and never married. Jo knew it could all be fiction, even his name. It was getting dark but the streets were still full of people and well-lit. They had walked and talked for so long that many restaurants were closing up. Finally, they found an outdoor table at an Italian restaurant with walk-up service. Jo sat and watched people go by, enjoying the musicality of many world languages overlapping, as Micha went inside to order. He came back carrying a tray with two tall beers and a bowl of spaghetti arrabbiata with two forks. They smiled broadly at each other as he walked towards the table.

"I'm sorry this is not the fancy meal I wanted to give you in Zurich."

"This is really perfect, though." Jo said, and meant it. Micha grabbed a candle from another table and set it between them. They leaned in close to share the pasta, the warm night air and distant sounds of revelry their chaperones.

On the walk back to Balmer's, Micha took them on a slightly different route to show her his landscape design.

"This was a competition I won in '79. The subject was inclusion. We were challenged to make a garden design that more people could enjoy." Micha opened a small gate between two buildings that led into a large open area. She didn't feel nervous even though they were in a more secluded area. Against her typical judgment, she trusted him.

"So I decided to design a Garden for the Blind. All of the plants are touchable, many are fragrant. I framed the garden with the auditory component of quaking aspens. You might also hear a few small wind chimes. The path is all one smooth level surface with rounded stone railings and placards in braille."

Jo walked along the path in darkness but for the bright moon, and explored the sensory garden. She smelled rosemary, lavender, and peppermint. Then gardenia and pineapple sage. Her fingers raked through lemon grass as the water in a small fountain purled beside her. She felt the Velcro tips of gomphrena flowers and the dense soft undersides of a rice paper plant. In the moonlight, she read a placard and learned Chinese star anise had been used to remove freckles, and her fingers glided across the braille translation below. She had never experienced anything like this place. All of her senses were awake and alive.

"I interviewed people with low vision while I was working on the design and something I heard again and again was their enjoyment of bold color contrasts. So, over here on this end, I created these tall panels with blocks of bright colors. And on the other end of the path, I made that black-and-white square panel. I'm relieved to see the paint is holding up."

"This is incredible."

"Thank you. I'm very proud of it, and I hear it is being well-used. I'm glad to see it has been tended properly. When I designed this garden I hoped the idea would spread and other cities would build gardens for the blind. I have heard of a project in Basel and one in Paris."

They left the garden and for the first time, their conversation stopped as they slowly approached the entrance to Balmer's. The courtyard was still active, but quieter, and tables were about half full.

"Would you like another drink?" he asked.

Jo didn't speak, but looked at him and shook her

head as she continued to walk to the hallway of the hostel lobby. He stayed next to her, but an almost imperceptible inch behind as they walked up two flights of stairs. Jo unlocked the door to her room and walked in, holding the door open for him. Micha lingered by the entryway, and then sat down on one of the pillows at the top of the bed, tan legs draped over the red-and-white checkered bedspread, as Jo brushed her teeth and looked at him.

He put his arms behind his head. "It is a strange feeling to know that I am right in the middle of an evening I will always remember," he said.

Jo wiped her mouth with a towel. "I know exactly what you mean."

"Do you promise you will remember me, Jo?"

"Micha. I think I might remember every single moment with you."

He stood and they walked slowly to each other. He put his hands on her waist and leaned down to kiss her neck. She reached her hands up to her hair and took down her bun.

"Micha," Jo hesitated as she felt his body pressing against hers. "I have to tell you. And I need to say it right now. This would need to be a condom situation."

"Yes, I agree."

"Good. That's settled," she said with relief.

"Should I pretend to go out and buy some or should we just use the ones I brought along in my bag? I have five."

They smiled at each other like teenagers. "I'm an optimist," he said, beginning to untie the shoulder straps of her sundress.

Five seemed to her like it would be enough so that he would never have to find out that she had some in her backpack as well.

35

"Look up at the sky," the instructions on Chris's laptop screen told him. It was after midnight and he was in his bedroom, so he skipped that step.

"Fuck!" he exclaimed, realizing he was getting chocolate from his airport Toblerone bar all over his keyboard. He got up and brought an antibacterial wipe back from the kitchen, trying to work a folded corner between the keys.

"Relax your forehead. Unclench your jaw." Suggestions popped onto his screen with a pleasing bubble sound. The site was called PeacePrize and it was a reward-based online mental health program.

Chris saw three dots appear on the screen and a message telling him he would be connected with an AI therapist shortly. He felt a knot of panic in his chest.

"For only $9.99/mo upgrade to live human therapist." Chris clicked yes.

"Click to allow camera access for video feed or choose avatar now." Chris chose an avatar. He gave himself blond hair and a goatee as a disguise.

"Therapist wait time is forty-five seconds..." Chris felt the panic again and stopped wiping his keyboard. He tossed the cloth over the side of the bed.

The computer made a loud ding and a three-inch square popped up with a young woman's face. She was mid-sentence.

"I'm sorry, what?" Chris asked.

"...do when conflict arises?"

"What do I do when conflict arises? Is that your greeting?"

Her face froze as the video feed lagged.

"Good evening. Are you in a safe place?"

"Yes," Chris answered.

"Did you answer yes?"

"Yes," Chris said again.

"Welcome to PeacePrize. Affordable, convenient online therapy from the comfort of your home. We are here so you are heard."

"Uhh. OK."

"My name is Allie. Let me start by telling you a

few things about myself."

Chris looked up at the ceiling. He looked back down when he heard her say she had four geckos. The screen went blue and she was gone.

"Working on updates. 3% complete. Do not turn off your computer."

Chris set the computer on the floor, masturbated, and fell asleep.

36

Jo and Micha had walked to the Interlaken Ost Station and gotten on the 10:00 a.m. train to Bern together. They were starving for any last time together, even one more hour, and so he planned to take another train to Zurich from Bern after saying goodbye. Jo watched his profile as he drew a small map for her on the back of a ticket.

"This is the parliament building. If you walk this direction, you will find stores and an open market. Stop for Laderach chocolate if you can. Then keep going this way to reach the Aare river. If you are a strong swimmer, you can take a float. The river is fast. So fast you won't believe it. This star marks an area where you could find a good dinner."

She was captivated by his long eyelashes. She

studied his elegant fingers as he pointed the pen around the map. He had strong masculine features and a shadow of dark facial hair, but in his tired morning face, she could see more clearly his fine angular bone structure. Delicate. She memorized him.

He leaned his head against her collarbone and held her hand. She thanked him for the map and traced her thumb across his knuckles.

"Will you be lonely, Jo?"

"Maybe in moments. But loneliness is not the same as solitude."

"That is true."

"I will have the memory of our night to keep me company."

He lifted his head and kissed her temple, pulling

her close to him. He nuzzled into her like he wanted to drink her into him and remember her scent forever. She was surprised a man could be so affectionate and expressive. It seemed like a role reversal, and confused her.

As they walked out of the train station, he pointed to some main roads she would need, and they lingered by a brick walled overlook just under a stone arch.

"I have a little more time before my next train. I could walk with you as far as the Aare, if you'd like?"

"Micha," Jo took a deep breath. "We will say goodbye here."

She willed herself not to cry. She imagined that not crying was the most important thing she would ever be asked to do. The fate of the universe depended on her not crying. She looked at him closely and inhaled through her nose, soothing all of the pin pricks behind her eyes.

"You are a beautiful person," she told him, "and I hope you have a very good life."

"My Jo," he said sadly, and hugged her, snaking his arms under her backpack and holding her tight.

After a long quiet embrace, she took a step back. She looked down at her feet and without looking up at him she turned and walked away.

Jo spent her day following the map he had made for her. She drank Chasselas wine and pulled melted cheese down a hot raclette iron onto a plate of pickles and steamed potatoes. She sat on the low stone retaining wall on the crowded edge of the Aare river, awash in overheard conversations in languages she didn't know. She watched her pale pink toenails under the water as the turquoise snow melt rushed across her feet.

37

Chris held a photo of his dad up to the light. He had to be about forty years old in the picture, but there was no date on the back. He was standing in the backyard at the grill and their family dog, Sammy, was at his feet. Bill looked happy and strong. Chris laughed ironically looking at the grill full of brats and steaks, knowing that a diet made almost entirely of meat was what ultimately killed him. Chris assumed his mother had taken this photo, but now he wasn't sure. It could have been his grandparents or even a friend. Maybe young Chris himself had grabbed the camera that day.

"Are you OK, honey?"

"Yeah, Mom, sorry, I'll be right out."

"What are you doing in there?"

Chris ducked his head out of the doorway of Eileen's bedroom. They had planned to watch a movie together and he had gotten her settled on the sofa in the living room. She had been making slow but steady progress after her stroke, but still needed almost full-time care.

"Sorry, Mom, just looking at some old pictures of you and Dad."

"Dear, you can bring them out here if you'd like."

"No, that's OK. Maybe another night. Just let me put them back where I found them and I'll be right out."

Chris opened the armoire and pulled out the velvet-lined wood drawer. He replaced the photos on the pile and straightened the row of other treasures. From the inside pocket of his fleece, he pulled out the ebony brush, which was wrapped in its leather pouch. He looked at the brush longingly.

"I want to paint my dad back to life. I want to paint another Bucks championship," he laughed to himself. "I even want to paint that nurse Jill. But where does it end? You have to let me rest now," he whispered to the brush. He pulled the long drawer all the way out and laid the brush against the back edge. He arranged a few more things in front of it including a small photo album, an envelope, and a pair of white leather baby shoes. He closed the drawer, shut the armoire doors, and went back out to the living room.

"Decide on a movie yet, Mom?"

"Can we watch *The Commitments*?" Her speech was still slightly slurred but he understood her.

"You bet. That's a great one." Chris leaned back and put his feet up on the coffee table. He searched through the menus on the TV until he found the movie.

"Oh, no dear, it's $2.99. Let's just watch something else."

Chris laughed. "My treat, Mom. Let's live a little."

Chris watched his mother as she watched the movie. She smiled and laughed, pointing at the TV when her favorite parts were coming up. She only fell asleep once, for a couple of minutes, and startled awake when the soul band started playing again. He had such respect for how hard she had been working on her recovery, and her attitude throughout. Chris felt grateful for this time with her, and didn't want to be anywhere else.

38

Grant sang along to "Mustang Sally" at the top of his lungs, using a ladle as a microphone as Jo walked into the diner.

Jo smiled and stopped in her tracks to stare at him. Everybody was turned to them, watching the show. After a few bars, more people joined in to sing the refrain. Jo's face was hot with embarrassment, but it was great to be back.

She walked the length of the counter, putting a hand over her face, and sat down at her stool. Dagmar reached to turn down the volume on the tape player.

"Welcome home, Jo!" she said. "Crazy Grant has had that song queued up for the last hour hoping you'd stop in today. You pretty jetlagged?"

"Welcome back, kid," Grant said, walking by and slapping her back with his dish towel.

"Thanks for the serenade, Wilson," she laughed. "Yeah, I feel a little out of sorts, but not too bad. I got home around midnight from Chicago and slept pretty well, actually." Jo looked at the menu. "Can I have a BLT?"

"Sure thing, gal. You have to tell me every single detail later, OK?"

"Of course," Jo said. "For now, I will just say it was spectacular." Jo knew Dag would never hear every single detail. One special part was to be locked in her treasure box. Tucked away to take out and look at, only occasionally, in quiet moments for the rest of her life.

Jo realized Nancy Miller and her husband, Bob, were sitting next to her.

"Hey, Jo, I heard you're quite the bridge player," Bob leaned in front of Nancy to tell her.

"Ha, not really. That was a fun night, though. We'll have to do it again sometime. I'll host next time."

"How was your trip?" Nancy asked.

"Pretty amazing. I'm so glad I went."

"Do you have any pictures?"

"I hope I got some good ones. I'm dropping off my film later today."

"Remember the pharmacy has free doubles on Tuesdays."

"Oh, right, thanks. I'll wait then."

"Jo, how on Earth did you manage to be away

from the flower shop for so long?"

Jo paused, feeling a little defensive. "It was just a week...I didn't...yeah I guess that was a tad long to close the shop. Especially in the summer. The whole thing was pretty spontaneous."

"Well, I suppose people without children can behave that way," Nancy said and turned back to her plate. Jo didn't know how to respond to that. Nancy was right, but that didn't mean it should have been said aloud.

"Pros and cons to everything, I guess," Jo said, and began to eat her BLT.

Nancy lowered her voice and leaned in. "You should know, Jo, that while you were gone, Grant spent some time with Brooke McMaron, Heidi's sister. They sat next to each other at Heidi's wedding last month."

Jo whispered back, "Good for him. I've only met her once, but she's hilarious and gorgeous. Why are we whispering?"

Nancy sat back straight on her stool. "Just thought you'd like to know, is all."

"And now I do." Jo rolled her eyes and then realized Nancy could see her in the mirror across from the counter.

Dagmar walked over carrying the guest check pad. "Anything else for you today, Jo? Slice of peach pie?"

"Actually, I wonder if I could buy a whole pie to take back to the store with me. Paj, Sawm, and Mai are coming over this afternoon for a meeting."

"A meeting? Sounds very official," Dag said. Grant was also in earshot and Jo could tell he was listening, too.

"Hey Grant? Come here a sec."

"What's up?" he said, leaning over and resting his elbows on the counter.

"So, when I was in Switzerland I saw an idea that I'd like to try in my back garden. But it's going to be a big project and I will need to hire a lot of help."

"I'm listening," he said.

"I'm having a meeting about it at the shop at 3:00 p.m. Can you come?"

"I'm there."

"Just so you know, I'm going to try to get these plants in the ground yet this fall, and so it might involve some weekend hours, too."

"Even better. I'm saving for a trip and I could use all the hours I can get. I'm in."

"A trip?" asked Jo, surprised.

"Yeah," he spoke more quietly now. "I decided I want to go to Vietnam someday. Saigon. It might take me a few years to save up. I started an envelope. I guess when I have a lot, I'll put it in the bank. That'd probably be safer than keeping it in an envelope. I don't know. I've been thinking about it. I guess you inspired me."

Jo looked at him thoughtfully. Grant was always so much more than she assumed or expected. So much more than she knew. She watched him as he wiped down the counter, reminding herself sternly to treat him with great respect. They were not the same, but they were equals.

September

September

39

Burning lungs and leaden legs. Sweat in his eyelashes. Chris had run from his condo to see the sunrise at the marina, planning to head south along the lakefront and double back to his office. He could shower there and he kept extra clothes in his office closet. His first meeting was at 8:00 a.m. Chris regretted ever taking a day off from running, let alone the past year. He knew it would be much easier in a couple of weeks if he stuck with it. His slight hangover and the wind in his face were doing him no favors. But the sunrise was worth it. On the horizon, peels of tangerine and Spanish pomegranate sat on the frayed denim tablecloth of Lake Michigan. Chris stopped to watch, leaning over and breathing hard, hands stretching out the bottom hem of his shorts.

By the time he was cleaned up and walking down the hallway to the conference room, some employees were already seated at their computers and a few were still coming in off the elevator. About half of the employees were working from home on a daily basis. Chris said hello to the two women at the reception desk. The turnover rate had been so high in recent years, he had given up on learning their names. He reached for an apple from the bowl on the counter between them and brought it to his mouth to take a bite.

"You're kidding me," said Chris.

"Oh, yeah, we got kind of tired of refilling it."

"We have fake apples now?"

"Yeah, but they're cute, right?"

"It's September. It's literally September. In

Wisconsin. And we have fake apples. Is this my real life? Am I really standing here right now? They're not even wood, for fucksake."

The women stared at Chris, patronizingly. "Would you like some apples delivered, sir? Do you, like, really, really love apples?" The ladies snickered to each other. One pretended to place a call on her headset. "Hello? 1-800-apples? We have an emergency." Chris set the painted plastic apple back in the bowl, took a mint instead, and continued walking to the conference room.

"There he is! Hey, big guy," yelled Jared.

"Hey, guys," Chris extended a low wave and took his seat at the table. He leaned back to look in the koi pond, now wondering if the fish were also plastic.

"Alright, now that we're all here, I called this meeting because we really need to figure out what we're doing in northern Arizona. Guys showing up to jobs are getting mixed messages from corporate. Lotta missed opportunities on these accounts because we don't have our ducks in a row." Scott shuffled papers while he was speaking and eventually queued up a slide deck of photos on the projector.

"This is the pinyons again?" asked Jared.

"Yeah, pinyons and junipers. Hydraulic decline. I guess the main question out there is: Are we giving the go-ahead to clear-cut?"

"Ka-ching!" Jared blurted.

Chris spoke up. "I was reading up on this issue last night, and it's a lot more complex than we've been treating it. There's some research now showing some of these groves actually get stronger after a brief drought. Almost like the trees learn and adapt from it so they're better prepared for the next one."

Jared rolled his eyes. "Right, right, we all know about the magical freaking trees. Talking to each other, knitting sweaters together underground, blah blah blah."

Chris ignored him. "I just think we have to keep making these decisions on a case by case, tree by tree basis. It's totally reckless for us to give some broad permission for our guys to clear-cut anytime there are signs of hydraulic decline," Chris said firmly.

He continued. "And another thing. In this room right now I see two lawyers, three software engineers, and one media flack. I gotta ask, why don't we have an arborist in here? A botanist? Hell, even a firefighter would probably know more about this than we do."

"Chris, dude, you've got your colon in a knot

lately, bro. Do you have any idea the number of accounts we lose when we go 'tree by tree' like it's a goddamn game of Pick-Up Sticks?"

"I hate to say it, but Jared is right," Scott added. "These aren't Ward Cleaver homeowner accounts. These are cities and townships. State parks contracting with us. Thousand-acre farms and ranches. If we go case by case, FELL becomes barely profitable. I've run the numbers again and again, trust me."

"Well, then I say we have to revisit the idea of planting a tree for every tree we cut down, like we talked about when we first started this company," Chris said, looking down at the papers in front of him.

"Ha, that again," Jared said. "Boys, I think someone needs to go back to math class." The men at the table laughed. "Income/Expense on that idea didn't work in year one and it doesn't work in year seven. Sorry, Al Gore. That's an inconvenient truth."

Chris didn't hear much in the rest of the meeting. He angled his chair so he could see the koi fish swimming around the low bubbling fountain by the window. He imagined pulling cool blue rivers of paint across Arizona, his brush hydrating each thirsty tree to save them from the chainsaws and felling machines. Phthalo Blue. A touch of Raw Umber. Yes. They would like that. They would drink that up. Chris smiled to himself and felt refreshed.

The rest of the day passed in a blur. Telling his assistant he had an appointment at 3:00 p.m., he walked outside, shoes chomping over the first autumn leaves on the sidewalks. He turned north and walked six blocks to an old carpeted two-story professional building next to a classic Milwaukee diner. He sat in the lobby of Sightline Psychotherapy, waiting for the man Sue Donovan had recommended.

"Chris? Nice to meet you. I'm Lucas. Come on in."

40

Jo set the Cat Stevens album *Teaser and the Firecat* on her turntable and turned up the volume. She opened her back window wide and ran down the stairs to greet everyone in the garden.

The Lor family was already back there, starting to weed and clear brush in the first dim light.

"Six o'clock in the morning? Jo, this hurts!" Grant and Brooke walked into the garden carrying a basket with a calico cloth bundle.

"Hi guys! What do you have?" Jo reached in the basket to take a peek.

"Fresh-baked apple cinnamon muffins. Piping hot. Dagmar insisted I bring some over."

"Wow, thanks, those smell amazing. But is this even early for you, Grant?"

"Not really. Most mornings I'm already at the diner by now. I was just kidding you."

Jo looked at Brooke. "But it might be early for YOU, right?" The women laughed.

"It's fine! I've got my overalls on and I'm ready for anything," Brooke said.

"Well, I can't tell you how much I appreciate this. I'll have you out of here by 8:00 a.m. This was the only time I could get everyone here at the same time. I want to talk about the general plan, and then after today, people can work whenever they have time."

"I love the idea for a garden for the blind, and I'm happy to help, truly," said Brooke. "My dad is stopping by in an hour to talk to you about the concrete work. I was telling him about the plans and he thinks his company might be able to donate some time to pour the paths."

"Seriously?" Jo's jaw dropped.

"Absolutely! But he wants to talk to you about whether you'd prefer bricks or something. Sorry, he was rambling and I didn't really listen," Brooke laughed.

"Wow, Brooke. Thanks so much. I can't wait to talk to him." Jo saw Grant look over at Brooke adoringly.

"Now if I can just get your dad out fishing with me, he'd be just about perfect," Grant teased her, and the two of them walked over to stand by Paj, offering her a muffin.

Jo talked to the group about the design plans she had made, showed them the plants that had already arrived, and discussed zones and placement along the future path. She paused at points to allow time for Mai to help interpret for her parents. Jo knew Paj understood almost everything, but she wasn't sure how much English Sawm knew. She would need a lot of advice from him as the project progressed.

"I'm still waiting on four aspen saplings for the corners. I could only afford young ones, but after a few years, I hope those will add a really beautiful canopy of sound as people walk along the path. There's enough sun back here that their shade shouldn't be a big problem. I will also have wind chimes and maybe a fountain if I can figure that out."

The group worked hard that first morning together. They laid wood planks along a border that would later be the concrete path. They defined the space for raised boxes of fragrant herbs, beds for scented flowers and touchable plants of many varieties. The weeds were overwhelming, but many hands made quick work. Perennials would be planted soon, and Jo would order annuals in the spring to fill things in. Paj had ideas for information about the plants to be engraved on the placards. She knew medicinal remedies and cosmetic applications. She had information that Jo had never read before in her library research. Mai knew a folktale about lavender that she wanted to include on a placard, as well. Jo had already contacted a school for the blind in Madison about doing the braille translations.

At the end of the shift, Jo called everyone over to thank them. As the group stood looking back across the lot, they could start to see the bones of her special garden emerging. She thought about Micha and his dream for the idea to spread to other places, and here it was, having jumped the Atlantic.

Later that day, Grant popped his head in the back door of the store to say hello before picking up the flower orders for delivery.

"That was fun this morning, Jo. It's gonna be a really cool place back there." He turned to start lifting the boxed bouquets into his car.

"Oh, actually, hang on, Grant. I'm just finishing one more." He walked into the shop and over to her worktable.

"Geez! Who died? That's enormous!" he remarked.

"It's not that big!" she laughed. "I actually made this for Brooke to thank her for her help. I thought maybe you could take it to her." Jo finished arranging the sunflowers and asters in a large blue vase, tucking in a few stems of Queen Anne's lace and lisianthus.

"No, seriously, Jo, that's like hotel lobby big."

"Grant! Stop, it is not! I just really appreciate her help. That's all."

"OK. But why don't the rest of us get one? Hmm?"

"Well…I guess I just want to make sure she… knows I like her." Jo looked up at Grant.

Grant looked at her suspiciously. "Is this something I should put in my 'women are weird' file and not think too hard about it?"

"That's not a bad idea," Jo said, nodding.

Grant picked up the vase and pantomimed his knees buckling under the weight as he walked to the back of the store. He looked back at her and smiled as he kicked the door open. No wink.

41

Eileen held tightly onto Chris's arm as they navigated the garden path through the courtyard of Liberty Acres. This was their first walk outside together since her stroke, and she insisted on attempting it without her walker. Her purse was over his shoulder, and he had wondered why she thought she might need it, but he didn't question it.

"Mom, I've been meaning to ask you about that paintbrush of Dad's you gave me."

"Have you tried it out? Is it useful, honey?"

"Oh, yeah, yeah, it's really nice. I did actually use it. I wasn't sure if I should, but it looked like Dad had used it before, right?"

"Yes, I think so. I really don't remember. It was so long ago."

"Do you know anything else about it? Like where he got it?"

"I'm sorry, dear. I don't know anything about it. It was just always in that drawer. When you said you'd been painting recently, it jogged my memory that it was there."

Eileen stopped and took her time stepping around an uneven drain grate. Chris held her steady.

"You're doing great, Mom."

"Well, thank you. I don't feel like I'm doing great. To be honest."

"Just take one step at a time. We can stop and rest at any of these benches. Don't be a hero."

"I'm just so sorry about all this."

They were quiet for a minute as they passed another group on the path walking the other direction. A man in a wheelchair was being pushed by his adult daughter, who herself looked like she was old enough to live at Liberty Acres. The man's head was tilted to one side and his hand was by his mouth. Two grandchildren, or maybe even great-grandchildren, ran along in front of them. Nurse Jill walked a few yards behind carrying a clipboard, and said hello as she passed.

"Let's sit, Mom." Chris helped Eileen to a bench and put out his arm for her to hold while she lowered herself down.

"Look, Mom. You have nothing to be sorry about. I don't want you to think that anymore, OK? I'm happy to help you. You'd do it for me, right? You HAVE done it for me."

Eileen was quiet. "It wasn't supposed to be like this. I was supposed to have a lot of children. Bill was supposed to outlive me. You weren't supposed to be the one stuck here. Dealing with everything."

"Well, yeah, and I was supposed to stay married. Have kids. The best laid plans, right?"

"I just want you to know how much I appreciate you."

"I do, Mom. I know. I wish I could do more for you. But I think we can be grateful you sold the house when you did, and that I live here in Milwaukee. The guys are always talking about moving the FELL headquarters, but I really don't see them doing it as long as Giannis is in town," he laughed.

Chris helped her stand and they continued walking past the raised garden beds in wooden platform boxes. Residents used these to plant vegetables and flowers each summer. Most of the boxes were overflowing with ripe tomatoes, bell peppers, and basil plants. One was filled with zinnias planted in rainbow rows.

"How have things been at work, dear?"

"Well. Gotta admit. Not awesome."

"I'm sorry to hear that. Is there anything that can be changed?"

"Huh. That's the big question."

"Do you ever think about leaving?" Eileen asked cautiously, looking at Chris.

Chris stopped at the next bench and helped her sit down again. They were parked in front of a row of hummingbird feeders.

"Leave FELL? I wouldn't even know how to begin. There is so much tied up in the shares and the corporate structure. It's just really complex."

"I understand. Well, I don't. But I can imagine it's not like quitting any old job."

"Yeah, basically Scott and Jared would need to buy out my equity. I don't think either one is in a position to do that. I can't picture even having that conversation. We built this thing together. They'd never forgive me. And I would feel like I was abandoning this creature we made."

"Can you imagine being at FELL for the next twenty years?" Eileen asked.

Chris felt a lump in his throat and couldn't speak. The idea of twenty more years at FELL made him nauseous. He had a hard time understanding how he would get through *one* more year, let alone the rest of his career.

"Honestly, no. I can't."

"I remember your dad used to say that sometimes it just takes twenty difficult minutes to save yourself twenty difficult years. I would add that sometimes it's really just more like twenty seconds."

"I wish it were that easy, Mom. I don't know. Maybe you're right. Maybe I should talk to my lawyer and see what options I have."

Chris and Eileen continued walking, every motion slow and careful, back to the elevator to return to her apartment. The doors closed and Chris pushed the button.

Eileen held the bar and looked at Chris. "You could just drop off the keycard."

Chris looked at Eileen and smiled. She started reciting the list of simple ideas from "Fifty Ways to Leave Your Lover."

"I get your point, Mom," he laughed, but then became serious. He crossed his arms and looked straight ahead. "Something's amiss, Chris," he said aloud to himself.

42

Hearing a sizzling, Jo wiped her hand on a dish towel and reached behind her to turn down the burner slightly.

"Jo? You up there?" Grant called from the back staircase of the shop.

"Yeah, I'm here! Just getting some soup started. Come on up." Jo finished chopping the bell peppers and onions, and added them to the bubbling butter in the pot on the stove. She reached for an ear of corn and started to pull off the husks and silky threads just as Grant appeared in the doorway.

"Dang, it smells good up here. Just letting you know I'm done for the day. Mrs. Taylor wasn't home, so I set the flowers by her side door in the shade."

"Perfect. Thanks, Grant. Thank Sandy Duncan for me too, please."

"Ha, will do." Grant lingered in the doorway. "Whatcha making?"

Jo held out an ear of corn to invite him to help her shuck. "Corn chowder."

Grant stood next to her at the counter pulling the leaves off the corn. He reached across her to grab the knife, setting the ear vertically in a shallow bowl and slicing off the kernels. They fell into the bowl in connected rectangles of white and yellow.

Jo turned around to stir the other vegetables. Grant walked over to her record player, which had stopped, and chose Simon and Garfunkel's *Concert in Central Park*. He had only been in her apartment a couple times, and she felt he was being awfully familiar. He also wasn't talking, which was highly unusual for him.

"Is there something else you need, Grant? Did I forget to pay you or something?"

"No, no, it's not that." He stayed facing away from her for a beat and then turned to walk back to the kitchen. Jo was finishing the roux, adding cream and chicken stock to the pot. He was making her nervous and she wished he would just come out with it.

"OK. So here's the thing. Brooke is moving back into her Madison apartment this week. You know she's starting law school."

"Yeah, it's great. I'm so impressed with that lady."

"Well, I know Wednesday is our golf night, but I was thinking I might take Brooke out to dinner. For like a send-off."

"Oh, my gosh, Grant. Is that all? You can't golf on Wednesday?" Jo laughed. "Yes, I think I will survive. And of course you two should celebrate. Starting law school is a big deal!"

Jo stopped stirring, the wooden spoon frozen in place, as she realized something he might be trying to tell her. Maybe he wasn't just talking about this week. Maybe he was trying to tell her they couldn't golf anymore at all.

"Oh, OK. Thanks, Jo. I might take her out to The Muskie Club or somewhere really nice. What do you think?"

"Brooke seems very agreeable. I'm sure she'll be thrilled wherever you take her."

"Yeah, you're probably right." He reached for the knife again and started cutting a stack of three crispy bacon slices into small pieces. Jo moved down the counter to put some space between them.

"Say, Grant. I was thinking. It's probably not a good idea for us to golf anymore, just the two of us."

"What do you mean? Why not?" He sneaked a bit of bacon.

"Oh, I don't know. It's just a small town. I wouldn't want Brooke to feel funny about it, or for anyone to say something to her." Jo dumped the full bowl of corn into the pot and adjusted the heat. She pulled open the oven door to warm up some bread.

"But we're just friends. You and I are just friends."

"I know, Grant." They turned to face each other. She could tell he was getting agitated.

"I've only heard you say we're just friends 700 times, Jo." He was raising his voice slightly. "So it must be true, right? So, what would be wrong about playing golf together?"

"Maybe we could play as a foursome. With Brooke and Dagmar. Or Brooke's dad."

"Brooke doesn't golf."

"Well, look. I don't know. Just go have a fun dinner this week and we'll figure this out later. It's no big deal, really. Summer is almost over anyway."

Grant picked up a dish towel to wipe his hands and threw it back down on the counter. Jo turned to the stove and continued to stir the chowder. She heard him close the door and walk down the stairs. She turned off the burner and heard his car drive away. She reached up to her cupboard and got one bowl. She opened the silverware drawer and got one spoon. Dunking the ladle in the soup, she thought of Grant serenading her in the diner just a month before. She used a clean towel to wrap around the hot bread to take it out of the oven and cut herself a slice. She carried her meal to the table and sat down to eat. She lifted the first spoonful and blew across the top, watching the steam swirl into the low light from her western window. The harmony echoed in the sound of silence.

October

43

Murder of Lady Sweetgrass: *Majestic 800-year-old live oak felled without cause in east Charleston. Gig workers from FELL, Inc. have not yet been reached for comment at this time. This is a developing story.*

Chris took a drink of iced tea and continued to scroll through articles and photos about this incident that had now reached national news. The waitress came outside to where he was sitting on the long side piazza, and set down his plate of shrimp and cheddar grits with okra.

"Storm might be coming in. You OK out here for now?" she said as she rolled down striped vinyl rain shades on two ends of the porch. "This should help block the wind for you. Just give a holler if you want to move inside. There's plenty of room at the bar."

Chris looked up and nodded to her, beginning to watch a video clip that was starting to gain traction.

"This tree survived wars, hurricanes, fires," the woman said, speaking through tears. "And it's gone. Just like that. Overnight. This doesn't even feel like my Charleston anymore. What is wrong with people? Lady Sweetgrass was part of our heritage. One idiot with a chainsaw." She waved her hand at the camera and turned away.

On the way from the airport to his hotel, Chris had driven by the site of the tree, and he could see mourners were starting to gather. People were leaving flowers, photos, and sweetgrass baskets by the heap of logs and brush. Most of the main trunk was still standing. The jagged cuts looked apocalyptic. From what he had read, the FELL crew was alerted and aborted the job immediately, once people realized what was happening, but too much damage had been done. At that point, they had to continue cutting limbs for safety reasons as a crowd gathered beneath them, phone cameras aimed like muskets.

Chris flew down right away, and part of the FELL communications team would be joining him the next day. Scott said he'd try to get there, but he was busy handling another smaller media disaster in Savannah. Chris hadn't heard from Jared, whose philosophy was they were a software company and nothing more. He had no interest in micromanaging arborists or apologizing for the connections facilitated by ones and zeros.

"Hey, Shelly, it's Chris. Look, I think this is going to turn into a much bigger problem down here. People are gathering by the tree like it's Prince or Kobe. Give me a call when you get a chance."

"Jared. It's Chris. Look, man, this thing in South Carolina is blowing up. You're the only one in Milwaukee right now and we're gonna need all hands on deck. Check your email, I sent you a document with the FELL history on the guys who worked on this job. I need you or someone to triple-verify that info. Call me back ASAP."

Chris knew he wouldn't hear from Jared. At best, he would pass the message to his assistant. But Chris was struggling to make sense of what had happened on that job site and grasping for any information. Four FELLers had shown up to the site. Two of them had worked on jobs together before. All four had great ratings and long histories with FELL. One had done over 300 tree jobs with no negative reviews. None of the four had criminal records beyond a couple speeding tickets. It just didn't add up. How had they made such a grave mistake?

Thick clouds muffled the yellow glow of the moon and Chris heard the rain start to intensify. The wind rocked the heavy bottoms of the roller blinds and water bounced off the white railings of the piazza. Chris put his phone in his jacket's inner pocket and carried his iced tea inside to sit at the bar. Sobriety seemed necessary on this ghostly night.

44

Jo felt the first drops of rain as she walked to her car. She decided to back the Citröen right up to her parking alley door so she could keep the flowers and herself dry as she packed the hatchback with bouquets. Grant had finished his delivery shift for the afternoon and gone home, but she needed to do a final run to Edelweiss Country Club to deliver sixteen centerpieces for a Rayovac corporate banquet that night. Days were getting much shorter and the coming storm was accelerating the dying afternoon light.

She took six trips back and forth to her cooler to load the bouquet boxes into her car. She was using a double-decker wood platform Grant had built to be able to fit all of the vases. She stepped back to admire the display before closing the hatch. Ten thousand tiny petals, ready for the dance. Ever-wizardly farmer Carol had dropped off buckets of the season's final snapdragons and dahlias the day before. In cream, orange, and fuchsia, their petals spiraled in flamboyant scoops. Jo had arranged them with chrysanthemums in bright gold, mauve, and burgundy. Each vase had stems of ornamental purple kale and lime green sedum, with eucalyptus from her own garden filling in contrast. She had tucked in a few eggplant varietals grown by Sawm Lor that looked like tiny green pumpkins. Jo gave the thickly loaded structure a little shake to check everything was secure and closed the hatch.

Loading the car had taken longer than she planned, and when she looked at her watch, she was shocked how late it was. The flowers needed to be there by 5:00 p.m., thirty minutes away, and it was 4:15. She started the car, scolding herself for not building in more time on this order. She knew better. She turned on her lights and drove out of town, not slowly.

With about three miles left before the turn into the country club, the clouds finally opened in earnest and the light rain became an outright downpour. Jo's wipers couldn't keep up with the deluge and she considered pulling over to wait it out. But she had driven this route to the country club dozens of times and she knew these roads well.

Grateful for the breather of a stop sign on the country road, Jo looked down at her watch again. She was relieved to see she still had fifteen minutes, and she pressed the heels of her hands against her temples telling herself to calm down.

It sounded like an explosion inside her own car. And then darkness. Jo's small white hatchback was slammed at full speed from behind by a Chevy Silverado. Her car spun 180 degrees into the intersection and was struck from the side by a Pontiac Trans Am.

A martin flying over the crash, disturbed from his perch on a wire, purple wings outspread, would see two roads forming an ancient cross. The cross was made of stained glass, with headlights and taillights projecting beams through the facets. Before hardening, the clear molten glass had been dyed by ten thousand delicate flower petals in every color of autumn.

45

Chris pushed his empty glass toward the bartender as his ears perked up to the conversation between the men sitting next to him.

"Oh yeah? Small world. I used to do jobs for FELL, too. I quit a couple years ago."

"Refill on your iced tea, honey?" the bartender asked. Chris nodded, wanting her to stop talking so he could listen in.

"Iced tea?" The man next to him turned and addressed Chris. "Naw naw naw, not here ya don't. You gotta have a Rusty Dragon. It's their specialty."

"What's in it?" Chris asked.

"It's pretty close to iced tea. You probably won't notice the difference," he said, slapping his friend on the chest as they laughed.

The waitress rolled her eyes. "It's Drambuie with Fireball whiskey and a splash of sweet tea. You up for that tonight, hon?"

Chris hesitated, and he could tell the men were watching him. "Sure, why not? When in Rome."

"There ya go!" The man shook Chris by the shoulder. Chris had never understood the point of these situations. The positions men put each other in to prove they weren't soft. It had confused him since he was a young boy, but he knew exactly what to do and how to navigate these moments. It was one of his most well-honed skills. The art of compliance. He took a drink and winced.

"Say, did I hear you say you've done some jobs for

FELL?" Chris asked.

"Yeah, I did a few dozen jobs. I'm in construction now, so I'm out of that game. Why? Do you do FELL gigs?"

"Yeah, I've done a few," Chris lied.

"You a climber or a bucket baby?"

"Uhh, both. Depends on the job."

"You're not the guy who axed Lady Sweetgrass, right?" the other man leaned forward to ask him.

"Ha, no, not me. I actually live up in…Chicago," Chris lied again.

"Corey. Nice to meet you. This is my buddy Jake. Just met him tonight at the dart board." The men exchanged firm handshakes.

"Yeah, we're all lucky we didn't touch that job with a ten-foot pole. Those guys have their heads on platters right now."

"Truth," Chris agreed. He paused, not wanting to give away his position. "I really gotta wonder how they made that mistake." He took a sip of his Rusty Dragon, looking straight ahead at the men's faces in the mirror behind the bar.

"You kidding? Come on, you know what it's like on FELL jobs," Corey said.

"Right? Every job was like 'Down, baby, down!'" Jake added.

Chris nodded, letting them talk.

"What do they expect? You prune or treat and get $300. You fell and get $3000."

"At least!" Jake interjected. "I had one job on a big

estate where I went home that day to eight grand dropped right in my checking account. These property owners don't give two fucks. Most of them don't even live there."

"Another round," Corey called to the waitress and she brought three more Rusty Dragons and a bowl of spicy pecans.

"I remember my first job with FELL. Me and two other guys showed up. I had just finished my associate degree, but hell, even I knew nothing was wrong with that tree. It was a hemlock. Real beaut. So the one guy goes up to the door and starts scaring the shit out of this woman. Telling her this tree was gonna fall on her house in the next big storm. So she signs off on the removal. She was grateful!" Corey took a long drink, ice cubes hitting his teeth.

"So, these guys are laughing, already counting their money. What am I supposed to do?

Somehow stop this from happening?"

"Right. Tough spot," agreed Chris, starting to feel sick.

"These fuckers made me hold the chainsaw. They were on the ropes. I was shaking. I was fucking shaking when I made that first cut. I remember I couldn't even talk to my girlfriend when I got home that night. I just blacked out the world."

Jake spoke up. "Same here, man. Those first few jobs were such a mind fuck. You gotta just tell yourself those trees were coming down eventually. And hey, I paid off my wife's nursing school loans with FELL jobs. Plus a trip to Cancun. I'm not complaining!" The two men clinked glasses and held them out to Chris. He complied.

"Well, the guys who KO'd Lady Sweetgrass will be fine anyway once this dies down. All those jobs are insured through FELL," Corey said.

"Yeah, but for now they might want to move or change their names!" The men laughed.

Chris had stopped listening. Numbers were rolling across his brain. Just an hour before, he had been reading the data on the number of FELL jobs matched in Charleston in October. He estimated the percentage of trees potentially felled without cause based on this conversation. Total number of trees lost. Times the number of markets in South Carolina. Times fifty states. Times twelve months. Times seven years.

Chris set cash on the bar and stood to leave.

"No! My man! We're just getting started!"

"Sorry, guys, I gotta meet someone at a bar downtown." He lied again.

"Alright, alright, go get that dick wet, brother."

"Nice to meet you guys." Chris turned to leave. He walked the length of the old oak bar, feeling unsteady and starting to sweat, yearning to collapse. He burst out the door into the blustery downpour and walked to the end of the piazza, stumbling down the three steps to the parking lot. He fell onto all fours, rocking back onto his calves, crying and heaving into his hands. The rain drops grew bigger and colder. The wind pushed him as he braced his body with an open palm on the pavement. He looked up, searching the sky. He only saw the branches of the sycamore tree above him, their outline in the shape of a crow. His hot tears coated his ears and ran down his neck. The wind tried again, harder this time, to pull him over. He complied.

46

The tarnished brass clock pendulum swung back and forth. A boxer's leather speed bag rebounded and worked towards a rest. The burlap sack of potatoes jostled in the back of her grandfather's wagon. Jo's vision started to come into focus.

"There she is. Did you sleep well?" The nurse was reaching her hand deep inside Jo's brown waxed canvas purse that hung from one strap around a doorknob.

"We found a phone number in your bag, ma'am. I took a chance and gave them a call. Just gonna put this card back where I found it."

Jo's eyes adjusted and she started to become aware of the room. Her head was throbbing and she felt sharp pains with every inhale.

"The doctor will be in shortly to speak with you. Can I get you anything? Apple juice? You want the TV on?"

Jo shook her head no. She started to reach behind her back to adjust the pillow but the nurse stopped her and helped raise the bed to a seated position. She set the call button next to Jo's hand and left the room.

"You walked between the raindrops, Miss Martin!" the doctor said loudly as he entered the room, lifting a page on his clipboard. "True miracle. How ya feeling?" Jo didn't respond. She stared at him, still trying to make sense of where she was.

"We'll need to keep you here for a few days to monitor your vitals and make sure there's no internal bleeding. But I think you're gonna walk right out of here. You've got a few cracked ribs, multiple contusions, and a concussion. Pretty bad sprain on your wrist. But that's all we're finding."

"How did I get here?" Jo asked, her voice scratchy and strained.

"Ambulance brought you up to Madison. Do you remember anything from the crash?"

"Rain. Two cars. Not much more than that."

"The cops who arrived on the scene don't know how you survived."

"Oh, my God. The other people from the crash! Did they make it?"

"They have some long recoveries ahead, but yes, they survived. It's been pretty miraculous all around," the doctor said seriously. "Someone was watching over you."

Jo closed her eyes and felt tears coming. She was so grateful everyone was going to be OK.

The doctor looked down at his clipboard. "The next few days will be very important. We should know by the end of the week if the baby will survive."

"Oh, God, there was a baby in one of the cars?" Jo clasped her hands over her mouth, realizing for the first time she had a chipped tooth.

The doctor looked confused. "Miss Martin," he paused and looked down again at her chart. "I'm sorry, did you not know you were pregnant?"

"What? No, that's not possible," Jo said, freezing in place.

"About ten weeks along."

"But we used…but I'm thirty-eight…I haven't

missed a cycle...this isn't possible."

"There can be some bleeding early in pregnancy that can be mistaken for a menstrual cycle. But I assure you, you are pregnant. Now we just need to hope the placenta hangs on tight. That little bugger really got his bell rung last night."

The room was spinning. Jo thought about Micha. She had no way to contact him. They hadn't even exchanged phone numbers. She immediately wanted to ask the doctor about abortion, but couldn't find the words. A feeling of terror poured through her veins.

"You'll want to contact your regular doctor right away. At your advanced age, he will need to monitor your pregnancy closely. But let's not get ahead of ourselves. For the next few days, just focus on prayers. I don't want to give you false hope, but I will say I've seen pregnancies hang on through much worse trauma."

"Thank you, doctor," Jo said quietly, stunned.

"Just get some rest. I'll be back to check on you in a few hours." He left the room and within a minute, the nurse was back with a big smile on her face.

"Ma'am, the doctor told me you just found out you're pregnant! I brought you a sherbet cup to celebrate. Hope lime is OK. Do you want orange? I can go back and get orange."

"Lime is good, thank you," Jo said in a daze.

"I'll give you some privacy. Just go ahead and use the phone on the bedside table to call your husband with the good news." She tiptoed out of the room while giving Jo two thumbs up.

47

The coyote looked at Chris, cocked his head, and then ambled back into the undulating field of blonde cordgrass, disappearing from sight. Chris balanced the sketchpad on the cockpit rim of the kayak, and pulled the pack of eight colored pencils from his fleece pocket. Two blue herons stood on the shore, not more than twenty feet away, probing the soft earth. The only sounds were the sparrows and warblers, and the occasional gentle breeze through the salt marsh. He began to sketch. He was surprised to find he was using every color he had, and for a scene that had seemed so monochromatic when he first paddled through it. He paused his pencil strokes to watch a small bird knock the spiked seed heads off a tall blade of grass. Chris startled as an otter flipped just to the right of his boat.

Chris had awoken early, his hotel room lights on, hungover and confused. He couldn't face the phone calls and emails. He didn't want to pick up the FELL fixers from the airport and drive them past the site of the tree. He didn't want to sit on a scenic veranda and expense a $400 lunch for the group as they strategized how to lie, yet again. He remembered his hotel loaned kayaks, and convinced the concierge to give him one, even though it was before the rental hours. Chris bought the drawing supplies at a 24-hour pharmacy in Charleston, and drove over the Ravenel Bridge to Sullivan's Island at sunrise. He stopped into an Exxon station to ask about directions to a good spot to put in the kayak. The man at the counter told him three turns to take to get to the launch, and Chris bought an iced coffee.

He hadn't been so fully immersed in nature like this in a very long time. Not even a glance at his phone in hours. Like slowly and gently untangling a knot in a child's hair, he could feel his anxiety loosen and release, strand by strand. As he watched the tall grass bend in the breeze, he felt oxygen filling his lungs and reaching his cells. He felt his shoulders drop and his pulse slow down. He watched a daddy longlegs crawl across the front hatch cover of the kayak, and had no impulse to flick it off. Chris recognized himself in the spider. He recognized himself in the egrets and fiddler crabs. In the ripples of the brackish water. Even in the eyes of the coyote, an ecosystem invader and a nuisance, of whom he was afraid.

48

Dagmar and Grant ran into the hospital room, both trying to be the first one in the door. Dag looked terrified and Grant looked disheveled.

"Jo! Oh, my God, Jo," Dag reached out to her bed, trying to hug her tightly while being extremely gentle at the same time. Like a child holding a beloved china doll. "You have no idea the scare you gave us." Dag burst into tears.

"Rocky, there you are. Sure is a relief to see you, kid." Grant's voice caught, and he set a hand on Dagmar's back to comfort her.

"Please don't tell me my new nickname is Rocky," Jo looked at him and smiled, reassuring him she was OK. She quickly held a hand up to her mouth, remembering her chipped tooth. She was suddenly self-conscious of her appearance, and tried to smooth her hair and tuck it behind her ears.

"You guys didn't have to come all the way to Madison. That sure was nice of you, though." Jo's eyes welled up, overwhelmed by everything, and aware of the secret she now carried.

"Oh, honey, don't cry. It's going to be OK. We can help you with anything you need."

Jo cried harder. What had she done to deserve such good friends? How would she ever tell them? What would they think of her?

"Is it about the Citröen?" Grant asked.

"What?" Jo looked up at him, wiping her eyes.

"Yeah, I'd be sad, too. Your car folded like a wet paper bag," Grant said, and Jo winced. "She's toast. But don't worry about it! I was thinking you could use Danny Kaye until you can find something new."

"Danny Kaye?"

"Yeah, my mom's K-car. It's just sitting in their driveway. Mom doesn't drive anymore and she already said she'd be glad to loan it to you."

"Really, Jo. It's all yours if you want to use it. As long as you need," Dag encouraged her.

"That would be extremely helpful. Thank you. Tell your mom she gets free flowers for life."

"No problem at all, Rocky. I'll give him an oil change and drop him off behind your shop tomorrow. When are they letting you out of here?"

"I'm not sure. Probably by the end of the week

if everything stays stable. The doctor says I was really lucky."

"I'd say it was a blasted miracle. My buddy Nick was the first cop on the scene. He said the guy who hit you was hammered. Blood alcohol .25. He had already hit a guard rail a mile back. Crashing into you probably saved his damn life."

"Oh shit! Edelweiss Country Club! The flowers!" Jo exclaimed.

Dagmar and Grant looked at each other and grinned. "Did Jo Martin actually just swear? Is that what just happened here?"

"Oh, geez, sorry." Jo shook her head.

"I'm sure the flowers were stunners, Jo. But right now they're pulverized in the ditch of Highway O," Grant said.

"Rayovac must have thought I really dropped the ball. I'm so embarrassed. Ugh, and they had already paid me, too. I have to get them a refund and an apology right away."

"Jo, Jo, slow down. You don't have to run a business right now. All anyone cares about is that you're alive. Don't devote any energy to all of these little details. Your only job is to rest and let your body mend. OK?" Dag took her hand.

Jo took a deep breath. "OK, Dag. Thank you…I just feel like my world has turned completely upside down. Honestly, I'm still having trouble understanding what has happened."

"Hey, Rocky, maybe those ditch flowers will set seed and it will be like an accidental roadside garden!"

"That's a nice thought, Grant," replied Jo, thinking that wasn't really how seeds worked, but appreciated his positivity.

"Are you really calling her 'Rocky' now?" Dagmar asked, annoyed with her brother.

"Just for now. Just while she's nursing those shiners."

"It's OK, Grant," Jo said. "You know I like your nicknames."

"See?" He turned to Dagmar and stuck out his tongue. "And hey, it's a compliment! Remember, Rocky won the big fight."

Jo thought that wasn't quite how she remembered the end of that movie.

November

49

"GOAL: One trillion trees conserved, restored and grown globally by 2030." Chris sat on the curb looking at his phone in front of Liberty Acres and swiped through the menus on 1t.org, TrillionTrees.org, and PlantWithPurpose.org. He had gotten an alert telling him the pizza guy was arriving shortly, but the driver must have taken a wrong turn. He texted Eileen to let her know it was delayed, but he would be back upstairs soon. Chris found the drop-down menu to schedule recurring monthly donations and selected $150. He saw the Prius round the corner of the front parking lot and quickly changed his amount to $1500. He wondered how many trees that amount of money would help plant each month. And if it could even make a dent in the damage that had been done by FELL.

"Are you Chris? Here ya go." The man pulled the pizza out from the insulated red rectangular bag. "Have a good night, bro."

"You, too. Thanks." He watched the man get back into his Prius and retrieve a lit cigarette from the dashboard air vent, taking a long drag and exhaling out the open window. He peeled away, almost hitting the corner bumper of a wheelchair transport van.

Chris carried the pizza inside the automatic security doors and up the elevator to Eileen's floor.

"Whoa! Pizza night?" Jill was standing in front of him as the elevator doors opened.

"Zaffiro's pizza and cribbage. It's a Schwarz family tradition," he smiled at her.

"Well, that sounds like a pretty nice Saturday night to me," she said warmly.

"I agree. Although my mom plays cribbage like a mafia boss."

Jill laughed. "I always thought cribbage was a gentleman's game."

"Ha! Etiquette masking ruthlessness."

"Well, have fun. Eileen has been doing amazingly well. It's been so great to see her getting back to her old self. She's a fighter." Jill stepped onto the elevator as Chris stepped off. "Say, what does she like on her pizza?"

"Everything but fish," Chris replied. Jill nodded approvingly and the doors closed. Chris had an impulse to push the button quickly so the doors would reopen and he could ask Jill to join them. But he turned and walked down the hallway to his mom's apartment.

"Ahh, there he is." Eileen sat up straighter in

her chair and rotated a rolling table over her lap. "Honestly, I thought I could smell the pizza coming down the hall!"

"Mom, I didn't realize I got the twenty-inch. You might have some leftovers tomorrow for puzzle time with Martha."

"Chris, honey, look in the second drawer next to the stove. I think there's a pizza cutter in there. Maybe you could cut these in half so I don't make such a mess."

"Sure, no problem, Mom. Hang on."

"I'll deal your cards, dear."

Chris walked over to the living area, set a plate of pizza in front of his mom, sat down on the sofa and put a roll of paper towels on the coffee table.

"Honey, what were you starting to tell me about

changes at FELL? Is that something happening soon?"

"Oh, yeah, I was just saying after that whole thing in Charleston, there has been a lot in the works. We'll see. I've laid out some plans for a pretty big overhaul. But so far, we just keep having meetings and going in circles."

"What do you think stands in the way of making some of these changes?"

"I don't know. Like, one thing we really need is a few full-time staffers in our biggest markets. Not all gig workers. We need eyes on these jobs before anything is cut down. I actually want to put body cams on every FELLer for a few months until we feel we have a handle on the scope of the problem.

"So, is it just about money? Finding the labor?"

"Yes, both. Sometimes I think it's Jared who always puts profits first, but I'm starting to think Scott is just as bad. He's just nicer about it. Those two always do a good cop-bad cop thing with me and end up getting their way."

"15-2, 15-4, 15-6, and a pair is 8, and the rest ain't great." Eileen pegged her points.

"Pizza's pretty good tonight. Surprised it was still hot," Chris said.

"It's very good. Crust is crisp. Well, I'm glad to hear things might have a chance of improving at work, dear. I know these travel situations have been difficult for you. People really do get so sentimentally attached to trees. I remember in our neighborhood, the Palmers lost a big old sugar maple in an electrical storm. Neighbors sent them condolence cards and brought them casseroles. Really!"

Chris chuckled. "Oh, yes, I believe it. Now add 500 years and sprinkle in some southern superstition, and you'll have an idea what it was like down there…15-2, 15-4, and there ain't no more."

"South Carolina really is a beautiful place. Your dad and I spent a long weekend there once for an anniversary. He could sit and watch the salt marsh for hours. That Lowcountry food is something else, too."

"Agreed. Hey, Mom, I'm gonna use the bathroom before the next game, OK?"

"Sure, honey, go in my room. Sorry if it's a mess."

Chris walked into Eileen's room and leaned against her dresser, surprised how the mention of his father had affected him. He went into the bathroom and held his hands under cool water, looking at himself in the mirror. He could see his mom's armoire in the background of his reflection. His heart was beating fast. He couldn't look away.

"Chris, you're acting like that's where she keeps the heroin," he said to himself. "If you want the brush, just go get the freakin' brush." He flushed the toilet to mask the sound of the wardrobe latch, and reached into the back of the long drawer, pulling out the leather pouch. He tucked it in his back jeans pocket as he left the bedroom, quickly walking to the kitchen pretending like he needed a glass of water. He stuffed the brush in the pocket of his jacket hanging from Eileen's coat tree.

"You want a glass of water, Mom?"

"No, thank you. I would be up all night if I had water right now."

Chris sat back down on the couch and heard his phone vibrate on the table in front of him. He flipped it over to see the alert. It was a text message from TrillionTrees asking him to check his account.

"Hang on, Mom. Sorry for doing this. I think I just got a fraud alert, I'm just gonna check it quickly."

"Take your time. I need to rest from moving my peg so far down the board anyway," Eileen kidded him.

Chris logged back into his account and read the alert. It was a personal message from someone in the organization asking him if he meant to contribute the large amount of $1500 a month or if it had been done in error. He wrote back that it was in fact an error, and he would like to change it to $15,000 a month.

50

Mai set her backpack on the floor and danced around the store in her forest green corduroys. Jo had started to open the shop for limited hours each day and was forced to give up her lone wolf lifestyle as she needed all the help she could get. Her wrist was still immobilized, and she was very tired most days. She couldn't yet carry heavy buckets, and was having concentration problems. She had hired Paj to make bouquets, man the cash register, and help with other tasks around the store.

"How was school today, Mai?" Jo asked.

"It was fun. I like my teacher. He brings bugs to school."

"Bugs!"

"Today he brought a walking stick."

"That sounds fun. I always loved science."

"Me, too. But my favorite part of the day is after school when I get to walk to your store and see my mommy." Mai's infectious joy was such a gift during this difficult time. It was delightful to have a child around the store.

"I have a yellow fan for you, Miss Jo." Mai held out both of her little downturned fists. "Pick a hand."

"A fan? How could you fit a fan inside your hand?" Jo touched the fist on the right. Mai opened her hand to reveal one perfect, bright yellow ginkgo leaf. Mai started giggling. "I found it on the sidewalk."

"What a well-made fan, Mai," Jo said as she pretended to cool off her face with it. "A fan for a fairy queen, I declare."

Mai leaned in to whisper, "I had one in both hands."

"I'm going to take this upstairs and put it in a safe place," Jo told Mai. When she came back down, she set a plate of warm, pumpkin-hickory nut bread on the counter for Mai and Paj. She had been baking more since her crash, trying to contribute and thank her friends in any small way she could. She wasn't used to relying on anyone. Mai took a large slice and it broke in her hand, falling to the floor.

"Miss Jo!" she gasped. "I'm so sorry!" Paj came out from the cooler to see the mess.

"We will clean this! Mai, you be more careful," Paj scolded her.

"It's so crumbly…it's not your fault, dear. Please take a new piece." Jo quickly bent down to clean the crumbs and felt a rush of blood to her head.

She stood up and braced herself on the stainless steel prep table. Paj walked to Jo and took her arm.

"Slowly, Miss Jo. Slowly," Paj said quietly. Mai looked worried.

Grant walked in the front door and the three of them pretended everything was fine.

"Hey, Jo, those four aspen saplings finally arrived," he said excitedly. "Do you think there's still a chance yet this fall to get them in the ground? It's been below freezing most nights."

Jo thought about her wrist and the task of digging large holes in nearly frozen ground. She couldn't bring herself to ask one more favor from the team that had worked like crazy since her accident to get the Garden for the Blind built and planted.

"Grant, I don't know. Maybe they'll be OK root-bound in the garage over the winter and we can deal with it in the spring. You're right. I think the ground is almost too frozen now."

"Pshaw. You think I have these big muscles just to impress the ladies? I can dig through that barren tundra out there."

"Grant," Jo shook her head. "You'll kill your shoulders. Don't even worry about it. We'll do it in April."

"Paj," Grant said, "what do you think? You're the expert. Can I still get the saplings in the ground and watered in? Will they survive?"

Paj, still holding on to Jo, shyly answered him. "Yes. Even the latest autumn day holds life. It won't be easy. Dig a few inches deeper than you think you should. Sawm can come tomorrow and help you. It will be a warmer day."

"I knew it! Thanks, Paj. See, Jo? The professor has spoken. No arguments. Sawm and I will get those colts in their stables tomorrow. Four corners of the garden, right?"

"Right," Jo said, relenting. She noticed Paj was blushing at the compliments.

So many times since her accident, Jo had thought about the biblical definition of the word grace. She had survived when there was no apparent way to survive that crash. Luck? Or divine, unmerited favor. The drunk driver had survived, too. Her friends were giving her hours upon hours of help that she didn't deserve and could never repay. There would be one last warm bonus day at the very end of the fall, weeks past the harvest. The saplings could tuck their roots into a safe home for winter and, by some miracle of nature, thrive. And Jo Martin, old and bruised and a card-carrying sinner, had not lost the baby.

<h1 style="text-align:center">51</h1>

Lucas walked into the room ahead of Chris and pulled the strings on the Venetian blinds. The room took on a yellow glow from the tree outside. Chris sat in his regular spot on the window end of the worn leather sofa. Curling carpet under him, stained drop ceiling over him.

"Wow. Quite a fall we've had, huh? That ginkgo is still holding on. Rain is coming in tomorrow. That will be the end, I'm guessing." Lucas grabbed a spiral notebook and took his place in the wingback chair.

"That's a great tree."

"Yeah, this building is falling apart, but I don't think I'd ever want a different office. Ginkgos have been around since the dinosaurs. No living relatives. I feel like he watches over me."

"I once read there were ginkgo trees that survived the atom bomb on Hiroshima," Chris said.

"You're right. I've been there. Six of them are still standing today. Outerlayers were destroyed, but somehow there was an inner core of cells that still held life."

"Damn."

"Yeah. That's the will to live, man. Not to be underestimated."

Chris was quiet, thinking about what it might have been like for the Japanese people when they realized those trees were coming back the next year. To see buds. Green.

"There's a plaque by each tree now," Lucas added.

"Hope."

"Exactly. Hope. That survival story can give us hope on an individual level after our personal traumas, and also give us hope for the planet itself."

"It's like the Earth saying, 'Do your worst, humans. We'll still bring the bud.'"

Lucas laughed. "That's a good way to put it. The planet should make bumper stickers."

Chris looked out the window and appreciated the tree in a new way.

"So. How have you been the past couple weeks?" Lucas looked at him with engagement.

"In a nutshell, struggling."

Lucas nodded. "Is it OK if I ask about your fingernails?"

Chris looked down at his hands. His nail beds were stained and caked with brown and green pigment.

"Yeah. You can ask," Chris paused. "Let's just say I went on a bit of a bender."

Lucas was quiet and Chris continued, curling his fingers into his palms.

"So. Yeah. I'm just gonna say it. That's why I'm here, right? What's the point of lying to your therapist? Who does that?"

"Everyone."

"Everyone?" Chris chuckled.

"I think so, yes. But it doesn't mean progress can't be made. The healing in a situation doesn't always hinge on a perfect verbal account of events."

"Well, that's good to hear. Sometimes these things are kind of a blur anyway."

"Absolutely."

"OK. So, since I've been back from the whole Charleston cluster, I've had this desperate anxiety around replacing the trees. I mean, Lucas, for fucksake, this is on the order of two million trees. How am I supposed to sleep at night?"

"It's heavy. It's very heavy. It's normal to seek atonement, even when we're not the perpetrator."

"But I am the perpetrator. FELL is me and I am FELL. I can't put this on anyone else."

Lucas was quiet and jotted something in his notebook.

"I bought thirty blank canvases. Maybe forty. I

don't even remember anymore. My whole car was full. And then I got wasted. Glenlivet." Chris stopped and looked at his hands.

"Go on."

"Yeah, so then I painted for about ten hours. Straight."

"What did you paint?"

"Trees. Tightly packed. Trees. Like a forest that had been planted as a windbreak in a farmer's field. Intentional. Geometric. I hung them all around the room. They filled the walls on four sides. It looked like corduroy wallpaper."

"Is it still there?"

"Yeah. It's still there."

"And I'm gonna assume you used the ebony brush?"

Chris looked down. "Yes," he answered quietly.

"Do you remember what you were feeling while you were painting?"

"Progress. Like I was bringing trees to the world. Like I was climbing out of a hole I had dug. Inching out from a dark tunnel. Not a tunnel. A grave."

"When you think about it today. Right now in this moment. Would you say that each tree you painted manifested a real tree on the Earth somewhere? Because you painted them?"

"No," Chris shook his head. "I'm not insane. Well, I am. Obviously. But no. I am well aware I don't have magic powers or a magic brush."

"Chris, have you ever heard of animism?"

"I don't know. Maybe? Is that like when animals

have human souls and stuff?"

"And objects. And places. It's basically the belief that all things are animated and alive. A river, a blanket, a rock, weather, even words."

"So, this is what I'm doing with the brush? Is that what you're saying?"

"I just want us to try to put this in the context of the practices of many world cultures and religions. Almost all, in some aspects. Especially indigenous populations. The people who have been here the longest. And groups like the Hmong, who have lived closest to nature. Do we think they're all 'insane,' to use your word?"

"Of course not."

"Right. Of course not. OK. So, is it possible you have assigned a living spirit to this brush? Maybe as a way to keep your dad alive, too?"

"It was his brush."

"I know."

"I mean. Maybe. It seems logical. He held it. He created with it. Whenever I see it, I think of him. You know, I want to show him my paintings. I want to ask his advice. So many times I want to pick up the phone and ask him something and then I remember."

"So, as long as the brush is alive, then so is he."

"I mean. I guess that makes sense. It just seems so childish. Like a stuffed animal coming to life."

"But you are a child. You will always be his child."

The two men were silent.

"Chris, I'd like to talk about the day you decided to go to the art store and fill your car with canvases. The day you decided to paint a thousand trees."

"4850 trees."

"Do you remember anything specific that happened before that? Maybe that morning? Or the night before? Feel free to look at your calendar or your text threads. I just want us to think about triggers in your life and how we can reduce those, too."

Chris took out his phone and started scrolling through emails and messages.

"I had a morning meeting. I was working from home. Nothing weird that I can see. Texts with a few high school buddies. Just bullshit about the Packers. Fantasy football."

"Take your time. Just look at everything."

"Ha. Well. Here's something. An old friend sent me a text to tell me my ex-wife had a baby."

"Remind me when you two split up?"

"Long time ago. Ten years. Total starter marriage. I mean, I did love her. Don't get me wrong."

"Do you still love her?"

"No. She's great. She's the best. I fucked it up. But that was a long time ago."

"What did you feel when you found out she had a baby?"

"I knew she had gotten remarried. I wasn't shocked. She always wanted kids. I think I was happy for her."

"OK. Happy for her. Anything else?"

Chris thought for a moment. "Well. I guess I'll describe it like this. You know when someone dies? You know they're dead. I mean, you KNOW they're dead. They're not coming back. But then maybe something happens months or even years later that makes them more dead. Like, you lose a watch they gave you. Do you know what I mean?"

"I do. A little self-disclosure here…before my mom died, she bought my toddler a bunch of clothes. Most were way too big. Eventually he grew out of the last thing she had bought for him. It hit me hard."

"Exactly. Well it was like that. When I found out she had a baby with him. Of course I knew we were divorced," Chris laughed a little. "But it was like we were divorced…harder."

Chris looked at the ginkgo tree again. He inhaled deeply and exhaled slowly. The wind blew and he could see leaves flying off to the side. The tree looked noticeably more bare than when he had walked into the room just an hour before. The yellow glow in the room was dimmed to gray. The intensity of the ginkgo's blazing handshake had loosened its grip, ever so slightly.

52

Tidy, organized piles of dried grasses and grains lined the long prep table. Jo had collected rusty bristles of broom corn, olive arcs of millet, soft linen hare's tail grass, braided wheat, and bright blonde beads of flax. At the far end of the assembly line, she had filled three big jars with some specialty items to be used more conservatively. One held stalks of smoky mauve quinoa. Another jar was packed with intricate scabiosa seed pods, only the size of shooter marbles, but that could rival Buckminster Fuller's geodesic domes. The last jar overflowed with tiger orange capsules hanging on bittersweet vines. Even though it looked like a lot, Jo knew how fast it would all go once they started building bouquets, and she had to make sure every order could be fulfilled. Jo had already stuffed the shallow ceramic pottery bowls with folded layers of chicken wire to prepare to make the Thanksgiving centerpieces. Her wrist was still bothering her, and she was grateful when she saw Paj come in the front door to start her shift.

"So cold!" Paj exclaimed, as she worked to pull off her mohair cape. She carried a large jar of a leafy sloshing liquid. Jo looked at it curiously.

"Isn't it? I'm shocked by the cold, every single year. Sometimes I think I have convinced myself it won't happen," she laughed. Paj set the jar down by the cash register and joined Jo at the prep table.

"I'm so glad you're here, Paj. I have all the vessels prepped, but my wrist is starting to kill me right now."

"You rest, Miss Jo. Just tell me what to do and I will finish them all for you."

"I honestly don't know what I would do without you and your family, Paj. I am just so thankful for you."

"I thank you too, Jo. I like to work here, and now that our harvest is done, I can be here whenever you need me."

"I am afraid I lean on you too much."

"I promise to tell you if it is too much work for me."

"Paj, I was going to wait until after the holiday next week, but I've decided to raise your pay to six dollars an hour. Starting today. I hope that helps to show you how much I appreciate your hard work."

Paj was quiet and kept her eyes on the prep table.

"OK, let's make one template bouquet together

and then I will let you work on making the rest."

"What is template?" Paj asked.

"Template is a model. Ummm...an example. A guide. You can make the rest like this one."

"Yes, thank you. I understand now. Template."

Jo set a cobalt glazed stoneware bowl on the table and the two women worked together to cut grasses and grains to size to fill in the base. Jo placed the more colorful specialty items around the center and sides in a natural, garden-like composition. She bent down to eye level to check the sight lines. She showed Paj how to place her elbow on the table, fist straight up, to make sure the height was low enough for people to see across a table. Jo removed one spray of flax that was floating too high and stuck it in the side instead.

"What do you think?" Jo asked.

"Very good." Paj nodded. "People will eat turkey and have a conversation."

Jo laughed. "Exactly, Paj."

Paj lifted three bowls onto the table and started filling them methodically, sliding them down the row as she went. She made quick work and they were all perfect. Jo was impressed.

"Paj, will you be OK if I go upstairs and lie down for a little while?"

"Yes, ma'am. Please rest. Take this." Paj went to the front desk and lifted the jar of liquid she had brought.

"What is this?" Jo took the jar and held it up to the light.

"Raspberry leaf tea. It is very good for you."

"Oh, wonderful. Thank you, Paj."

"I have seen bred heifers eat all the leaves from the raspberry vines. It will help things to be easier."

Jo kept focusing on the jar and didn't want to look up and meet Paj's eyes. She knew. Paj knew about the baby. Jo wasn't showing yet, but somehow Paj knew. Jo felt embarrassed and self-conscious.

"Thank you, Paj." Jo swallowed hard. "How can I make more of this when it's gone?"

"Just crush a handful of dry raspberry leaves and fill the jar with boiling water. After a few minutes, you can drink. Add ginger or honey if you like the taste. Now you have the template."

Jo smiled, still not looking up. "Thank you, Paj. I will do that."

Jo turned and walked up the stairs to her apartment. She set the tea on her kitchen counter. She lay down on her sofa, curled to her side, and pulled a blanket up from her feet to her chin. Jo thought about the term "bred heifer" and cringed. If Paj knew she was pregnant, it was only a matter of time for everyone else. Jo would need to tell them soon. Hot tears formed and she closed her eyes, pulling the blanket up tighter. Seemingly overnight, and in spite of her most strenuous denials, it had gotten so cold.

December

53

"Chris. It's Jill at Liberty Acres. Call me back when you get this."

"Great," Chris sighed. His mom had been doing well, but he knew setbacks were inevitable. He finished sending an email, stood up to close his office door for privacy, and walked over to the windows to call Jill back. The shore of Lake Michigan was beginning to freeze, and the water looked dark and choppy. Only a few walkers dotted the footpath, bundled tight with scarves and down coats. The retractable wings of the art museum were closed up securely. Jill answered on the first ring.

"Hey, Jill, it's Chris Schwarz, Eileen's son."

"Yes, hi, Chris. OK. So, Eileen has had a fall, but

don't worry, she is just fine."

"A fall? Where?"

"Well, she slipped on the ice. It was too cold this morning for the salt to work and our guys hadn't been out to sand yet."

"Where the hell was she going?"

"She said she was going to buy you a wreath. The scouts had set up a booth in our parking lot for a fundraiser, and Eileen was afraid they would sell out, so she skedaddled down there first thing."

Chris put his hand over his eyes and shook his head in frustration. "A wreath? For ME?"

"Yes, Chris," Jill was smiling. "But she's fine. Not hurt, just a little shook up. I mean, it's kind of sweet, isn't it?"

"Jill," Chris laughed. "I'm a single man who lives in a condo. Last night I had a banana for dinner."

"Are you telling me you're not a wreath guy?"

"I'll be there in thirty minutes. And no, I wouldn't say I'm known as a wreath guy." They were both laughing. "See you soon. Thanks, Jill."

Chris got his car from the parking garage and drove to Liberty Acres. The roads were worse than they had been when he left that morning. A layer of sleet quickly covered his windshield. He could feel his brakes stutter and re-engage at each stoplight. He stopped at a drive-thru window and bought a large caramel latte for his mom.

When he arrived, Jill was in the lobby talking to another resident. They nodded and waved to each other and he went upstairs.

Eileen's door was propped open and she called for him to come in when he lightly knocked.

"I am so stupid, honey."

"Mom, you're not stupid."

"I knew it was a bad idea the moment I stepped outside. Is this for me?" She took the coffee and looked delighted.

"Don't worry, it's decaf."

"Yum. Chris, you are so sweet to me. Here, go take money from my purse."

Chris ignored her. "Are you hurt? How did you land?"

"Fortunately, right on my rump."

"You might be a little sore tomorrow. Do you have ice?"

"Oh, yes, Jill mentioned ice. Ironic, right? Ice is the cause and the cure?"

Chris helped her adjust some pillows and get more comfortable. The door to her apartment was still wide open and Chris looked up to see Jill walking by. They caught each other's eyes for an instant. Chris stayed a while and watched a talk show with his mom. Standing up to leave, he handed her the remote and tucked a blanket around her feet.

"Just call or text if you need me, Mom. I'm gonna head home instead of back to the office."

"Thank you, dear. Drive safe, honey."

Chris kissed her on the forehead and said goodbye. He was a few yards down the hallway when he heard her yelling to him and he ran back urgently.

"What?! Are you OK?"

"Your wreath, dear. Take your wreath."

Chris stifled a laugh and picked it up from the kitchen, looping it over one arm.

"What a beauty. Thanks, Mom."

Chris got on the elevator and saw Jill rounding the corner. He put out his hand to hold the doors open for her as she jogged to make it inside.

"Well, well, well," she said, smirking. "Looks like we have a regular old Wreath Guy in our midst." She pressed the lobby button. The elevator doors closed but it didn't start moving.

"Haha, very funny. Yes, it was all worth it. And supporting the scouts, no less." Chris looked up at the elevator numbers, wondering why they weren't moving.

"It'll just be a minute, I hope. These elevators have been weird lately. If someone is in the other one, then this one stalls. Of course this would happen at the end of my shift," she said, rolling her eyes.

Jill reached over to feel the top of the wreath. Chris inhaled her lemon scent. Combined with the evergreens, he felt like he was in an extremely antiseptic porno scene. She looked up at him and he wondered if she could read his mind.

"They sell over-the-door wreath hangers. This one doesn't seem to have a loop for a nail, but you could just add one." She took a step, even closer to him, and pushed the floor button again. She didn't return to her place, but instead stood facing him.

"You think a wreath guy doesn't know about door hangers?" he asked, kiddingly, and in a voice a notch quieter than before. She looked up at him, lips open slightly.

"Sorry. I didn't mean to galsplain," she said, her eyes not leaving him.

Chris reached up and touched the side of her neck. Her collarbone was too perfect. She didn't pull away. He leaned down and kissed her deeply. She kissed him back.

The elevator started to move and they backed away, looking at each other intensely.

"Would you like to get some dinner?" he asked.

"Yes, I would. Will it be a banana?"

"It might be. If you play your cards right."

Her nostrils flared, refusing to let herself smile, as they stepped off the elevator together.

54

Jo unfolded the heavy wooden ladder and adjusted its position in her front windows. She wired layers of pine boughs up and down the A-frame, covering the front and back sides. She tied in branches dripping with blue juniper berries, short spikes of spruce, and bright tendrils of gold mop cypress. She could almost feel her immune system strengthening with each inhale. A customer had once told her that the smell of rosemary and pine helped ward off the winter blues, and over the years she had come to believe it.

Jo went to the basement and brought up a box of glass-cylinder vases she had wrapped in papery white birch bark, and gently set them on each step of the ladder. She filled every vase with branches of bright red winterberry. At the top of the ladder, Jo used a small easel to prop a bracket fungus that she had found on a walk in the woods. Having once grown in the shade around the base of a dying tree, it now held the exalted role of angel wings.

"And the last shall be first," she thought to herself as she reached to place an upright pinecone in the center of the large mushroom topper. Jo walked over to the cash register and used a bit of rubbing alcohol to remove the sap from her hands, and headed next door for lunch.

"Whoa…something is different," Jo said to Dag as she took her seat at the counter.

"Little bit of a mess right now. I guess we're finally doing that no-smoking section thing. Grant has been moving tables around and trying to figure out the best way to do it that'll tick off the fewest customers."

"Adjust we must, right?" Jo thought about her

parents, who had learned of the dangers of smoking way too late. "Cup of chicken noodle, please. And…a plate of fries with gravy."

"You got it." Dag headed to the kitchen. Grant walked in the front door and shook the snow off his hat.

"Hey, Jo, I just went to mail a letter and you might want to know there's a line outside your door right now."

"A line? Of people?"

"No. Snapping turtles. Yes, people!" he laughed and flicked the back of her head.

"Jo, it's gonna be awhile on those fries. Gotta heat up the grease again and dip a fresh batch." Dag said, setting down Jo's cup of soup.

"Actually, I'll skip the fries. Sorry, Dag. Sounds

like I'd better head back to the store," she said, starting to eat quick spoonfuls of her soup, trying not to burn her mouth.

Jo left and saw there was indeed a line of about ten people standing outside her door. She greeted them and turned the key in the lock, welcoming them inside. They all went directly to the back of the store and took wreaths from the coat hooks Jo had affixed to a long board of beechwood.

"Word is out, huh?" Jo said to the first woman in line at the cash register.

"Wreaths always start the same day you put up the ladder tree in the window. I wasn't about to be skunked again this year," said the woman, referring to the "sold out of wreaths" sign that Jo would be hanging in a few days. She had thought one of these years she should reconsider her ten dollar price point, or simply make more, but the desperate flurry of demand was a fun tradition for her. Jo knew constants could be reassuring to people, even if they could be improved upon.

The next woman in line had six wreaths looped around her arms. Jo felt slightly annoyed at the hoarding.

"Wow, six!" Jo said, hoping a reason would be given.

"Is that OK? I volunteer in the children's cancer wing at the university hospital and I wanted to hang one by each nurse's station." The woman handed her a Visa card.

"Oh, my. Yes, of course it's fine. In fact, I have to call in any charges over fifty dollars, and Visa is so busy around the holidays, I usually have to wait on hold. I'm just going to charge you for four of those and then I won't have to call it in."

"Oh, I couldn't possibly accept that."

"Please, it's my pleasure. Just look behind you," Jo whispered. The woman turned around to see a line of people with faces of impatience.

She smiled at Jo. "Very kind of you, ma'am."

Jo greeted a steady stream of customers the rest of the day and had to break occasionally to bring out more wreaths to restock the hooks. Even though she was tempted to hang the "sold out" sign in the window at the end of the day, she decided to stay up until midnight every night that week instead. She listened to Bing Crosby, Nat King Cole, and The Flying Pickets. She built magnificent wreaths and breathed in the fortifying scent of pine.

55

"I'm glad we're getting the break-up etiquette out of the way on our fourth date," Chris said, pulling apart a warm sourdough roll and reaching for the butter.

"It's important!"

"No, I agree," Chris laughed. "Rejection is a really crappy part of the whole enterprise, no matter which side of it you're on."

Jill nodded. "Isn't it? So, I meet some guy for a beer, and the odds are it won't work out. Of course those are the odds. We all know that rationally. But you go, you chat; it's fine. No big love connection. So, what then? Either you just ghost out or you have to send some awkward text like, 'You're really great. I just don't feel a connection.'"

"That is the worst text. Have you sent that text?"

"A few times, yes." Jill laughed and took a sip of her water.

"Don't send me that text." Chris shook his head, smiling.

"OK, I won't. What is your preferred method of rejection? I think a good Band-Aid rip is the kindest way in the long run. They can move on. It's crystal clear."

"I agree in theory. But it sucks so hard. Just don't send me that text. I already like you. A lot." Chris surprised himself with this admission.

The waiter set their plates in front of them. Jill looked excited to see her meal of spaghetti carbonara, and Chris enjoyed watching her face light up. She seemed to take great pleasure in simple things, and it was contagious. He took a drink of his gin rickey and felt a warmth he hadn't felt in a long time. Only a few days until Christmas, the restaurant was strung with lights and pleasantly crowded. They had a cozy wood booth for two.

"Are you still OK with just water, miss?"

"Yes, this is perfect. Thank you."

Chris lifted his drink to indicate he'd like another. "Whenever you get a chance. Thanks."

Jill leaned forward to look at his dinner of chicken piccata, green beans and roasted potatoes. "Wow, that looks amazing, too. You ordered well, sir," she said, holding up her water to toast.

Chris reached his glass to meet hers. "Thank you for joining me. I know things are busy with the holidays." He paused. "Did I mention you look beautiful tonight?"

Jill looked down at her outfit and shook her head shyly. "I will just say thank you. I'm working on accepting compliments."

"By the way, I meant to ask you last time…I noticed you haven't ordered any drinks on our dates…I don't want to pry, but is there any history there? Pregnant?"

"Haha, no. Not pregnant. I actually don't drink." Jill waved her hand towards Chris's drink. "But you do you! I don't care at all."

"Oh, OK. Good to know. That's cool. Healthier, for sure." Chris felt slightly self-conscious, and also wondered if this difference would be a problem. He had always dated women who drank. A lot.

"So…I guess I'll just tell you the story. Just so you don't wonder if I'm in AA or something." Jill paused and adjusted the napkin in her lap. "So, my mom was a genetics professor."

"Wow, cool."

"Yeah, I always idolized her when I was a kid. She and my dad would drink with their friends, but I never thought much of it. But one time when I was sixteen, my dad was out of town, so my mom invited me to come with her to a faculty party at her colleague's house. I felt really special. They all treated me like such a grown-up. I remember I wore my mom's pearl earrings."

Chris was listening and trying not to eat too much so he could pace himself with Jill, who had set her fork down.

"That night, my mom had drink after drink. She started talking really loudly and thought everything was hilarious. At one point, she bumped into a vase and caught it with her free hand. Cheering like she had caught a touchdown pass. I remember people looking at me…I guess I would call it pity. The looks they gave me."

"Wow. And you were sixteen?"

"Yep. So, finally I found her purse and told her we needed to go home. I made up some excuse. I had just gotten my license and I had to drive us through a blizzard to get home. I was trying not to cry the whole time, clinging to the steering wheel. Just so mad at her."

"Damn. Yeah a night like that would leave an impression." Chris looked at his drink and it didn't seem quite so appealing at that moment.

"When I finally went to bed that night, I promised myself that I would never drink. And I never have."

"Never?"

"Not even once." Jill went back to eating her meal, and the weight of the story seemed to be lifted.

"Hey, thanks for telling me all that. I'm sure it wasn't easy."

"We still need to agree on a plan," she said, changing the subject.

"A plan?"

"Yes. Chances are we will have to break up eventually."

Chris laughed. "Oh that! You are a realist."

"I am. But I'm still hopeful."

"That's good to hear." Chris smiled at her.

"For a while I had come up with this perfect way to reject people. It worked every time," she said.

"Really? You could monetize that! How did you do it?"

"OK, so it goes like this. I would say, 'Hey, Chris, there's nothing great about this conversation. I've gone on a few dates with someone else recently, and today we decided to give it a try in an exclusive way. You're a great guy, and I really enjoyed our time together. Nothing is missing here other than timing.'"

"Wow. Good last line. And was there another man?"

"Not at all. But every time the guy responds with, 'Hey, thanks a lot for your honesty, and congrats!' And I never hear from them again."

"That is crazy and I can see why it works so well."

"Yep. Because what I've realized is a lot of guys don't care about my opinion at all. So, they won't go away because they think I made a mistake. But if I insert another DUDE into the equation, then it's like, 'Oh! Got it. Bro code! Now HIM I respect.'"

"Sounds accurate. This would not work as a way for me to reject women. If I said, 'Hey, I've been dating this other woman,' it would activate her competitive streak. She would say I was a player, but then continue to text me for weeks trying to lure me from this woman she now feels she needs to beat. At the very least, she would write 'You know where to find me,' with a winky face."

Jill laughed. "While the feminist in me wants to tell you you're wrong, I've seen women act like that too many times to disagree with you. I'd like to think I'd handle it well, but I would probably stalk your social media later to try to find her picture. Seems so silly when I say it out loud."

"So, what's our plan to hack the system?" Chris smirked. "We can perfect this thing."

"Hey, I've got an idea." Jill sat up straighter, her eyes sparkling. "What if the dumper gives the dumpee some sort of treat. And we do it without saying a word. But we will know this particular treat means it's over. Maybe leave it in the mailbox or doorway. And the dumpee agrees to just let it be and not probe for an explanation or try to convince you otherwise."

"I like that idea VERY much. In no small part because when you get dumped, it helps to have a treat. And we could pick a treat that would be slightly difficult for the buyer to find, to make them feel a little pain. Like not just a plain old brownie."

"Yes! That's perfect. So, what's our treat?" Jill asked.

"Molasses cookie?"

"Yummy, but too easy. Let's see…how about one of those black licorice pipes?"

Chris almost spit out his drink. "Do you even like

those? What, would we have to order one online? Wait for the circus to come to town?"

Jill laughed. "OK, yes, maybe that's a little hard to find."

"I've got it," Chris said. "A black and white cookie."

"Nice! Like the ones in New York," Jill nodded strenuously. "I think I've seen those at some bakeries in Milwaukee. Might have to make a couple calls. I think that's actually perfect."

"I think we're geniuses," Chris said.

They locked eyes and smiled at each other. Jill set down her fork and leaned back. "I have a good feeling about this."

"I'm almost looking forward to it."

56

Paj dipped the long-handled brass mold into batter and then into bubbling oil. She deftly slipped the hot rosette cookie off the mold and bent it into a more perfect shape while it was still pliable.

"How are you so good at this?" Dagmar asked Paj, watching her finish making an entire tray without a single mistake. "When I'm on the rosette line, I break half of them, and I'm Norwegian!" Dag spooned batter onto the greased *krumkake* griddle. Nancy stood to her right folding the hot circles around a wooden cone form.

"This is just like *kanom dok bua*. I make *dok bua* since I was a girl. It is lotus blossom cookie. The mold we dip in oil is the same."

"Is the batter recipe the same too, Paj?" Jo asked, listening in from her end of the table where she was mixing lard into the *sandbakkel* dough. Martie worked beside her pressing balls of dough into small tins with her thumbs.

"Almost," replied Paj. "In Laos, we use coconut and sesame, too."

Brooke and her sister Heidi stepped away from the *pepperkaker* production table to admire Paj's rosettes. They started laughing and everyone looked up. Grant, wearing his mother's faded red ruffled apron, was holding the powdered sugar shaker over the tray of rosettes and tapping it along to the song on the radio, which happened to be "Oh, Pretty Woman," by Roy Orbison.

"Grant, oh my goodness!" Brooke exclaimed, laughing but looking embarrassed for him. He batted his eyelashes at her and put one hand on his hip.

Mai ran over and started dancing next to him. "Mercy!" Grant sang, as he handed Mai the sugar shaker and lifted her up by the armpits to finish dusting the cookies. Every year the prep party after hours at the restaurant was great fun, but this was the best one that Jo could remember. The diner was a box of warm light on a pitch black street, its front windows fogging slightly in a luminous haze of love and revelry.

The song ended and everyone went back to their stations. "Grant, you sure have a woman's touch!" Martie said, still laughing.

"Baking cookies and delivering flowers!" Grant's father chuckled. "I raised a regular Joe Namath."

"I was actually just reading an essay by Susan Sontag," Jo said as she stirred the dough. "She said, 'What is most beautiful in virile men is something feminine; what is most beautiful in feminine women is something masculine.'" She looked up and thought she saw Grant blush.

The room was quiet. Jo looked around, self-conscious, and saw Brooke and Heidi exchange a glance. She knew she had overstepped. The quote had sounded flirtatious, or something close to that, and she didn't mean it to be. Jo pinched her eyes closed, scolding herself for not thinking before she spoke. For being arrogant and trying to sound smart. The big sweater she had worn to cover her growing body now felt ugly and too hot. Ten years older than Brooke, she knew they must see her as a desperate old crone, trying to steal Grant. A predator. She didn't fit in this room and she didn't fit anywhere. She stared at the dough and stirred harder, willing herself not to cry, wishing she could rewind the last thirty seconds.

Grant's mother walked backwards through the swinging kitchen doors carrying a large tray of White Russians in Styrofoam cups, and a plate of pickled herring and Triscuits. She set the tray on a low table and handed Mai a cup with chocolate milk and a cinnamon stick. Mai carried it carefully so as not to spill on her new Bugs Bunny sweatshirt. Everyone left their prep stations and gathered around the table. Jo hoped no one would notice she wasn't drinking. She stood at the back of the group, wanting to disappear.

Dagmar pressed play on the *Beach Boys Christmas* album. Grant raised his cup. "Thank you all for coming to help out again this year. We joyfully carry on the traditions taught by our grandmothers and great-grandmothers. With love and warm memories, *Skål!*"

"*Skål!*" "Cheers!" Everyone raised their cup and gestured to each other one by one.

Sawm, who was sitting at a table next to the circle, raised his cup too and Grant jogged over to clink it.

"So, Sawm, what do you think of your first Norwegian cookie-making party?" Grant asked.

"Very good. Very good. Happy people," he said.

"I'm glad you're here, my man." Grant put a hand on his shoulder. Paj and Mai sat down with Sawm in the booth.

Sawm held up his cup. "We thank you. Everyone. And to Miss Jo, we thank you one hundred times. My family was pulled out of the ground. Now we have new roots growing. You say cheers and we say *zoo siab!*"

Jo barely heard him. She didn't hear the gratitude and the compliment. She wasn't able to see everyone turn and smile at her warmly. She couldn't see the good that she had done, at one time or another, for every person in that room. She didn't know how hard they had prayed when they heard she had been in a car accident.

All she could hear was the thunderous crashing wave of shame in her ears. She could see the turquoise wings of the halcyon, which had protected the calm waters in the days before the winter solstice, thrust and fly away. Jo could feel the fatigue in the tips of her fingers, desperately clinging to the torch-lit dory floating on the black icy water. She was nothing more than claws and salt, trying to prevent herself, at least for one more hour, from slipping next door to be alone in the dark.

January

57

Jill and Chris walked on the path along the Milwaukee River from the Fiserv Forum back to his condo. The sparkling crystals of precipitation hung in the glow of the streetlights. They walked at a slow pace, hand in hand.

"It doesn't know if it wants to rain or snow," Chris said. "Are you still OK walking?"

"Yes. It's a pretty night. We're getting close now."

"I wish I could have shown you a win at our first Bucks game together. They couldn't make a free throw."

"So close, though. Exciting game. I was a big Celtics fan as a kid. Larry Bird and the gang. So that was fun for me, too. Thanks so much, Chris."

"My pleasure. You're great company."

"It's always an awesome moment when I can make my brother jealous of my social life. He texted me like thirty times during the game."

"I'd be happy to get him some tickets. We always have extras kicking around to give to clients."

"Ha, that would ruin our cool break-up plans, though. Meaning, he wouldn't let me ever break up with you," Jill laughed.

"Damn, I keep thinking about those free throws." Chris clasped his hand over his forehead in frustration. "Brick after brick."

"They gotta switch to granny shots," Jill said seriously.

"Haha, what?"

"I mean it. The stats are better on underhand free throws. By a lot!"

"Yeah, I think you're right, actually. I know Wilt tried it one season and his conversion went way up."

"See? And can we guess why he quit doing it after a year?"

"Umm…because he felt like a sissy?" Chris laughed.

"Bingo. I mean, think about how crazy that is. You're in the NBA. Millions of dollars and fame on the line. And you make the conscious decision to play WORSE. To score FEWER points. All because of a myth about which shot is for grandmothers."

"Jill, I didn't know you were so passionate about the granny shot," Chris said as he put his arm over her shoulder and pulled her close. They stepped onto the elevator of his condo building and shook off their hats.

"I might write a manifesto."

"Please do."

"The granny shot just needs better branding. It's so symmetrical and powerful," she said, bending her knees and mimicking the arm motion.

"It needs a better name, for starters. Something cool like 'vintage arc.'"

"Yes, exactly. Or something very literal, like 'deep balls bucket.'"

Chris bent over laughing as he tried to put the key in the door.

"Johnny," Chris said, catching his breath, "Johnny,

go out in the driveway and practice your deep balls bucket, son."

"You'll never make it to the NBA shooting those sissy wrist flippers," Jill put her arms around his back and pressed her body into him, laughing as he opened the door. They took off their shoes and Chris turned on the fireplace.

"Did you clean? Looks great in here."

"Maybe a little. OK, come here," Chris said excitedly as he took her hand and led her into the kitchen. "I stocked up on NA options for you."

Chris opened the refrigerator and started moving things around to display the choices. "I've got ginger beer, sparkling water, and kombucha. This is Montmorency cherry juice. I thought that could be a good mixer with the ginger? I could also make you hot chocolate." Chris opened the cupboard to show her the spicy Mexican or peppermint options.

"Wow, Chris," Jill smiled at him. "This was really nice of you. You didn't have to go to all this trouble."

"I want you to like being here. If this isn't good, I'll get you anything you want. I have even more options for breakfast drinks," he laughed at himself.

"Should we do hot chocolate?" she asked.

"Boom. Love it." Chris started to heat up milk and pulled two mugs down from the shelf.

Jill used the bathroom while she was waiting. "Hey, Chris?" she asked, coming back into the kitchen, "You know, you've never given me a full tour of this place."

"I haven't?" Chris stirred the chocolate into

the mugs and handed one to her. "Sorry, no marshmallows. I'll get some for next time."

"Thanks. Yum." Jill looked over at the closed door of the spare bedroom. "Well, yeah, I just wondered if I could see the dead body room over there?"

"Actually, I call that the 'almost' dead body room. Good thing it's soundproofed," he teased her.

Jill drank her hot chocolate quietly, and waited.

"Yeah, OK. I'll show you. Just be nice, will ya?" Chris said this without need, since he had never known Jill to be anything but kind. He walked past her and down the hallway to his painting room. She stood beside him as he slowly turned the knob after a deep inhale.

"Whoa..." Jill walked to the middle of the room and slowly spun around, wide-eyed. "What on

Earth?" Her attention turned to the easel and the painting in progress. "Did you paint all of these?"

Chris nodded. His heart was beating fast as he waited for her reaction to his secret.

"Unreal." Jill walked from painting to painting, taking it all in. "Chris, why didn't you tell me you are an artist? These are incredible."

"I..." Chris couldn't speak. He felt like a heavy weight was lifted, and he wanted to share every part of this with her, but didn't know where to begin.

"Well, it doesn't matter. I'm just so glad you're showing me now. I love this one," she said, standing below a canvas full of trees. "I think it's my favorite one. The colors remind me of a children's book I loved called *A Tree is Nice*."

"Oh really? I don't know that book. I'm glad

you like it." Chris went to stand next to her. Her lemon scent still captivated him. "It's actually one of a…series…I guess I'll call it. I donated the rest of them to the elementary school down the block."

"That's so cool. I bet the kids love them."

"Yeah, they hung them all around the perimeter of the library, above the bookshelves. The librarian had me come visit the classes like I was some local artist or something."

"You are, though! Chris, honestly, these paintings look beyond professional."

"Well. Thank you. It's been quite a journey. A few ups and downs, to say the least."

She turned to him and put her arms around him, snuggling in close. "You contain multitudes, Chris Schwarz. I can't wait to learn you even more."

The idea of such a beautiful generous human "learning him" scared and excited him. How could he be ready for such an opportunity? Could he ever truly open himself up to her fully? He hugged her closer and inhaled her goodness. As if they could read each other's minds, they both set their mugs down on the chair. Their bodies found themselves intertwined on the floor. The overused rippled tarp, the protective cover, was their canvas.

58

Jo dipped a soft rag in a cup of milk and water. She gently shined the thickened, fleshy leaves of the succulent plants lining the shelves of her store. Even her plants that thrive on neglect needed a little care sometimes. She rolled one cart of jade plants in terracotta pots closer to the south-facing windows, and snipped a few dead leaves from the pots of agave. Realizing it was after closing time, she walked to the front door to turn the sign around. She startled at the sound of a loud knock.

"Martie! Is that you? Come on in!" Jo said, catching her breath after the scare. "I'm so sorry I didn't even see you standing there until you knocked. It's so dark tonight."

"I knew I would frighten you!" Martie laughed.

"My students say this hat makes me look like a yeti."

"What are you doing out in this cold?" Jo asked, reaching to hang a basket of trailing yellow sedum from a hook above the cash register while holding in her stomach.

"Oh, I don't know. Kip is at his mother's in Dubuque this week, so I've been going home after school to an empty house. I was just thinking you might want to go get fish fry with me? I haven't seen you in awhile…I guess I've been a little worried about you."

"Worried about me?"

"Well, just a little. You haven't seemed like your outgoing self lately…but I know it's winter. I don't know. I've just been thinking about you."

Jo didn't know what to say. Martie wasn't wrong,

but she was surprised anyone had noticed. The front door opened suddenly again and both women jumped.

"Oh this is perfect!" Dag shouted. "Martie's here, too!" she yelled to the car on the street behind her.

"Dag, what on Earth?" Martie asked, with a hand on her chest.

"Get in the car! We have two extra tickets to the Bucks game in Milwaukee tonight! Come on!"

Jo and Martie looked at each other. Neither had time to think about all the reasons not to go.

"I'll go get my coat?" Jo said sheepishly.

"That's the spirit!" Dag cheered.

"This is crazy," Martie added.

"Not as crazy as Sid's defense! Playing the Celtics tonight. Let's see how he holds up to Bird."

Jo ran upstairs and back down just as fast, carrying a Tupperware container of blondie bars and a bag of apples.

"Road snacks," she said, smiling, as she worked herself into the rest of her winter coat. Giddiness turned to panic as the three women stepped outside and Jo realized the car Dag had been shouting to was Grant's brown Oldsmobile. Was Brooke in the car, too? For some reason, she had assumed it would be Dag's husband, Tom, driving them. Dag and Martie climbed in the back which left a seat for Jo in the front next to Grant. No Brooke.

"Yes! Road snacks! We need fuel for the MECCA, baby!" Grant exclaimed as Jo sat down and closed the door. She laughed and started to relax.

Dag leaned forward. "Our parents gave us these four tickets for Christmas, but Tom is sick, Brooke is kaput, and Mom and Dad said they'd rather stay warm and watch it on TV."

"Wait. Kaput?" Martie asked.

"Yeah, she dumped me," Grant said casually.

"Dumped? Really? Oh, sorry, Grant. That's never a good feeling," Jo said, empathetically.

"Thanks. It's OK. Probably for the best," he said, sounding a little sad.

Jo opened the Tupperware and Grant reached to take a bar. "Can I ask what happened?"

"She's a snob, that's what happened," interjected Dag from the back seat.

"Dagmar!" Grant laughed. "We've been over this.

Brooke is a very nice person. I was just not quite her speed."

"Ha! Her speed? Brooke should be so lucky," said Martie.

"I still think it was the alpaca scarf," said Dag.

"I got her an alpaca scarf for Christmas," he told Jo. "Apparently, Brooke's friends made fun of it."

"Why? That's a nice gift."

"I don't know. I could tell her friends always thought I was a hick. But it's not like it was from MY alpaca," he laughed.

"But you do know the farmer, Grant. It wasn't exactly Pierre Cardin," his sister teased him.

"Huh. That seems like a really dumb reason to break up," said Jo.

"Yeah. But I know it was more than that. The bottom line is I'm thirty-five. I want to get married and have kids. Our parents had four kids and a house by this age. She's got different ambitions right now. Law school. Who knows after that." He sounded sad again.

"I'm sorry it didn't work out, Grant. Even if it's for the best, it's still hard."

"Thanks. She was a good one." He reached for another blondie bar.

"Her loss!" Martie said cheerfully. "We get to ride to the game in the luxurious Sandy Duncan, and Brooke is probably home studying tonight. Something dumb like torts. Right, Dag? You wouldn't want a snob for a sister-in-law, anyway."

"Do you even know what torts are?" asked Grant.

"No, but I know they're lamer than a Bucks

game," Martie said emphatically.

Dagmar muttered something indecipherable and reached up to the front seat to grab an apple and a bar.

Grant laughed. "What was that, sis?"

"Torty Bitch."

"Dagmar!" Jo turned around and pretended to cover her ears.

"What? Grant isn't the only one who can give people nicknames," she laughed.

The car skidded slightly and everyone's attention turned back to the road. Grant adjusted the radio as they entered the range of Milwaukee stations. The conversation had stopped and Jo felt a nervous wave oscillate through the air. She knew an honest moment was available. It was right there for the taking. She felt her difficult news just about to come out. She could say the words and it would be done. She would start by saying, "I have to tell you guys something and this is very hard for me to say." Yes, that would be how she would start.

"Hey, what did you guys think of the Apple Macintosh commercial during the Super Bowl? Kinda creepy, right?" Grant asked.

"I thought it was cool. Like Orwell? Felt ominous, though. I didn't really get it," said Martie.

And just as quickly as it arrived, Jo's moment was gone.

59

Lucas used the stylus to touch some options and handed the tablet to Chris. Inserting his credit card into the Square reader, Chris selected a 20 percent tip. He didn't know if people were supposed to tip for therapy, but after so many sessions there was no going back now. He stood up slightly to hand the tablet back to Lucas, and adjusted a pillow behind him before settling back in. Lucas had closed the blinds on the gray day and turned on three lamps instead of the overhead lights.

"Hey, I wanted to thank you for recommending Agave Grill. My wife and I tried it last week and it was fantastic."

"Oh awesome! Glad you liked it. Yeah, Jill and I ran past that place so many times. I'm glad we finally made a reservation. Great menu," Chris nodded.

"You two run together?"

"Yep. That's part of our morning routine when she stays over, if the weather is decent."

"Sounds like this is a pretty healthy relationship?" Lucas asked.

"So healthy it feels like I'm in a commercial," Chris laughed. "Definitely different from what I'm used to. She's…I mean…she's astounding."

"You sound like you might be in love," Lucas said, smiling.

"I'm in something. Honestly, I don't know how I got so lucky. Makes me nervous."

"In what way?"

"I'm just…waiting to find out what will be the thing that makes it end. There's always a thing."

"Does she have any opinions on what we talked about last time?"

"Leaving FELL? She just wants me to be happy, but I have a feeling she would be very supportive if I quit. It's hard to explain to her all the history with these guys. Everything I've put into this company. I can tell she doesn't understand why I would stay at a company that profits from cutting down healthy trees, and then covers it up."

"I think that would be hard for most people to understand."

"Yeah. I know. You're right."

"Generally, I never encourage clients to leave jobs. It can be very destabilizing. A job isn't just a job.

It's often a person's friend group and support network, their daily routine, financial security, health care, sometimes even their gym. But I want to ask you a few questions, because I feel like your situation is a little different."

"OK, shoot."

"Would you be able to pay your bills for a period of time while you look for a different job?"

"Yes. No problem."

"Are the terms you discussed with your lawyer things you can live with?"

"Not quite. I don't want to leave FELL in the same mess it is now. I'm hoping I can use my profit-sharing as leverage to guarantee some changes I've been lobbying for. We'll see. It's all up to Jared and Scott. I just can't predict how they would react to all this."

"Do you think your friendships with Jared and Scott would be over if you leave?"

"Yes, but these aren't friendships. These have been mutually beneficial contractual partnerships. These are men with whom I happened to go to college. I won't see that part as a loss, trust me."

"Do you have any ideas about what you'd like to do going forward?"

"I think about it a lot. I don't know exactly. But I see the honest work that Jill does every day, and it's humbling. It's so authentic. There's no spin. There's nothing phony. I think there has to be something out there where I'm using my skills in a way that's not hurting anyone. Or hurting the Earth. Right? That has to be out there."

"Chris. Does FELL feed you?"

"No. FELL is starving me. That's the easiest question you've asked."

"Did I ever tell you about my bathroom mirror?"

"I don't think so."

"My dad was my high school basketball coach. Small high school. We weren't good. But my senior year, we were actually winning some games. Then we won some more. So, eventually we're in a regional championship game. I know that doesn't sound like a big deal but it was, like, everything."

"No, I get it. Those games can seem like the whole world."

"So, we have this time-out, twenty seconds left in the game. We're down by one."

"That's a lot of time."

"It is, but here's the thing. In that time-out, my dad says to us: 'Boys, it's later than you think.'"

Chris was quiet, picturing this crew of small-town boys. Imagining Lucas as a gangly teenager playing the game of his life. Chris gave the coach an epic mustache.

"A couple turnovers. Some sloppy mistakes. Then my buddy Jay sends me a perfect pass. Jay and I were the only two Black kids in the conference. We were always looking out for each other. This pass was like a bullet across the court. There was too much time on the clock. But I had a great look."

"I really want this to end well," Chris laughed.

"I took the shot. All net. We're up by one. We got the steal and ran out the clock. The students stormed the court. Only time I've ever seen my dad cry."

"Wow. Damn, I love high school hoops. Nothing like it," Chris said. "Wait, I thought you said this was about your bathroom mirror?"

"It is. So, I've kept those words taped to my bathroom mirror ever since. The words my dad said in that time-out." Lucas paused. "It's later than you think."

Chris looked down at his lap, thinking about that message. Thinking about FELL and his career. Thinking about his mom. Thinking about Jill. Thinking about the planet.

"Chris. You know I don't give advice. That's not my style. But I think you know what I'm trying to say."

Chris looked up at him and nodded. The two men, having led very different lives, both broken and rebuilt too many times to count, sat together quietly in a small cozy room, in a dingy professional building, just down the street from a massive frozen lake.

"I need to shoot my shot."

"I think it's time."

Chris felt scared, but exhilarated. He knew Lucas was right. As he thought about the path he would need to take in the next few weeks, a vision of thorny brushwood appeared in his way, but his mind remained calm. He saw himself jump powerfully and soar over it all.

"Thanks for the assist."

60

"My students just finished a unit on Robert Indiana, the man who designed this floor," Martie said, reaching across Jo's lap to take another handful of popcorn from Grant.

"I don't know about him. Crazy cool floor, though," said Jo. "So vibrant. I haven't been to a Bucks game in years."

"The king of pop art. He's the same guy who did the LOVE sculpture. After we learned about him I had the students design their own gym floors."

"Martie, why did I never have a teacher like you?" Dagmar lamented.

Grant pointed at the yellow center diamond outline. "That is actually two huge letter M's. Can you see it? M for Milwaukee."

"Oh, wow, I hadn't noticed that. It looks like an Aztec rug or something. I love the color palette," said Jo.

"Yeah, he kept it a secret the whole time he was painting it. All these tough guys were freaking out. Public money, you know? And a lot of it," Grant said.

"But then everyone loved it, right?" asked Dag.

Grant nodded. "Oh, yes. Huge hit. The players love it too because the opposing teams get confused by it and step out of bounds."

"I must say I like the irony that all these sports fans are forced, for two hours, to stare at what is basically an art installation," Martie laughed. "It's like culture osmosis for jocks."

Grant cleared his throat. "Yeah, it's like what Jo was saying at the cookie party. The best part of something masculine is actually the feminine part. Or something like that."

Grant could see Jo looking at him but kept his eyes on the court. "What? You think I don't listen to you?" He turned and winked at her.

Dag stood up. "I should really use the ladies' room before halftime is over."

Jo and Martie stood to follow her and Grant pulled his knees to the side to let them by. "Hey, Dag, can you bring me back an RC?" He handed her a dollar as she rolled her eyes at him. The women walked up the stairs and around the bend of the arena hallway to the bathroom. The line was short.

"Guys, I'm actually dying," Jo said urgently. "Do you mind if I go first?"

"No, of course! Go ahead," Dag said, pointing to a stall that had just opened up. She exchanged a quick glance with Martie that Jo didn't notice.

As they made Grant contort himself to retake their seats during the most exciting play of the game, he impatiently asked them what had taken so long. Dagmar shushed him and said the line had been long. He was about to berate her for forgetting his soda, but stopped himself when he saw that Jo's face was red and puffy like she had been crying. He turned his attention back to the game and worried he had done something to offend her. And it was true she had cried. It started the moment her friends had confronted her about the pregnancy as they washed their hands at the sink. And Jo would cry some more, plenty more, when she finally tucked herself into bed that night. Because they had stood in the bathroom and hugged her tight. And they had told her it would be OK. And they stroked her hair and told her the tyke would play at her feet while she arranged flowers. And they made her understand she wasn't alone. And they told her this was a lucky child to have Jo as a mother. Of course Dagmar and Martie were cross with her, but only because she had kept it a secret. They argued with each other, too, about who would take Jo to her next doctor's appointment and who would get to be the first to babysit. Yes, Grant was right that she had cried. Swollen rivers of tears, as the salt of her shame was expelled.

February

61

"I don't usually love polenta, but that was crazy good," Jill said as she flopped down on Chris's sofa and patted her belly.

"Make room, I need to stretch out, too." Chris climbed on top of her and comically took his time squashing her as he rolled across and spooned in behind her body.

"What are you, a steam roller?"

"Beep, beep, beep, beep…"

"No way you can flatten these boobs, Mr. Schwarz," she said seriously.

"I can try, though," Chris said as he rolled back on top of her as she giggled. "Beep, beep, beep."

"Usually I hate Valentine's Day, but I must say this one has been quite fun."

"I agree. Sorry we had to eat so late. I should have tried to get a reservation weeks earlier. I'm not used to having a girlfriend."

"I liked it. It felt very cosmopolitan to eat late. But I'm thinking we need to come up with a safe word to use when we're too full to have sex. Not saying that's the case right now, but it's close," she laughed. "You might not get my best moves tonight."

"Yeah, there should be a page in the *Kama Sutra* where both people can be on the bottom somehow."

"Right? Why is that not a thing?"

"How about 'polenta'? For the safe word."

"Perfect. We will use it sparingly," she said, and kissed him deeply.

"Do you still love me now that I'm an unemployed loser?" Chris asked.

"I think I love you even more," she said as she wrapped her legs around his butt and snuggled her face into his neck. "I'm so proud of you. I know these last few weeks haven't been easy."

"Thanks. Handing over most of my equity was not ideal, of course," he laughed. "But now they're contractually obligated to the changes I've been wanting, at least for five years. I feel really good about it."

"I think it was a huge coup, Chris. Money is the cheapest thing there is. And now you're free to find something that truly feeds your spirit."

"Oh, hey, I got you something," he said as he

pushed into a plank and got up off the sofa.

"I got you something, too! Nothing big. Hang on, it's in my bag."

"Here, open mine first," she said as they sat back down. She handed him a flat pink box, about the size of a wallet. He untied the bow and lifted the lid.

"Oh, cool. Are these seed packets?"

"Yes! Sweet peas! I thought I could help you start them inside this spring and then we can move them outside to your roof garden after the last frost. But if that's too much of a mess, we can do it at my place."

"No, yeah, let's do it here. I love it. Thank you." He kissed her and put the top back on the box.

"They're from this small farm in Washington's

Skagit Valley that has been collecting heirloom flower seeds, trying to rescue these nostalgic old varieties. You won't believe the scent."

"I can't wait. You just tell me what supplies to get and I'll be your student." Chris handed her a present wrapped in newspaper comics, about one foot square.

"OK, now before you open this, let me explain. So, I went to buy you flowers today, and honestly it all sucked. Everything looked the same. So cheesy. It just didn't seem worthy of you. You're so natural and beautiful. I just couldn't buy you something so commercialized and conventional. OK, you can open it now."

"Yeah, flower shops aren't what they used to be. Now it's all shipped in from who knows where." Jill unwrapped the newspaper and saw a blank white canvas.

"So I can paint you flowers."

"Oh, Chris." Jill seemed truly moved. "I would love that so much."

"Or anything you want! It doesn't even have to be flowers. I just want you to think of something that makes you happy and I'll paint it for you."

"Wow, Chris. This is so great. Thank you."

"No dick pics."

Jill laughed. "What? Darn. OK, fine." She set down the canvas on the coffee table and attacked him with a hug.

"I can do it now?"

"Right now? Sure! That would be fun. And it will give us time to digest before we go to bed."

"My thoughts exactly," he laughed. He took her hand and they walked to the painting room. He grabbed another chair from the kitchen and Jill sat down next to the easel.

"I feel super special right now," she said, almost bouncing in her seat.

"Well, so do I. Just close your eyes and think of something that would make you happy. Something that you've been wishing for."

Jill was quiet and thought for a minute. "Hmm, the winter is kind of dragging on, and I could really use some sun."

"Sun. I can do that. What else?"

"What about a boat...a warm day...calm water... maybe a ladder off the side so we could go swimming. Is that possible?"

"Now you're talkin'."

"Maybe it's late afternoon. You know how the sun gets kind of glimmery on the water. We've been out there for hours and we're really tan. Maybe we're drinking lemonade and getting kind of hungry. There's probably a restaurant nearby where we can dock. You know that kind of day?"

Chris reached for his dad's ebony brush. "I really want that day with you, Jill." He looked at her sweet face, hopeful for all the moments ahead for them together.

"Well, since we live right by an enormous lake, I think we can find a way to make it happen this summer," she laughed.

"Will you hate me if I admit I'm looking forward to seeing you in a swimsuit?"

"Ha! See, this is what people get wrong about

women. I love to hear YOU say that. I just don't want to hear that from my boss or some guy at Walgreens. Make sense?"

Chris laughed. "Noted."

Jill watched with admiration as he prepped the canvas and started creating the scene she had described. She got lost in the sea he was painting. It looked so real and yet ethereal. Too perfect for this world. The boat rested on the waves and looked to have the slightest rocking motion. The angle of the sun was exactly how Jill had imagined.

Her trance was broken by the sound of Chris's phone. "What do you think?" he asked, setting his brush down.

"Chris, it's magical. Truly. This is the nicest gift. Your talent is unreal."

"I'll let it dry for a few days and you can take it home." His phone buzzed again.

"You can answer that. I don't care."

Chris looked at his phone. "It's just Scott and Jared FaceTiming. They're in Hawaii at the moment, on my dime," he laughed.

"You've gotta answer it. Come on!"

"OK, fine. Now you'll see what bozos these guys are." Chris dragged the slider to accept the call.

"Brooooooooooooo," Jared shouted into the phone. Chris quickly lowered the volume.

"Scott, come here! You gotta show Chris that marlin!" Scott came into view, dragging the large fish across the floor of the boat by the dorsal fin and bill. Chris could see at least four women in the background, none of whom looked like Scott's wife.

"We're just off the coast of Oahu. Eat your heart out, my man!" Jared yelled.

"Take a screenshot," Jill whispered. Chris looked at her, not understanding, and turned back to the call.

"That's great, fellas. Looks really nice there. Have fun," Chris said, wanting to wrap it up.

"What's in the background, man? Are you at a museum, you fairy? What time is it there? Damn, your girl must have you whipped."

"Alright, Jared, I gotta go. And by the way, you might consider catch and release next time." Chris tapped the screen angrily and ended the call. "Sorry about that, Jill. I'm so glad to be done with that world."

"It's OK; I grew up listening to my brother's friends talk. I get it. Plus, I already know I have you whipped," she teased him.

"You really do," Chris agreed as he tickled her playfully.

"I just wanted you to get a screenshot!" Jill said, frustrated.

"Why?"

"The boat, Chris! This was their boat. Like, exactly." She pointed at the painting in front of them on the easel.

It was hard to deny. "Wow," Chris said, without affect.

"I mean, even the low afternoon sun was the same. Isn't that a crazy coincidence? I actually just got the chills."

A terrible feeling came over Chris that he would never get to have the boating day with Jill next summer. Somehow that special day had been given away. Or stolen. He had wanted so badly to warm her, and instead she was chilled.

62

"Stop, stop, stop. I've got these," said Grant as he jogged across the store and lifted the heavy crate from Jo's arms. "Geez, did you cram enough pots in here?"

"Thanks." Jo shook out her arms. "Yeah, orders have been nuts this year." She bent down to pick up another crate. "I just need to make some room in the cooler so they don't pop open too quickly before people can get them today." Jo slid ten pots of bubblegum pink hyacinth down the shelf in her cooler, and filled the space with pots of paperwhites. She had potted the bulbs and forced them to bloom indoors in the windows just in time for Valentine's Day. Some years she had miscalculated the bloom time by a couple days and it cost her dozens of sales, but this year was just right.

"Here, let me do that." Grant walked into the cooler and started lifting pots onto the shelf. "Lordy, it smells like a perfume factory in here. Let me get that," he said, taking a water bucket from her hand.

"My word, you're being awfully chivalrous this morning, Grant," she laughed.

"When I'm here, there's no need for you to do all this lifting, Jo." He held the door for her as they stepped out of the cooler.

"My wrist is all better, though. You don't need to worry about me. Isn't your breakfast shift about to start, anyway?"

"Just take it easy, OK?" Grant sounded irritated. Jo froze.

"Grant."

He turned to face her. They looked at each other and didn't speak. Jo walked over to the desk behind the cash register and took a drink from her water glass. She crossed her arms and rested her hip on the side of the counter, looked back up at him, and sighed.

"So, your sister told you?"

"Told me what?"

Jo didn't answer.

"Why you're mad at me? No, she didn't tell me. You mind cluing me in?"

"Mad at you?" Jo asked, confused.

"Well, ever since the Bucks game, you've been weird around me, and I wish you'd just tell me what I did wrong."

"Grant..."

"Look, I know I say stupid stuff. I'm a guy. I'm always making jokes. But Jo, I'm sorry for whatever I said. I've been trying to think back on every conversation. The only thing I could think was when I said that cheerleader looked like she might tip over. But it was just a dumb joke. She just looked a little top-heavy, is all. You know, like I was worried for her safety." Grant chuckled and then caught himself. "But look, I'm sorry. I know I gotta cool it with that sort of comment."

"No, Grant. I didn't mind that. I'm not mad at you. Not at all."

"Well, then what is it? I feel like you don't even want to be around me lately."

"Grant. I have to tell you something. Dag, Martie and Paj already know. And I'm sorry I didn't tell you earlier. I just couldn't find the words."

"Damn, Jo. You're scaring me. You can tell me anything." He walked over to her and stood across the counter from her.

Jo looked out the window. The store was about to open for the day and the rush would begin, probably not letting up for hours.

"What is it, Jo? Are you sick?" Grant looked terrified.

"No, Grant." She turned back to look him directly in the eye. "I'm pregnant."

63

Chris raised each of the blinds higher and turned on more lights in the apartment. He carried a floor lamp across the room and plugged it in closer to Eileen's chair.

"Any better, Mom?"

"Yes, thank you, dear," she said as she leaned closer to her magazine. "I don't know how to describe it. It's just harder to read lately."

"Jill said she set you up with audiobooks after your stroke. Do you want me to put some more on your phone?"

"Maybe later. I just want to do one crossword to prove to myself I'm not becoming addled."

"Trust me, Mom. You're still sharp as a tack."

"I just feel like it's always something. Now it's my vision. What will it be next month? This darn body is failing me, slowly but irrevocably. Like dominos falling through molasses."

"That sounds messy. Did someone spill the molasses on the dominos or what happened there?" Chris teased her.

"Haha, very funny, yes, even my metaphors are getting disabled. Let's talk about something more fun. How are things with our Jill?"

"Jill's great. We're headed to Chicago for the weekend. Just to hit the Art Institute and a couple restaurants. We discovered we're both big Edward Hopper fans."

"It seems like the more you two get to know each other, the more you find you have in common.

It's so nice to hear. I always liked her. She's a consummate professional but also very kind."

"Yeah, I can't seem to find anything wrong with her. And for once, I'm not even searching for flaws anymore. It feels like being with my best friend."

Eileen clasped her hands together and brought them up to her chin. "Oh, Chris, I don't want to get ahead of ourselves, but I have to say my mind starts thinking about grandchildren. Ah! I know I'm not supposed to say that."

"Well, hate to disappoint you, but that's probably not going to happen."

"Why not?"

"Well, for starters, I don't want kids. I thought you knew that."

"I know you've said things like that in the past, but I always thought it would be different when you met the right person."

"Yeah, it's just not in the cards. I'm not dad material."

"I think you'd make a great father, Chris. Truly."

"It's just not the life I want, Mom. Call it selfish, or whatever. I like my freedom. And I think this is a pretty bleak future to bring kids into, frankly."

"Have you talked to Jill about this?"

"No, it hasn't come up."

"I think you better talk to her, Chris. I know for a fact she wants children."

"How on Earth would you know that? Or are you just making an assumption that all women want children?"

"No, that's not it. I don't want to violate her confidence, but we had a conversation about a year ago that makes me think you two really need to discuss this. Soon."

"What, so she just knocked on your door last year to drop off a flyer about new COVID restrictions and she just happened to mention that she wants to be a mother?"

"Chris. Honey. I'm just looking out for you. Please trust me on this."

"Well, it doesn't matter anyway. I had a vasectomy after my divorce."

Eileen looked at him, stunned.

"What? Don't look so shocked. There are actually human beings in the world who don't want to have kids." Chris stood and walked to the kitchen, dumping out his coffee. He pushed the dining chairs close to the table, one by one, a little too forcefully.

"That's your business, honey. I understand. I certainly didn't mean to put any pressure on you. I just didn't realize you were so serious about it. Now I know." Eileen couldn't hide her disappointment.

"It's OK, Mom. I'm sorry I got short with you. I know it's not the news you wanted to hear." He returned to sit on the sofa next to her chair.

"Chris, I'm going to tell you this thing, and I'd prefer you don't tell Jill you know about this. But I realize you will want to be honest with her, so I'll leave that up to you."

"What is it?" Chris asked, concerned.

"About a year ago, Jill was in my apartment helping me with my new dietary plan when my meds changed. She got up to get a glass of water from the kitchen and she had a dizzy spell and almost fainted."

"She did? What? Why?"

"I had her lie down and asked if I should call someone for her, but she told me it was just a side effect from her injections."

"Mom, what are you talking about?"

"Chris, she told me she was doing IVF treatments. She had decided she wanted to try to have a baby on her own using a donor, and she was starting to prepare her hormone levels."

Chris didn't speak. The walls of the room seemed to lose their solidity. He could barely hear his mother, as if she were behind glass. He knew Jill would leave him.

"I hope you can see now why I really think you need to have a conversation with her about the topic of kids."

64

Jo turned the sign in the window to CLOSED and locked the door, exhausted. She had sold every single pot of flowering bulbs except one, which she had pulled off the shelf earlier in the day when she saw a small crack in the side. She turned off the overhead light and brought the pot over to a work table to fix it before she went upstairs for the night. The small lamp on the table was the only light in the store, and it felt much later than it was. Jo had forgotten to eat all day and was thinking about calling to have a pizza delivered. The financial windfall from the big day was a relief and would help her pay her bills until the spring rush started in a few weeks. The cost of her trip to Europe and the garden project had made for a particularly tight winter, but she thought she would have enough extra money now to shop for a crib and some baby clothes. If the roads were decent, she planned to drive to Madison on Saturday to visit Gimbels. It was one of many times in her life she was missing her mother, thinking how much fun they would have had picking things out together. Jo shook the soil free from the cracked terracotta, cupping the unruly bulbs, and placed the confused mass into a new pot. She held the old pot up to the light to see if she might be able to glue it or if it was a lost cause.

"Oh my God, Grant, you scared me!" Jo said, as she held her hand up to her heart.

"Sorry, Jo. The back door was unlocked. I thought you heard me come in."

Grant stood at the end of the long wood table. He looked tall and strong. He was wearing a white Oxford shirt, gray wool pants and a black leather belt. Jo could smell his cologne and it looked like he had just shaved.

"You look nice. Date tonight?" she asked, looking down at the tube of epoxy, realizing she should just scrap the repair project and go upstairs. Grant had been pretty quiet when she told him her news that morning, but he seemed to take it in stride. He was supportive and didn't ask any questions about the father. It was a relief to tell him, but she didn't really have the energy to discuss it with him further at that moment. She also wished he didn't smell so good.

"Jo," he said, sounding nervous.

"What is it?" She stopped what she was doing and turned to him.

"You know I'll always be your friend, right?"

"Oh, Grant. Yes, of course. I know. I shouldn't have been so worried to tell you about the baby. I'm sorry I didn't tell you sooner."

Grant set his hands on the wood table and leaned against it. He worked a small knot with his thumb, as if he were trying to polish it smooth.

"Are you OK?" Jo asked.

"Marry me, Jo," he said without looking up at her.

"What?"

"I love you, Jo. You know that. Don't you know that?" He still didn't look up from the wood.

"Grant," she said, sadly.

"It'll be a good life. I promise you that. I've saved a little money, but I can do better. I'll get another job. There's a lot of construction up in Madison and I'm a fast learner. Maybe we can stay in your apartment for awhile until I can buy us a house. I'll give you a good life. I'll take care of you. Dammit, Jo. You know I love you." His voice caught and his eyes welled up.

"Grant," she said quietly, walking to him and hugging him tightly. They didn't speak for a long time.

Jo gently pulled away and reached up to lift his chin with her hand. "I could never do that to you, Grant. Raise another man's baby?"

"Don't think of it like that, Jo. I would love that child like my own. You don't have to worry for one minute about that. Everyone would think it's mine anyway," he laughed a little and so did she.

"Well, you're probably right about that part. People have thought we've been sleeping together all year," she wiped her eyes and took another step back from him.

"We could have more kids, Jo. It would be great. I'd give them all nicknames and teach them to fish. Please, Jo. It's a good life. Right in front of you. Take it."

"Grant, I'm thirty-eight."

"Plenty of time."

"Ha. Not really. I think this is my one shot. My one child."

"You don't know that."

"There's something else you should know. I was married before. When I lived in Wausau. I got divorced right before moving down here."

"I don't care. None of that matters. I wouldn't want to get married in the church anyway. We'll do it our way. What about up at Stewart Park? It's snowy but we can make a big arch of cedar boughs. How about we do it at night with an aisle of luminarias? Some chairs for family and a few friends. Really simple. We can do it this weekend. It's not supposed to be very cold." He sounded truly excited. "Then we can come back to the diner for a little party."

Jo looked down at the repotted pink hyacinth bulbs, leftover but renewed. When she looked up he was holding a ring.

"Oh, Grant. That's beautiful."

"It was my grandmother's ring. I asked my mom for it today. She loves you. They all do."

"I love your family, too."

"See? It's perfect. It will work. I promise you, Jo. I won't let you down."

A movie played in Jo's mind of a life with Grant. A life as a wife and mother in Mount Horeb. She had watched that movie a hundred times.

She had written the messages on cards from flowers sent from husband to wife. She had seen them eating in the diner and overheard their conversations. She had seen the wives at the grocery store. So many times she had wanted to be one again. She had wanted to play a part in that movie. It would be so easy to say yes.

"Grant. I can't tell you how much this means to me. That you would do this. You know I love you too, right?"

"Don't do this, Jo."

"All marrying me would do is prevent you from meeting the woman you're supposed to be with. It would prevent you from having the kids and the family you deserve to have, and *will* have."

"Jo, no. It's you. I know it's you."

Jo looked back down at the table. "Grant, do you

see these flowers? They're pretty, right?"

"Yeah."

"But there's something not quite right, don't you think?" she said seriously. "Not quite like field-grown flowers."

"No, they're great. What do you mean?"

She shook her head. "The color isn't quite as vibrant. They won't last very long. The stems are weak. The smell seems unnatural."

Grant listened, confused.

"The thing is, these flowers were forced to bloom. They had to grow trapped in a pot, with no direct sunlight. Only what they could grab through a window, in the low slanted light of a Wisconsin winter. No rain, just water from the sink. And it shows. Yes, they're pretty. It's a wonderful solution. A trick, really. But there is nothing like flowers that have grown in the field, under the blue sky and the summer sun."

"Jo, what are you saying?"

"You deserve that kind of life. That kind of love. And so do I." She looked down and cradled her stomach with her hand. "An honest life. The kind of life that can breathe and send down roots deep into the earth. A life that can be battered by a soaking storm, but stand back up the next day at sunrise, even stronger and refreshed." Slow tears were streaming down Jo's face now.

"You don't have to say any more," Grant said, looking down at his feet and putting the ring back in his pocket. "Your divorce? The man who let you go? He was an idiot."

"Grant, this doesn't change the love we have for each other. That will always be true. Always."

Grant walked to her, put his hands under her arms, and gently lifted her onto the work table. She didn't resist. He pulled her towards him and hugged her close, his arms folded around her back. She wrapped her legs around him and draped her arms over his broad shoulders. She felt his head nuzzle tight and rest on her shoulder. She rubbed her hand up and down the back of his crisp white shirt as he finally heaved the tears he had been holding back for the entire day.

March

65

"We cannot break up in a George Webb."

"Chris, we're not breaking up. I just need time to think."

"Sure sounds like we're breaking up." Chris took another forkful of pie and shook his head. They had stopped at the diner for a late night snack on the walk home from a Tracy Chapman concert at the old Pabst Theater. It had been a magical night. He wished he had just let it be.

"Look, Chris, it's good that you brought this up. We had been having so much fun the past few months, I guess I just didn't want to have to think about it. But you did the right thing. I know you love me. You don't want to waste my time." Jill looked sad and thoughtful.

"I do love you."

"I mean," Jill sounded like she might cry, "would you ever consider having your vasectomy reversed?"

Chris paused, considering her feelings and his possibilities. Giving her false hope would be the easiest and cheapest thing to do. It would buy him some time. Thinking back, he was ashamed he had done it before with other women. "Jill. Right now I just can't see that as my path. I know it's hard to understand. I'm sorry. I just think I owe it to you to be totally honest about this."

"No, you're right. I appreciate it. All we can do is approach this with integrity. Both of us. I'm thirty-six. I really want children. Being a mother has really been my one life goal. I know that might seem old-fashioned or small. But it's true. Even a few months in the wrong relationship could mean the end of that dream. It just sucks for women."

"Sucks from where I'm sitting, too. I don't want to lose you. I wish I could give you everything you've ever wanted. You're the best thing that's ever happened to me." Chris steepled his hands and rested his forehead against them, breathing deeply, trying to cool his pain. He had known this was coming for weeks, but had been delaying the conversation.

"Chris, I don't ever want you to live an inauthentic life. I would never want to change you," Jill said sincerely. "But can I just ask why you don't want kids?"

"I want to say it's because I'm selfish. I like my weekends. I like to do what I want," Chris said, not quite believing it himself.

"Chris, you're not selfish. I've seen how you care for your mom. And care for me. I think parenting would come naturally to you."

"Maybe. I don't know. I've felt this way for as long

as I can remember. My therapist would say it's about my father."

"What about him?"

"I don't know. I guess I'm just afraid. Like maybe I could never live up to my dad. Like I don't have it in me."

"I wish you could see what I see, Chris."

The restaurant was nearly empty. Jill and Chris sat quietly together at the counter and watched a few last revelers walk by outside the big windows. They both wished time could stand still.

"I wonder if we look like *The Nighthawks* to those people walking by," Chris mused.

"What do you think *The Nighthawks* were talking about?"

"This."

66

The lumberyard had delivered the four large panels of marine-grade plywood. Jo had moved the displays in the rear of her store to make room for them on the floor while the primer coats were drying. Each panel was six feet square, and would fit into the vertical metal frames Grant had built the past fall. The frames stood at the terminal ends of each leg of the walkway in the Garden for the Blind. Jo remembered what Micha had told her about people with low vision enjoying the experience of bold color contrasts.

After months of indecision, Jo had been inspired by a beautiful, little embroidered dress she saw Mai wearing to celebrate the Hmong New Year. Jo bought a bright fuchsia paint color for the first panel, a vibrant shamrock green for the second, and a lemon yellow for the third. Three coats of paint were now dry and cured. The panels would stand up to the weather but be easy to slide in and out of the frames when touch-ups were needed. In the corners of each panel, Jo had started to add a few finely detailed floral elements that reminded her of the embroidery in the dress, using the Norwegian brush stroke technique of rosemaling.

Jo knew she wanted the fourth panel to be a dramatic black and white contrast, and the design choice felt important since it would be placed in the final frame of the path. It would be the last impression as people left the garden. She considered painting the outline of a daisy. She thought about a peace sign. After spending an afternoon at the library, poring over images in design books from many different cultures of the world, including charts of Samurai crests and alchemist symbols, Jo decided to paint the yin and yang. She understood the ancient Chinese symbol to mean there is duality in everything.

The yang was light, active, dominating, hot and strong. The yin was passive, intuitive, cold and dark. One was expanding and the other was contracting. The white side held a smaller circle of black, and the black side held a smaller circle of white, to mean that everything carries the seed of the opposite. Jo planned to rotate the symbol 90 degrees on each solstice and equinox, like a clock through the four seasons.

She squatted on the panel in her socks, using carefully measured pieces of twine as the radii, and light pencil marks to outline the borders of the symbol. Her rapidly growing body was limiting the time she could spend down on the floor, and her balance while painting was becoming unreliable. Despite the large tarp under the panel, she was not looking forward to opening the can of black paint.

"Knock knock...Jo?"

"Back here!"

"Hey, I didn't see you down there," Grant said. "I brought you a ham melt and a snickerdoodle. I figured once you started painting, you wouldn't want to take a break." Grant set the brown paper bag on the floor beside her.

"Thanks, Grant. That was really thoughtful." She noticed Grant had been coming in the front door lately, which seemed formal, but she was relieved they were being friendly and getting back to some version of normal.

"This will be really cool," he said, standing over her, looking down at the lightly outlined design.

"Thanks. I'm happy with how they're turning out." Jo stood up and took a step back from the boards to look at her work.

"Pretty chilly in here with the windows open, Picasso."

"Don't remind me," she laughed, rubbing her upper arms. "It was too cold to do this out in the garage, but I didn't think paint fumes were exactly good for the baby."

"Just give a holler when you're done painting and I'll do the varnish coat, OK ? That stuff stinks. It's supposed to warm up by the end of the week and I can do it out back."

"That might not be a bad idea. Thanks, Grant."

"Oh, hey, are the placards ready?"

"Yep. They'll be attached to the railing at wheelchair-height and include braille. They're scheduled to be installed before the ribbon-cutting in May. I can't believe this is actually happening."

"It's a really special garden, Jo. People will love it. I guess a couple good seeds were planted during that Switzerland trip, huh?"

Jo looked at him and was delayed a beat before she realized what he meant. He winked. She burst into laughter and pretended to attack him with little punches in his ribcage as he put his arm over her shoulder.

67

Chris peeled off his soaked socks and mud-caked running pants. It was a rare 50 degree day, with plenty of sun, but the roads were still laden with dirty slush. The clean path along the lake had been the one stretch of reprieve where he didn't have to watch every step for slick spots, but the sharp wind pushed him back into the neighborhoods. He piled his clothes on the bathroom floor, set his phone on the sink, and stepped into the hot shower. The dirty water ran down his legs and swirled at his feet. Chris closed his eyes and let the water hit his face and warm his red ears. He hadn't heard from Jill in a week, since their talk at the diner about kids. She said she needed some time. He stole a glance at his phone through the shower door to see if he had any alerts and shook his head, frustrated at himself, as he turned back to the water. He had felt sick about it all week, and was doing his best to stay distracted.

Chris dried off and put on a T-shirt and sweats. He grabbed a kombucha from the fridge and sat down on the rug in his living room, which had become his makeshift office. Printouts of job applications, versions of his résumé, and headhunter bios were scattered around his laptop. He tried to sit cross-legged but couldn't do it for more than a minute. Finally he reached for a pillow from the sofa and lay on his side on the floor, with his laptop propped on the diagonal against his knees. Chris had discovered it was much harder to look for a job with no office equipment or administrative assistant down the hall. He had already gotten many calls and emails about positions at tech start-ups all over the country. But he had no interest in diving back into the same pool he had just climbed out of. He was looking for something totally different. Staying in Milwaukee would make sense, so

he could easily help his mother, but he was
searching in Madison and Chicago, as well.

Chris picked up his phone and ordered a falafel
dinner to be delivered, and a second meal
of chicken shawarma to eat the next day. He
researched a few companies that interested him
and found himself distracted by YouTube every
few minutes. He stood up to stretch and heard
a knock at the door. It seemed too quick for
his food to have arrived, and they would have
to be buzzed in to get upstairs anyway. Chris
checked the peephole and didn't see anyone,
so he decided not to open the door. There had
been recent thefts in the building, including two
bikes, and people were on edge. He sat at his
kitchen counter, feeling nervous and unsettled.
He wanted a drink, but he had poured everything
down the sink after Jill's story about her mom.

Twenty minutes later, he got a text alert that his
food was almost there. He stepped into his slides

and grabbed his keys to go downstairs and meet the driver in the vestibule. When he opened his door, he saw a brown paper bag on the floor by his feet. Inside the bag was one black and white cookie wrapped in cellophane. Chris closed his eyes and inhaled through his nose, searching for the lingering scent of lemon hanging in the air, but it was gone.

68

The phone rang and Jo turned onto all fours to climb up off the floor of her living room.

"Oh, here honey, let me help you," said Martie, standing up and walking around the partially assembled crib to give her a hand.

"Thanks. I feel like an elephant. I'm coming!" she called to the phone as she jogged ungracefully to the kitchen.

"Hello?"

"Is this Jo Martin? This is Doctor Kiesau calling you back."

"Oh, hello, Doctor. I'm so sorry to bother you."

"No problem at all. My nurse said you've been having some pain?"

"Well, yes, it's just this feeling above my ribs. It's hard to explain. I keep thinking it will go away and then it doesn't," Jo glanced over at Martie, who looked worried.

"At this stage in your pregnancy, what you might be feeling is indigestion. Or you could be having some false contractions. Either way, it's nothing to worry about. You're still a few weeks out."

"OK that's what I thought. I just called because… oh, never mind. I won't worry about it."

"Because why, Ms. Martin?"

"Well, I just wanted to make sure you saw in my chart about the car accident last fall."

"Let me see here." Jo could hear him rustling

papers. She nervously adjusted the five daffodils in the vase on her kitchen table.

"Yes, I see it here. Looks like you broke some ribs but the rest of the scans were clear."

"Right, that's what they told me. That was up at the hospital in Madison. I've just been a little worried, and the pain seems to persist day and night."

"My advice is to try to relax. Put your feet up. Sounds like your emotions are getting the best of you. Baby will be here in due time."

"Yes, doctor. I will try. Thank you for the call." Jo hung up and poured herself another glass of raspberry leaf tea.

"What was that all about?" asked Martie, helping Jo sit down on the sofa.

"Oh, I don't know." Jo dragged a line across the top of her stomach. "Right in here I've been having some pains lately. And sometimes in my shoulder too. I think I'm just getting paranoid. Doc Kiesau didn't seem concerned."

"Should we go to the clinic? I'll drive you."

"No, no, it's fine, Martie. Thanks, though. He thinks it's just some false contractions."

"That's not uncommon. He's seen every pregnancy in this town, so I guess he would know."

"Actually, I don't even feel it right now. See? It's nothing."

"This is such a sweet little crib, Jo. Is it birch?" Martie asked as she screwed the pale wood spindles into the frame.

"It's ash. I love it, too. Did I show you the sheets?"

Jo stood up and walked to the linen closet. "Can you believe these?" She brought them over to show Martie.

"Oh, my goodness," Martie giggled. "Are those pea pods?"

"Yes! Is this the sweetest thing you've ever seen? For my little sweet pea," Jo said as she held the soft crib sheet up to her cheek.

"And you're really not finding out the sex?"

"Nope. It doesn't matter one bit, and that will be a fun surprise."

"Dagmar and I have a bet. I say girl, she says boy."

Jo laughed. "What did you bet on it?"

"The *Thriller* album," Martie grinned. "Grant has that album and Dag is jealous."

"And if you win, do you get *Thriller* too, or did you ask for something different?"

"No, *Thriller*'s fine," she laughed. "My students will think I'm cool."

"You and Dag are so funny."

"We have a name pool at the restaurant, too. Everyone put their guess in a bowl."

"Oh, didn't I tell you? I already decided on Billie Jean."

"What? Oh, haha, very funny, Jo. Oh, my God, are you OK?" Martie rushed to her side and took her arm as Jo winced and doubled over.

"Yeah." Jo breathed deeply. "Yeah I'm OK." Jo stood back up slowly and held her stomach with her hands.

"Are you sure we shouldn't go see the doctor?"

"No, no, I just need to sit down. He suggested putting my feet up."

Martie helped her adjust pillows around her back and feet. Jo watched as Martie finished assembling the crib and rolled it into the corner of the living room where Jo had hung a mobile. Martie lifted the small mattress and set it inside the crib. It looked cozy and warm.

"Should I put the sheets on?"

"That's OK. I'll do it later," said Jo, feeling a little left out of her own special jobs. "Thanks so much for your help today."

"My pleasure. Now don't hesitate to call if you need anything."

Jo stayed in that place on the sofa for the rest of the afternoon. She talked to her baby about everything she had planned, and about her dreams for their life together. For a short while, she fell asleep. When the heat kicked on, she saw the mobile dance in the draft, and imagined her baby looking up at it, cooing in delight. She set her hands on her belly and felt the reassuring little kicks and stretches. The light eventually dimmed in her apartment as the sun started to go down. That day, with her tired feet propped on pillows, Jo did three things she hadn't done in a very long time. She rested. She sang a lullaby. And she prayed.

April

69

Chris set a mug of spearmint tea on the table next to Eileen's chair.

"Careful, that's hot, Mom."

Eileen nodded and didn't say anything.

"So, I'll probably go back to your apartment and roll one more cartful over today, but then I'll come back on Saturday and do the rest. Sound OK?"

"What day is it today?" she asked.

"Thursday. I can come tomorrow, too, if you want, I just have an interview in Madison so it might be pretty late when I get here."

"No, no. Saturday is fine." Eileen clasped her hands in her lap and looked toward the window.

"I'll get everything all set up for you, Mom. Don't worry. I know this is a big change."

"Yes," she said sadly. "Of all the problems I imagined for my old age, and I imagined a lot, I never pictured macular degeneration."

"You're gonna learn new ways to do things. I'll be here every step of the way."

"It's just so scary to not know how fast it will go. I'm so terrified I'll wake up one morning…"

"Mom, that's not what your doctor is telling us. They'll do everything they can to slow it down."

"I don't know what I'll do without reading, Chris. Books have been my best friend. For my whole life."

"I know, Mom. I'm just so sorry this is happening." Chris sat on the sofa next to her and took her hand.

"You said there's some device?" she asked.

"Ha! Mom, there are devices up the wazoo. I will get you all hooked up. There's this big screen we can get you that will magnify any text you want. I can get you anything on audiobook. Your phone has a ton of apps designed for low vision. You can wear a little voice recorder on a necklace so you can make a grocery list for me. We will figure it out. You can even *write* a book if you want."

Eileen's eyes were tearing up. "Thank you, Chris."

"My tech background will finally come in handy," he laughed. "First things first, though, OK? I'm gonna get all your stuff over here, and get you settled and comfortable. I know this has been sudden. Really sorry I forgot your robe yesterday."

"Liberty Acres sure didn't waste any time pushing me over to The Fields. Nice bump in their paycheck, too."

"Mom, I really think they have your best interests at heart. Usually I'm skeptical of this sort of corporation, but everyone involved in this decision has been kind and patient. They're looking out for you."

"You won't see our Jill much anymore now that I'm over on this side."

Chris didn't respond. He reached to pull the tea bag out of the mug and carry it to the trash can, holding his hand under the drips.

"By the way, honey, what's the job? Your interview tomorrow?"

"Oh, yeah, I'm kind of excited about it. So, there's this global initiative to plant a trillion trees by

2030. The governor just got on board and will be pumping some funding into it. So the Wisconsin chapter is hiring for a few positions."

"Hmm. Sounds interesting. I've always liked that governor."

"Me, too. It could be a really good fit for me. We'll see. Hopefully they can overlook my FELL baggage."

"I would hire you, honey."

Chris laughed. "Thanks, Mom. Is this what they call 'A résumé only a mother could love?'"

"I think you're going to impress them. I'm just sorry it's been such a crazy week for you, dealing with me. Can you hand me that tea, honey? I'm afraid I'll knock it over."

Chris reached for the mug and noticed on the

table next to it was a small mirror and a pair of tweezers. He took Eileen's hand and made sure it was closed securely around the mug. They sat together quietly as she drank her tea.

"Hey, Mom, can I help you tweeze something?"

"I can tell you're smiling, Chris."

"Can I help you tweeze something," he said again with a downturned mouth to make her laugh.

"Well, if you must know, I can feel these two pesky chin hairs and I was trying to pull them but kept pinching my damn skin so I gave up!" she said laughing, but exasperated.

"Mind if I give it a shot? Here, I'll have you hold my phone flashlight and we'll point it right at your chin." Chris handed her his phone.

"This is ridiculous," said Eileen, but did as she was told.

Chris saw about a dozen wiry white hairs and got to work, warning her before each tug.

"Does this hurt? Do you want ice?"

"Oh, no, these hairs have been pulled so many times before. The nerves don't even notice anymore."

With each hair, Chris improved his method, using his free hand to pull the skin taut, and grasping the hair closer to the base as he pulled.

"This is kind of gratifying. I feel like a surgeon," he said.

"Well, I'm glad someone is enjoying it. I will have to sign up for the salon services downstairs. We will not be making a regular habit of this, Chris."

"Why not? Hey, and I'm a painter, too. I think I could give you a helluva pedicure."

"This reminds me of something Susan Sontag said in her essay 'Notes on Camp.'"

"Mom, you will have to stop sounding so smart. I'm trying to be in charge now," Chris laughed.

"Let me see if I can get this right. She said, 'What is most beautiful in virile men is something feminine; what is most beautiful in feminine women is something masculine.'"

Chris leaned in close to her beard, only a few inches away, to grab the last short hair. "Do you think this is what she meant?" he smiled.

Eileen set down the phone light and placed her hand on the side of his face, feeling a fleeting brush with a moment from long ago. Touching, for just an instant, the warm round cheek of her little boy. With his curly blonde hair and high voice. "Yes, Chris. I do. I think this is exactly what she meant."

70

Jo stood in the doorway of the diner. The lunch rush was in full swing and almost every table was full. She saw an open stool at the far end of the counter and wished with her entire heart that she could go sit down. Order an open-faced roast beef sandwich and mashed potatoes. Chat with her friend. Take a slice of lemon icebox pie back to the store with her to eat later.

"I need help," she said, barely audibly.

"I need help," she said, again, wanting to cry.

"Something's not right. I need help," she said, much louder this time. She clutched her stomach and tried to stay standing upright.

The restaurant became quiet. Everyone turned

to the front door. The patrons, the waitstaff, her friends, and strangers. They stared at her and nobody spoke. Jo felt like a character in a sci-fi scene where everyone was frozen in place and she alone could move and walk among them.

Grant pushed open the swinging kitchen door and emerged balancing four plates on his arms. He saw Jo and blanched with fear.

"I'll get Sandy!" he called to her. "I'll pull her around front! Hang on, Jo!"

Dagmar rushed from behind the counter and supported Jo under her arms, leading her to the edge of a booth where two people were sitting. Jo didn't know them and they moved closer to the wall, looking confused.

"I think we're about to have one more Mount Horeb resident," Dagmar told them, smiling apologetically.

"But Dag. It's not time yet," Jo said quietly.

"Close enough, Mama." Dagmar set a hand on Jo's shoulder and reassured her. "Grant will get you up to Madison and Tom and I will be there in a couple hours. Is your bag ready?"

"No, I'm not ready at all." Jo put her head in her hands.

"I'll pull a few things together for you. Pajamas, socks, cold cream. Women have been having babies since the beginning of time without luggage," she laughed. "Baby is ready to meet you, and baby's the boss!"

"It hurts too bad, Dag. I'm scared. This doesn't seem right." Jo tried to breathe slowly but couldn't help but tense up in pain.

"It's normal, honey. This part will be over before you know it."

"But it feels like a knife. It doesn't come and go. It just twists."

"Here he is," said Dag, looking through the front windows. Jo stood with difficulty and they walked outside to the car. Grant ran around and opened the back door for her.

"Back seat? Is that good? So you can lie down?" he asked loudly and excitedly.

Jo climbed in the back of the Oldsmobile and lay on her side, knees bent in front of her. The sharp pain was exhausting. Unrelenting. Grant pulled away from the curb slowly, like he was carrying stacks of china tea cups.

Through the car window, Jo saw her apartment pass by above them. The curtains were closed but she could see she had left a light on. She felt dread in knowing she wasn't home, and with every mile she was further still.

71

The sweet pea seedlings, almost four inches tall, lined the windowsill in Chris's bedroom. He had removed the mirror from the back of his bathroom door and propped it against the window, positioning his easel to its right. He sat in his deep, comfortable bedroom chair, now facing the mirror, and contemplated the project. Chris had begun another series of classes at Sue Donovan's studio, and the assignment for the week was to paint a self-portrait.

Chris leaned forward to adjust the mirror and get more light on his face. Sue told them working from a photograph was expected, but a mirror would be more of a challenge. It was not the ideal chair for painting, and felt a few inches too low, but Chris wanted to include the gray bird toile fabric pattern in the background of the painting.

The worn, faded chair had been in the living room of his boyhood home and felt appropriate for the tableau.

Having more trouble getting started than usual, Chris's focus turned to the sweet peas. They looked healthy and robust. It was gratifying. He had watched some YouTube videos and come up with a germination method that seemed to work. He soaked the seeds in warm water, scored them lightly with a nail file, and after planting, he domed them with clear shower caps. Now the seedlings were tall enough to be growing freely, and in a couple more weeks when the threat of frost was gone, he would move them outdoors. He had a childish hope that someday sending Jill a photo of successful blooms would help win her back.

Chris looked at his face in the mirror. He had aged. The past year had felt like a decade. The lines around his eyes were deeper, and his cheeks were more hollow. But he had never felt healthier. He had never felt more at home and more like himself. He picked up a palette knife and began to mix the color for his skin tone. Chris had made multiple charcoal drawings of his face to work out problems before he started. His eyes had been the most difficult part, but he was confident now in his strategy. He toned the canvas to kill the pure white and he began to paint.

Chris chose warm colors for the foundation of the image, radiating an inner heat like the human body itself. He went back in and carved out details with cooler tones, working instinctually. He laid broad impressions onto the canvas, and when he felt a need for shadow or an edge, he fulfilled it. He paused to add a glaze to parts of his face to increase the luminosity, a technique used by masters who came before him. Studying great paintings in museums and books, and observing nature on his long runs, had been as integral in his improvement this year as painting itself. From both he had learned that a whisper could be more engaging than a shout. One fine brush stroke, perfectly placed, could move a wave or change a mood.

His eyes darted back and forth to the mirror, constantly adjusting for perspective and proportional balance. He thought about how quickly Artificial Intelligence programs could learn and micro-correct, and had to admit the human brain was still the most incredible machine. Chris set down his brush and leaned back in his chair to take an overall look at the painting. He would need to stop for the day soon because the light was changing on his face. He was pleased with the overall effect and felt it was a good resemblance. The eyes were the only part that wasn't quite right.

On a whim that felt like it was a conclusive test of his sanity, Chris picked up his father's ebony brush. With a slow careful touch, he dipped the pointed tip into a smear of Midnight Black. He tapped the excess onto the flat palette board, and leaned into the mirror to study his eyes. He realized the detail he had been missing. Turning back to the painting, he choked up on the brush and steadied his hand. He added thin, delicate circles around the circumference of his irises. He used his finger to soften the edges. He dipped the brush again, this time into Titanium White, and added a brighter light reflection to his pupils. He set down the brush and leaned back in his chair. He was satisfied. His eyes had come alive.

72

The doctor was backlit by fluorescent ceiling lights, obscuring his facial expressions. Grant grasped the sides of the molded plastic chair he was sitting in, tucking his thumbs under his thighs. He looked at the doctor's necktie. It had a pattern of small brown pineapples on a royal blue background, with about eight of them repeating before disappearing under the white coat.

"Sir, do you understand what I'm telling you?"

Grant didn't speak.

"The baby is alive. We think the baby will survive. The vitals look good."

Grant heard water in his ears. Like a gently babbling stream on a spring day. A chorus of high plinks and splashing burbles. The doctor's voice broke through only occasionally.

"...sign documents..."

The air register by Grant's feet rattled. He looked down at it.

"...splenic artery pseudoaneurysm..."

Grant reached down to pull the back of his sock up higher above his ankle.

"...attributed to labor pain..."

Grant wound his black Timex watch.

"...identify the body..."

73

After spending most of the day hauling the rest of his mother's belongings to her new unit, Chris had come back to the old apartment for one last load. He sat on the floor of his mother's nearly empty bedroom, checking the Masters leaderboard on his phone. He had spent hours boxing up old photos and paperwork. The large mahogany armoire would be donated to charity along with most of her other furniture. Chris was profoundly fatigued. He was sure he had inadvertently saved some garbage while discarding some heirlooms.

Ready to tackle the final drawer, he pulled a stapled document out of a faded yellow envelope that looked like it had been opened with a letter opener. He unfolded it and realized it was his adoption paperwork. A nervous bolt of adrenaline pierced his chest. He had never seen the official document before. His eyes scanned the information and froze when he saw that his birth mother had died in childbirth. His parents had always told him she died in a car accident. Without thinking, Chris picked up his phone and called Eileen.

"Hello?"

"Mom."

"Chris? Is that you? Are you coming back over?"

"Yes, it's me. I'll be there soon with the last load. But I have to ask you about something."

"By phone?"

"Look, Mom. I don't want to catch you off guard with this, but I'm looking at a document that says my biological mother died in childbirth. You guys always told me it was a car accident. I always thought she had met me and spent a little time being my mother before she died."

"Oh. Childbirth? I'm sorry I don't remember that, Chris. I thought they told us at the orphanage it was a car accident."

"Yeah, childbirth. Something about her spleen. How is this news to you?"

Eileen was quiet.

"Mom, I'm sorry. I don't mean to pile on. I'm sorry."

"It's OK, honey."

"There's nothing about the father. Just the word 'unknown'. I've never understood how that's possible. Unknown?"

"It was a different time, dear. Pregnancy out of wedlock was not something to sing from the rooftops. You have to remember this was in the heart of Reagan and the moral majority."

"OK, but regardless, he had to have known. And then he just decided he didn't want me. That's what happened. Or worse."

"Chris, please don't jump to conclusions. We just don't know. We weren't told anything about him. Maybe he died in the car accident, too."

"Mom! For chrissake, it wasn't a car accident!"

"Oh, geez, Chris. Calm down. I got confused. Give me a small break, could you? This is not exactly the easiest conversation for me either, you know."

"I'm sorry," Chris said gently. "I know, Mom. I'm sorry." Chris felt terrible for snapping at her.

"I have to admit I always wondered if he was married."

"My biological father?"

"Yes. It would explain why he didn't come forward to raise you."

"That's possible, I guess. Still a shitty, cowardly decision."

"Well, not every man is as good and strong as your dad was. Or as you are."

"Ha, well you're right about Dad. But I've got this chump's DNA."

"Chris, you can't think like that."

"Well, it's pretty hard not to think like that. I have to wonder if those doubts in myself are exactly why I lost Jill."

"Oh, Chris. Did you two break up?"

"Yeah. You were right. Kids are a really big deal for her."

"I'm sorry, Chris."

"Thanks. I suppose it's for the best."

"Chris, I know I've said it before, and it's no excuse, but it really was a different time back then. A man never would have been expected to raise a baby on his own. He wouldn't have been viewed as capable. I know it sounds crazy now. The church handled the adoptions in those days, and they wanted babies to be placed in homes with a mother and a father. That's just the way it was."

"You don't even go to church, Mom," Chris chuckled.

"We did then! Everyone did."

Chris was quiet and looked at the paperwork again. He had been eight days old when he was given to Eileen and Bill. He thought about how stupid he felt that eight short days of being "unclaimed" were still affecting him as a forty-year-old man.

"You know, if you feel like more information could be healing, you might consider submitting your saliva to one of those websites. Maybe you could find the chump."

Chris thought it was generous for Eileen to suggest that idea. He didn't tell her that he had already done that years ago. It showed Germanic and Norwegian heritage, and no DNA matches so far on the paternal side. The chump was a total mystery.

"Chris. I know it's not the answer you're seeking, but I want you to know there wasn't a day of your life that you weren't deeply loved. Your dad and I loved you before we met you. From the moment he and I fell in love with each other, we were waiting for you." Chris could tell that she was crying, and that every word was true.

74

Grant sat on the damp ground and leaned against a thick stalk of forsythia. A patch of irises were just beginning to sprout next to him. He unwrapped a sandwich from a large cloth napkin. Turkey and baby Swiss on pumpernickel, with pickles and a generous layer of stone-ground mustard.

"I thought I might find you back here," said Dagmar, walking towards him along one of the newly laid brick paths of the garden.

"Yeah. Sorry. It's still hard to be around people."

"I understand. The days are long right now," she said sadly, kneeling down next to him.

"Oh, here. Sit on this." Grant spread out the cloth

napkin and Dag sat down beside him, hugging her knees to her chest.

"What do you think will happen to this garden? To her building?" he asked, trying to fight back tears.

"I don't know. I think the State will get involved if they can't find a will. Dad said he asked his lawyer if he had heard anything, and he said it's still unclear."

"We've gotta save this garden, Dag."

"We will if we can. Don't worry about that now, OK? Paj and Sawm have been tending to it. Just take care of yourself. I'm worried about you."

"I called and talked to Doc Kiesau this morning. He had some more information from the hospital."

"I don't know if I want to know," Dag muttered.

"I still feel terrible that I dismissed her pain. I told her it was 'normal.'"

"He said it was the car accident."

"What?"

"Yeah. Can you believe it? There was some sort of bulge in an artery from the trauma of the crash. They missed it in her X-rays. The day she went into labor, it ruptured. No one caught it because the labor pains were the star of the show."

"She knew, though."

"Yeah. She told everyone that something wasn't right. When we got to the hospital she was almost begging someone to listen to her."

"I still can't believe this. I wake up every morning and remember she's gone." Dagmar put her forehead on her knees.

"Kiesau said he couldn't believe the baby survived. He's never seen a case like this where the baby lived."

"Did you hear it's some Catholic couple in Milwaukee?"

"Yeah. I heard," he said angrily.

"Grant, come on. Be real."

"What? I could have done it. I would be an awesome dad."

"You would. I agree. But there is no way they were about to give a baby to a single man who isn't even related. Absolutely no chance in hell."

"No one would even listen to me. No one even gave me a shot."

Dagmar put her hand on her brother's shoulder.

"Jo would have loved that you tried, Grant." She looked up at the forsythia branches arching over them, coated thickly with bright yellow four-petaled stars, open wide. "She would have loved that you tried."

May

75

"I'm Mai Lor. It's a pleasure to meet you." She shook Chris's hand and smiled warmly. "Please, sit." Mai took her place behind the desk and pulled up a page of notes about Chris on her screen.

"This is a beautiful office," said Chris, looking around at the dozens of lush green plants. He felt like he was in a conservatory.

"Oh, thanks. I've always had a bit of a green thumb. Feel free to come in and take a cutting any time you want. My door's always open." She scrolled through the notes and then turned her full attention to Chris.

"I apologize I wasn't able to sit in on your interviews. I've been overseas working with our

Thai and Chinese partners. But you come highly recommended from my team and this is truly just a formality. My main purpose today is to see if you have any questions for me before you begin."

"I'm just really excited to get started. I appreciate the opportunity to work for such an important project."

"I was told you'll be working primarily at the Milwaukee office, so you'll report to me. And any time you're at the Madison office, just ask Silas if you need help. You met them in the interview. Tall? Glasses?"

"Oh, yes, I remember Silas. OK, thanks."

"Your title will be Deputy Director of Technology Integration, and I think Dave went over salary info with you. You'll find working for a nonprofit isn't quite as glamorous," she laughed. "But I promise we will always have good coffee and lots of laughs."

"I can't wait."

"I've spent time in D.C. working on lobbying efforts quite a bit this year, and what I'm hearing is this app you'll be working on could make all the difference. Trillion Trees is a lofty global goal, but it's only possible when projects are tracked on the state and local level. We're hoping Wisconsin can not only catch up, but be a real leader on this nationwide."

"I'm ready," said Chris. The oxygen in the room seemed boundless.

"Feel free to work from home any time that makes sense for your life. As long as you and Dave are making good progress, it's not important where you do it. I was actually Director of Technology before moving to my current role, so I'm happy to help troubleshoot programming or website issues, too. Sometimes it helps to get a fresh set of eyes on things."

"Wow. Great, thanks. I admit I did research your bio and you've had an incredible career."

"Just getting started," she smiled.

Chris was in awe. He had a feeling he would do anything he could to impress her and live up to this opportunity. This second chance.

"On your way out today, you can stop and get your keycard and login info from Chloe."

Chris started to stand, sensing Mai was wrapping things up.

"Oh, one more thing," she said while standing and closing her laptop. "Once a month, the team does an outreach project. Not required, but they're usually a lot of fun. If you happen to be free Saturday morning, we'll be over in this small town called Mount Horeb, south of Madison."

"I know Mount Horeb! My dad used to take me to the Mustard Museum when I was a kid."

"Really? Ha! I actually grew up there. We took field trips to that museum," she laughed.

"Wow, that seems strangely complementary to the bratwurst factory field trip we Milwaukee kids did. And I am free Saturday. I'd love to be involved. What's the project?"

"Great. It will be a good chance for you to meet more of the staff. There is a really special sensory Garden for the Blind, tucked right behind Main Street. Once a year, we go help tidy things up and get it ready for the season. So wear something that can get dirty. Chloe can give you the details."

Chris and Mai shook hands again by the door. For a brief moment, he thought he saw in her eyes all she had to overlook in his history to give him this chance. What he felt in her palm was grace.

76

Chris found a parking spot on Main Street and could see people gathering under an iron arch next to a restaurant. He reached into the bag on the passenger seat and grabbed a water bottle and his sunglasses. The bag also contained a small amount of painting supplies, in case he had any time in the afternoon to drive around the driftless region. He hoped to find some rocky outcroppings and meandering streams to paint. He remembered a beautiful area where his dad had taken him trout fishing, but he wasn't sure he could find it again. Realizing he probably shouldn't have brought a one-time-use plastic bottle, he decided to leave it in the car.

"Hi, Chris!" Silas waved to him as he approached the group. "Come meet everyone."

Chris shook hands and tried to use mental tricks to remember names, but so far Silas, Dave, Chloe, and Mai were the only ones he was sure enough to say out loud.

"You won't believe this place," Mai said to Chris as she led the group down the narrow brick path next to the restaurant and opened the garden gate.

A handsome older man, fit and tan, with wavy salt-and-pepper hair, approached the group. He greeted Mai and hugged her tightly.

"We got a newbie on our hands?" he asked, looking at Chris and smiling.

"We do, indeed. Grant Morrison, meet Chris Schwarz. He's our new tech whiz in the Milwaukee office."

Grant shook Chris's hand firmly. "First thing I

need you to do, kid, is come move a boulder for me." Grant winked.

"He's kidding, Chris." Mai rolled her eyes at Grant. The rest of the staff had made their way over to a table of muffins and juice. Some were picking out gloves and rakes.

"Let me give you a tour, Chris," Grant said while clasping his shoulder. "We're damn proud of this place. I appreciate the help today. Great turnout. My wife and sister might stop by later. Maybe my kids, too. My wife's a judge up in Madison and this is her only morning to sleep in." He laughed. "At this age, I couldn't sleep in if I tried! But she loves her long coffee time."

"Relatable," Chris nodded. "How many kids do you have?"

"Three kids, eight grandkids. All good people. I'm a very lucky man."

Chris walked slowly around the brick path while Grant pointed out details and told him the history of the garden.

"Now usually you'd be hearing the audio on these placards as you walk by, but we've got the electricity off right now so we can give them a good scrub. But it's cool as hell. Same technology they use at the Rock and Roll Hall of Fame. But quieter," he chuckled.

"I love it. Great idea."

"Yeah, that was added a few years ago after we did some fundraising. State of the art. We figured out braille wasn't all that useful. A lot of people lose vision later in life, so they never learn it. Actually, a pretty small percentage of legally blind folks can read braille. Only about 10 percent. I think it's one of those myths that help sighted people think a problem is solved when it's not."

"Interesting. I never knew that. My mother has actually lost quite a bit of vision recently, so I've been learning a lot."

"I'm sorry to hear that," Grant said sincerely. "If you ever want to bring her here, come on a weekday morning. You'll have the place to yourselves. Good restaurant next door. Tell them Grant sent you."

They approached a corner and Chris looked at the bright painted panel covered with tone on tone floral artwork. The effect felt three-dimensional.

"Now these panels were Jo's idea."

"They're stunning. Who's Jo?"

"Oh! She's the person who started this garden. Back in '83. Her idea. She drew up the plans. I wish you could have met her." Grant seemed melancholy.

"It's all pretty amazing."

"Yeah, truly. A few years ago these panels 'went viral,' whatever that means. Apparently, some influencer was here and posted some photos of them. After that, attendance rates went nuts. It was like the world discovered us. The change of seasons is a big deal, too. That's when we rotate the wheel." Grant pointed to the yin-yang panel. "People come from all over. We had to get a bigger lockbox for the donations," Grant laughed. "It all goes to the Wisconsin Council for the Blind and also to Hmong Veterans of Wisconsin. Mai's parents helped build this garden. He was a Vietnam vet. Awesome people. They were great friends of ours."

Grant stepped off the path, bent down, and pulled up a small flower with tiny white bells. "You ever smelled this?" He handed it to Chris.

"Lily of the valley, right?"

"Hey! You know your flowers! These always remind me of Jo."

Chris and Grant rejoined the group standing under a tall aspen tree and listened to Mai give instructions. The team worked for two hours, clearing leaves and debris from the walkways and perennial clumps, weeding, and planting annuals. Two women on stepladders worked on touching up the paint and weatherproofing the panels. One of the metal frames needed tightening. Chris and Silas spent time dividing and replanting ornamental grasses. Chris was getting more confident with names and really liked the staff. Grant put out a second round of snacks on the table and people finished up their tasks in the garden, gathering again to have a cookie and say goodbye.

Mai addressed the group. "In a few minutes, we'll be doing The Release, so if you'd like to stick around for that, please do."

Chris looked confused, and made questioning eye contact with Grant.

"Hey, Mai," Grant called. "Not everyone knows about The Release."

"Oh! I'm sorry. Let me explain. OK, so the wonderful woman who built this garden, Jo Martin, was working back here one day and she discovered an old cistern. It's in the dead center of this garden, and has a stone on top you can twist and lift like a manhole cover. Of course, we don't want the public to know about that, so it's hidden with vegetation. We don't really know how deep it is. It seems to go on forever. I don't remember when we started doing this, but every spring we toss stuff in there we want to say goodbye to. Last year, I think I remember there were a lot of masks and covid tests." Everyone laughed. "Some people write something on a slip of paper. Or toss in a small object that's symbolic to them. Totally up to you. It's just a way of releasing something that's been holding you back, and a way to start fresh for the growing season."

About half of the staff went to their cars and headed home, but the rest stayed to do The Release. Chris decided to stay and watch.

"Chris," said Mai, coming up beside him. "Are you wondering if you've joined up with a bunch of witches?"

"Ha! Not at all. I think it's cool."

"Sometimes I wonder if most of the slips of paper are just the names of exes," she laughed.

Chris stood in the back of the group and watched as each person put something down the hole. It seemed to be a meaningful ritual, and one man became emotional as he let go of a scarf. He was comforted by a colleague. Chris tried to imagine the FELL team having such a vulnerable moment with each other and it seemed ludicrous. He realized his authentic self would be welcome here. These people would never want him to be someone he wasn't. The idea that had been tickling his brain finally came to the surface, and he quickly jogged to his car to get his father's paintbrush. He joined the queue and soon it was his turn. Almost everyone else had left the garden. Chris held the paintbrush over the cistern.

"Hey, hang on there. What do you have?"

"Grant! That's his personal business," said Mai.

"Sorry, yeah. Bombs away, Chris. I just thought that brush looked familiar." Grant stepped closer to get a better look. Chris held it vertically so he could see the details.

"Hey, Mai, come over here. You gotta see this."

Mai stepped around the thick vegetation to stand next to Grant. "Doesn't this look exactly like the brush Jo brought back from Switzerland?"

"Wow. I remember the ebony handle, for sure. Gosh, that takes me back. I think she actually used it to paint the ferns on the green panel. I haven't thought of this in so many years."

"Where'd you get that, son?"

"It was my father's," answered Chris, a bit startled that they had known of a similar brush. It made him wonder if it was more common and commercially produced than he thought.

"You sure you want to say goodbye to that beauty?"

Chris looked at the brush. He nodded. He had never been so sure of anything. He dropped it into the hole and didn't hear a landing noise. He saw nothing. It was as if the hole in the center of this plot of land was deprived of senses so that the surrounding garden could have them all.

77

Chris parked next to the bridge on the quiet country road and scrambled down the embankment to a small trail along the side of the creek. He wasn't sure this was the exact spot he'd been fishing years before, but it was close. He had left his painting bag in the car, but brought his water bottle. He felt like simply taking a walk, and maybe getting some good photographs. While the morning had been chilly, it was now sunny and 70 degrees. Chris unzipped his fleece and tied it around his waist.

Chris thought back on his morning with gratitude. He was confident he would be able to do good work for this organization. He made himself do a name/face inventory one more time to help solidify his new memory connections. The terrain of the trail was uneven and he took careful steps as he thought through the list of people he had met. Then he said each name aloud, picturing each of them and where they had been working in the garden. A chipmunk darted away from the path through some leaves and Chris startled. He started over from the beginning of his list, ending with Grant.

The trail wound away from the creek and uphill through the woods. Chris was aware that he was probably on private property now, and wanted to be respectful. He thought of the date and wondered about the hunting seasons, thinking turkey hunters might be out today. Chris looked down at his navy blue T-shirt and jeans. It wasn't exactly blaze orange. He decided to cut through the woods to return to the creek's edge instead of doubling back on the trail.

He stepped carefully down the hill, hanging onto trees and vines in the steep parts to keep his balance. The forest floor was dotted with violets, trillium, bellwort, and mayapples. He took great care not to step on the ephemerals, knowing how endangered native woodland flowers had become. Chris had always had an encyclopedic botanical memory, which had helped him when he started FELL, and helped him again in his recent interviews. But the feeling of walking among those same flowers and trees was so much more meaningful than a guidebook. It made him feel in his bones the need for preservation.

Chris reached an outcropping of rock and sat down on a flat surface, resting his feet on the layer below, and took a drink of his water. A nearby grouping of large rocks covered in moss and unusual ferns formed a doorway to the creek below, and he laughed thinking about how Grant had joked about hazing him. A cluster of white trillium skirted the rocks.

The afternoon sun drove a path through the trees

to where Chris was sitting. He closed his eyes and leaned back on the warm sandstone. He could hear the creek below him gurgling and plinking. He felt surrounded by a calm energy and slid deep into a daydream.

He pictured a kind, strong, curious woman. She was good and true. He knew she painted delicate ferns, in all shades of green, on a bright shamrock board. The fern was a symbol of solitude, which she must have revered. She made that art, and created that garden, not for herself, but to bring joy and sensation to people who lived in near-darkness. And because Chris wanted so desperately to shine a joyous light on his unknown birth story, he decided that she didn't use a brush she had bought at a store. He decided she used a very special brush. One of a kind, in fact.

For the next hour, in what would be his greatest masterpiece yet, Chris created Jo. He created a woman's life, lived simply, between the two brick buildings on Main Street. Using the few things that Grant had told him, his mind spun into being the details of one entire year. He imagined a summer adventure she had in Switzerland, and a dashing, intelligent man she met there. Dark hair, like his own. He must have been an artist or a designer himself, because when they said goodbye, he gave Jo the brush, to remember him by. To remember their special night. They thought it best not to exchange addresses or even last names. Their night had been a moment in time. A capsule of freedom. A bookend of youth. And Grant! Charming, funny Grant. He must have been Jo's best friend. And yes, Chris bet he had a little crush on her, but everyone did. Jo told Grant everything. So, a few days after Jo died, his heart in a million pieces, Grant went back to the hospital to say goodbye to the precious child. And he tucked the brush with the ebony handle in the soft folds of the baby blanket. He told the nurse it had been the baby's father's brush, and to keep it very safe. When the new parents arrived, meeting the child they already loved, they named him Christopher Michael.

Of course, Chris would not be able to hold onto his fantasy of Jo and Micha for very long. The next year, Chris would go back to Mount Horeb for the spring clean-up at the garden, now a married man with a baby himself, and he would meet the real Jo. A small spry woman, almost eighty years old and very much alive, would come outside to thank the group. Grant would smile broadly and tell her to climb in for a "wheelbarrow tour," turning to wink at Chris as he said it. Chris would laugh at himself remembering the story about Jo's life he had created. Little did this sweet old woman know that a complete stranger had imagined her swimming at a nude pool, surviving a grisly car crash, and having an international fling. Seeing the twinkle in Jo's eye, Chris was sure her real life had been even more spectacular. He was happy for whatever family she did have, even if he wasn't a part of it.

Another year after meeting Jo, Chris would finally learn the identities of his biological parents. They had been teenagers from a small high school north of Milwaukee. The girl had died of an infection soon after giving birth. The boy had struggled with addiction for decades afterward. Now a fifty-eight-year-old man, he was living with his second wife and her kids in Rockford, Illinois. At Jill's encouragement, Chris would send him an email. The man would reply with a request that Chris not contact him again, so as not to disrupt his current family. It was a kindly worded message, and a fair request that Chris respected. But he still lay his head in Jill's lap that night and cried.

Chris never reached out to him again, but he drove to Rockford on his fiftieth birthday and

parked across the street from the man's house.
While listening to a Brewers game on the car
radio, he watched his biological father mow
the lawn. The man's headphone fell out of his
ear and Chris saw him search the grass on his
hands and knees. He was stocky, tan, and looked
nothing like Chris. A teenage boy came outside
and didn't help the man search, but backed a
car out of the driveway and sped away. The man
found his headphone, and finished mowing.
Chris wondered if they were listening to the same
baseball game.

On the way out of town, Chris stopped at a diner
for a piece of blueberry pie. As he watched the
ice cream blur across the dark fruit, he felt lighter.
Freer. But he had to admit the old heavy yoke,
at times, had felt like a hug. He took a bite of
pie and stifled a laugh, thinking about how his
therapist, Lucas, had job security.

But resting on the warm sandstone in the forest,

after the first morning of garden work with his new colleagues as a forty-year-old man, Chris didn't yet know any of this messy difficult story. He simply listened to the applause of the leaves in the gentle breeze around him, and only thought of precious Jo and dashing Micha. Deep in the sun-dappled woods on a spring day, Chris had found an origin story. He had found a story in which he was never abandoned, and always loved. Though the story was ephemeral, it was no less transformative.

Chris turned his gaze to a cluster of trillium to his left. He saw the flower's three white iridescent petals and felt unity with his mom and dad. They had always formed a happy little team. He looked to the next flower and felt connected to his biological mother and father, too. He looked at the last flower and saw himself, Jill, and a child. The child had warm, round cheeks and curly blonde hair. Chris sat up straight, the colors came rushing in, and he was enrapt. He untied the fleece from his waist and used it to wipe his tears. He stood up and walked quickly down the last part of the hill to the stream. The path back to the road was easy to find now. He breathed full fresh inhales and moved with purpose.

He would show up at Jill's door that evening wearing a crisp white Oxford shirt and return the black and white cookie, now stale and hard. And he would tell her how much he loved her. And he would tell her he was ready. He would hold out one short stem of pale lavender sweet pea, and he would ask her for forever.

78

"About time you two showed up," Grant teased Dagmar and Brooke as they opened the garden gate.

"Ooh, cookies!" said Dag. "How did it go?"

"It went really well," said Mai, picking up the last few rakes and shovels. "Can you guys admit I have the best staff on earth?"

"Yeah, they're pretty great. And they look younger to me every year! I can't believe how many of them came, especially the ones from the Milwaukee office. That Chris fella seems like a hard worker."

"I think he'll be a good hire. I'm so glad he came today."

"You guys, this Chris kid had a paintbrush that looked exactly like the one Jo got in Switzerland. It was kind of eerie," Grant told them. "Remember that weird old thing?"

"Not really?" said Dag, helping to pack up the leftover food.

Mai lifted a bucket of soapy water onto the table. "The only reason I remembered it was because when I was a little girl, I used to pretend it was the brush from this old folktale my father used to tell me. Jo kept it on a shelf by the cash register and I would play with it when she wasn't looking."

"Oh I gotta hear this one!" said Grant, excitedly. "Sawm always had a great story up his sleeve."

"OK, let me try to remember it. I know I won't do it justice." Mai sat down on a chair next to the snack table and Grant, Brooke, and Dagmar sat on the bench across from her. Grant put his arm around his wife.

Mai closed her eyes. She took a moment to remember sitting on her father's cozy lap and tried to get his story just right.

"Once there was a poor young boy named Pab. He toiled in the fields for a cruel master all day, in exchange for food to help his family survive. The earth was dry and hard to dig. He was too small and weak to carry heavy loads, and his master would scold him and withhold his payment. Pab never complained. At night, by candlelight, Pab would draw beautiful pictures on scraps of rice paper using broken reeds and ash from the fire. He had no proper tools, but he could make cheerful scenes to bring smiles to his family.

"One day, Pab rested in the shade of a tree, out of the sight of his master, and an old woman approached him and gave him an exquisite paintbrush. She warned him to use it with great care. The next day Pab mixed pigments from berries and went to the town square. He used the brush to paint a picture he hoped he could sell for money or food. He painted a mountain valley, flowers, a blue sky, and a white bird. But when he put the final touch on the bird, it lifted off of the paper and flew away. He stared up at the sky in wonder. It was then he knew the old woman had given him a magic paintbrush. He ran home to tell his family, and painted them a table overflowing with meat, fruits and cakes. He painted toys and dresses for his sisters.

"Hearing a hard knock at the door, and knowing he had been found out, he escaped out the back door. He ran up into the hills overlooking the village. As he sat on a rock, holding his brush, looking down at the drought-stricken fields, he had an idea. When he sneaked back home later that night, he painted a cool, clean river meandering through the countryside, to bring water to the farms. It worked! And he knew then he must always use his brush for good.

"Pab's master had heard about the magic brush and told the greedy King, hoping it would bring him favor. The King sent soldiers to seize Pab and bring him to the castle. The King tried to use the brush to paint riches himself, but soon realized it held no magic when it was in his hand. So, he held Pab captive and forced him to paint. Pab was small and young, but he was smart. Smarter than the King, in fact. He painted a large, beautiful, persimmon wood boat for the King and his henchmen. They were pleased and climbed aboard. They sailed down the river to where it met the sea. This is when Pab, watching them from the window of the castle, added a violent storm to the painting, and they were washed out to sea, never to be heard from again.

"As Pab grew into a man, he became a great leader of his people. He was known throughout the land as kind and generous, and his village never went hungry again. Years later, after he had raised a good and true child of his own, he went far into the woods and buried the brush deep in the earth. He knew that the magic of creation was not in the brush at all, but inside himself."

The friends were silent for a moment, listening to the sounds of the garden.

"Gosh, that made me miss Sawm. I could hear his voice. Thank you, Mai. Kinda makes me want to drop a fishing line down that hole and bring the brush back up!" Grant laughed.

"Grant, I don't even want to know what you might paint with a magic brush," Brooke teased him as they all stood to leave.

"Well, folks, what do you think?" Grant asked as he turned to face the garden, arms outstretched. "Does this get the Jo stamp of approval?"

"Most definitely," said Brooke. "This place looks shipshape and ready for the season."

"When is she getting back, anyway?" asked Dagmar.

"A couple more weeks. She's in Florence for a few more days and then she'll be meeting up with Fern in Siena," Grant replied. "I can't remember where they go after that."

"Ha! She's still such a lone wolf. Her daughter is the only one she'll travel with," laughed Dag.

"I've gotten my foot in the door, too," said Mai. "In June, Jo and I have a lobbying event in D.C. for Hmong veteran benefits. She even agreed to stay in the same hotel with me."

"I honestly can't believe Congress still hasn't addressed this, after...what...fifty years?" Brooke marveled, disgustedly.

"Last year, they did approve veterans license plates and funeral expenses," said Mai. "Baby steps."

"Pfft. A pittance." Grant shook his head. "Shameful."

"It's a start, though. Jo has never given up on this, even after my parents were gone. She's been writing letters and lobbying for forty years."

"That's our Jo," Grant said with a soft smile as they started to leave the garden. "Hey, guys, you go on ahead." He waved his hand toward the gate. "I'll meet you next door. I just noticed the aspen placard didn't get scrubbed and I want to do that before we flip the juice back on."

Grant put on a pair of gloves, and dipped a rag and a small scouring pad into the soapy bucket. He used a gentle circular motion to remove the fine layer of dirt and pollen. Then he used the corner of the scouring pad to dig into the raised lettering, taking care to carve out the lichen in the edges so each letter was clear. He did the same with the lines of braille at the bottom. He dipped the rag in the water again and went back over the top to clear any remaining debris, and then refolded the rag to a drier section to go over the placard one more time. The sun shone through the new green leaves of the tree above, and glimmered against the polished golden words.

As you walk beneath the aspen tree, take a moment to feel the smooth white bark, marked with rougher dark patches from age. In many cultures, the aspen is a symbol of resurrection. It was said that wearing a crown of aspen leaves would give ancient heroes the power to visit the underworld and return safely. The aspen is a dancing tree of many colors that has captivated people for ages. If you wait for a breeze and listen closely, you might even hear applause.

The End